DOUBLE MURDER

His face illuminated by an occasional flash of lightning, he jimmied the lock without much trouble at all. Pulling a knife from a scabbard clipped to his belt, he walked through the ground floor. The lights were out. No one stirred.

Knife drawn, he crept up the stairway. He hoped Cady's daughter didn't sleep around. A man in the bed would probably raise a ruckus that would awaken the little girl. He'd wind up slitting the throats of all three. Pity. But he supposed it couldn't be helped.

A thunderclap resounded through the house as he reached the second-floor hallway. The door to his right stood slightly ajar. He peeked inside. A woman stirred under her bedclothes. He chuckled to himself. Tonight he would commit a double homicide. He would slit Sara Cady's throat and shatter Maxwell Cady's heart as well.

QUANTITY SALES

Most Dell Books are available at special quantity discounts when purchased in bulk by corporations, organizations, and special-interest groups. Custom imprinting or excerpting can also be done to fit special needs. For details write: Dell Publishing Co., Inc., 1 Dag Hammarskjold Plaza, New York, NY 10017, Attn.: Special Sales Dept., or phone: (212) 605-3319.

INDIVIDUAL SALES

Are there any Dell Books you want but cannot find in your local stores? If so, you can order them directly from us. You can get any Dell book in print. Simply include the book's title, author, and ISBN number, if you have it, along with a check or money order (no cash can be accepted) for the full retail price plus 75¢ per copy to cover shipping and handling. Mail to: Dell Readers Service, Dept. FM, P.O. Box 1000, Pine Brook, NJ 07058.

THE CON GAME

Ed Naha

A DELL BOOK

Published by
Dell Publishing Co., Inc.
1 Dag Hammarskjold Plaza
New York, New York 10017

Copyright © 1986 by Ed Naha

All rights reserved. No part of this book may be reproduced
or transmitted in any form or by any means, electronic or
mechanical, including photocopying, recording or by any
information storage and retrieval system, without the written
permission of the Publisher, except where permitted by law.

Dell ® TM 681510, Dell Publishing Co., Inc.

ISBN: 0-440-11403-9

Printed in the United States of America

May 1986

10 9 8 7 6 5 4 3 2 1

DD

For Janelle

Special thanks to Bob Mecoy, Linne Radmin, and Frances Doel for their support.

CHAPTER ONE

"No! No! He's going to kill me!"

Max Cady watched impassively as the woman screamed for help. In a few seconds a homicidal maniac resembling Mighty Joe Young would appear from the shadows, violently grab her mane of long red hair, and run a razor across her throat.

Max wouldn't see that, of course. You never see that kind of stuff on television. People have to *pay* five big ones to see that crap in movie theaters. Crap that gave weird ideas to equally weird people. Crap that Max Cady once earned *beaucoup* bucks from.

Max groped for the remote control box and eliminated the volume on the television set as the redhead vanished and a newscaster appeared. Cady switched channels and found himself watching Alan Alda, valiantly slogging it through a rerun of *M*A*S*H* for the umpteenth time. Cady didn't bother adjusting the volume. He knew Alda would make it through the Korean War intact, his vitriolic humor saving his sanity, showing us the better way and enriching the lives of all those around him.

Amen.

At 11:24 P.M. on this muggy New Jersey Monday, Maxwell Norvell Cady was wearing his unenriched life around his ankles.

He pushed himself up out of his battered leather armchair and stumbled into the kitchen, where he poured himself another drink. How many did this make? He had lost count after twelve. He stood before the refrigerator, swaying slightly, still wearing the spiffy lightweight suit he had taught in this afternoon. His face, normally heavily lined, was now positively crinkled. His eyes were puffy, their lids at half-mast. He didn't look like a teacher right about now. He looked like an aging palooka after one fight too many or a film *noir* private eye after a close encounter with a blackjack or, quite simply, a man resigned to the fact that his existence was slowly going down the toilet.

He had seen the newspaper around four o'clock.

The phone started ringing about five.

The TV news vultures picked up on the tabloid report by the end of the five o'clock report and broadcast the story, laced with heavy chuckling, in their "Faces in the News" section.

He had started drinking by six.

Tequila at first.

Straight tequila.

When that ran out he switched to gin and tonics. He had sucked up all the tonic water by nine and was now working on gin and orange soda.

He removed the bottle of Beefeater dry gin from the fridge and the last drops of Shasta orange. He poured the remainder of the soda into a coffee cup and filled it with the liquor.

He wasn't a big gin man but he appreciated the Beefeater people. They had the decency to explain what the hell a Beefeater was on the bottle's back label. How they were guards in the reign of King William the Conqueror (1066–1087) and did their best to keep the riffraff out of both the Palace and the Tower of London (although exactly why anyone would want to try to sneak *into* the Tower of London puzzled him, Max appreciated the Beefeaters' loyalty and the slightly sweet taste of their wonderful gin).

He staggered back into his living room staring at the rug on the floor. It had been on the floor when Max bought the house. Not exactly a homemaker, Max just let it stay there. He stared at the gummy surface. It might have been blue once.

The house itself wasn't anything to write to *Better Homes & Gardens* about, unless they were exceedingly hard up for mail. It was a one-story rectangle. At one time it had had grass in the yard. A previous owner had poured cement over it and now the exterior of the abode looked like an abandoned parking lot on the moon.

The interior was solidly nondescript, with walls bland enough to display either pictures of kids with big eyes or a 3-D portrait of Jesus. To Cady's credit he had neither school of art in evidence. A wall calendar. A bulletin board. A lot of cracks.

THE CON GAME

Max slid into the tattered leather chair and groaned. He hurt all over. Even his eyelids were pounding.

The phone was still ringing.

It hadn't stopped all evening. Since penitence was the name of the game at this point, he hadn't bothered to take it off the hook.

May the bells of New Jersey Tel absolve me of my past sins.

He slouched deeper into the leather chair as Alan Alda exchanged a mute joke with Harry Morgan. Max squinted at the screen. Klinger was in the outer office so he figured out that this was one of those episodes filmed after Radar had split. He could understand why Gary Burghoff had left the series. After a while, success, if it's the kind of success you never really dreamed of, can be a real pain in the butt. Coping with it, explaining it, ignoring it could become a twenty-four-hour job.

Max Cady had realized that eight years ago.

And, so, he had jettisoned his notoriety and abandoned his unexpected stardom.

And all had been right with the world . . . until today.

Up until eight hours ago Max Cady had been a fairly content human being. Forty-nine years old. Big. Burly. Quiet. More than a little burned out, with a checkered past history that frequent drinking made palatable, even humorous. Twice divorced—with a twenty-five-year-old daughter and outrageous alimony bills to prove it.

For the last five years he had lived out his life in the quiet suburb of Rohannan, New Jersey, teaching English in a parochial school, the all-female Our Lady of Perpetual Hope High School, holding his own against an army of Dominican nuns.

All that was bound to change now.

Max rubbed a few beads of sweat off his forehead and took a deep sip of his mind-numbing concoction. Christ, was it bad. Without thinking, he picked the late edition of the New York *Post* up off the coffee table. It was still opened to "Page Nine." Without looking at it, he began swatting it against his leg rhythmically.

He had memorized what was on the page hours ago.

Top of the page. Two photos. On the left a portrait of actor James Coburn wearing a battered trench coat and mauling a cigarette, playing a character named Jimmy Ammo in a motion picture called *Murder Me, Murder You*. (The flick on the tube with the redhead, the razor, and the simian in sneakers.)

On the right-hand side of the page was a snapshot of a fairly startled Maxwell Cady taken only this morning as he ambled from the school parking lot toward the front entrance of the ivy-covered building.

The headline: IN REAL LIFE, AMMO IS A TWO-FISTED TEACH.

Cady shut his eyes. Bad move. His chin dropped onto his chest and the room began to swim wildly. Max felt like he was tumbling through a black hole. His torso pitched forward. He forced his eyes open abruptly. He was anchored safely to the chair once again. Alan Alda, Mike Farrell, and Harry Morgan were sharing a communal laugh. Good. That meant the episode was over, the final commercial would be aired, and the late-night movie would materialize. *A Fistful of Dollars* with Clint Eastwood. If Clint Eastwood had been japed by the press outside *his* school this morning, he would have just walked over to that photographer and made him eat that camera. Piece by piece.

But Max Cady wasn't Clint Eastwood.

He wasn't even Max Cady anymore.

He was Jimmy Ammo, macho man, private dick, mauler of men and abuser of women.

He felt a circular burp bang around his chest. He hoped it was just gas. He'd hate to vomit all over the rug . . . not that it would make much difference. He hadn't been this drunk since the mess with Dorothy. That mess, in turn, produced Jimmy Ammo. Jimmy, in turn, caused this whole catastrophe.

Sometimes Dorothy used to say, shriek, actually, that disaster was Max's middle name.

"It's better than Norvell, anyhow," he would reply in a lame attempt at banter.

Twelve years ago, when Max and Western civilization had been a tad younger, Cady was making a decent living as a crime reporter for the New York *Daily News*. He specialized in covering works of sociological ingenuity that were so brutal and borderline pornographic that other scribes actively avoided them, fearing impromptu visitations from past meals.

THE CON GAME

(Favorite headline: BODIES RAIN FROM HEAVEN—"They looked like hamburgers," says eyewitness to rooftop arson spree.)

Cady, however, took it all in stride. It wasn't that he was an active oddball or closet kink, it's just that the excitement, the morbid flurry of activity that surrounded each one of these heinous acts kept his mind occupied . . . it kept him from thinking about real life.

His life.

Back then he had a marriage he knew was failing yet, for some reason, he was powerless to save it. Dorothy and he were one of those matches made on the rebound. Totally illogical. They both had been lonely. They both had been hurting. Blah. Blah. She had wanted security. He had wanted another body in the house. Neither got what they wanted so, in a way, it was a true exercise in matrimonial equality.

Back in those days he also found it impossible to communicate with his daughter, Sara. She was into hash, dating bikers, and playing Bowie's *Ziggy Stardust and the Spiders from Mars* at Mount Vesuvius volume.

He was working for a paper that wouldn't print the kinds of stories he *wanted* to write, stories that had flashes of insight and compassion. The kind of O. Henry to the nth power stuff that would make Pete Hamill and Jimmy Breslin media kings. And, so, he was forced to pen what amounted to extended headlines for a half-dozen years.

Twelve years ago he had thought that he was in a devastating rut. As awful as his existence seemed, however, he had taken some small solace in the fact that day-to-day living couldn't get any worse.

Wrong.

He and Dorothy split. Divorce time. It was messy, ludicrously painful. Max had been working the graveyard shift for months, roaming the streets until dawn. Tumbling, exhausted, into bed when Frank McGee was just clearing his throat on *The Today Show*. Dorothy was bored. He could understand that. But when she decided to have her affair she really outdid herself. She hadn't just chosen his best friend, she had chosen his *two* best friends. His marriage went kaput and a perfectly swell bowling team was fragmented forever.

Through some aberration of the judicial system, Dorothy was awarded custody of Sara. That didn't last long, however, in that his darling daughter ran off with the first pair of pants that paid attention to her.

Ah, romance.

Max grunted into his coffee cup as a group of banditos scared the oats out of Clint Eastwood's mule.

After the divorce Max turned to the bottle to work out his grief . . . and his typewriter. In between blackouts and black-and-blue evenings in nameless bars, he hacked out a novel, *Murder Me, Murder You*, a graphic tome about a boss who rapes and abuses all his female employees, threatening to blackmail them with a ton of compromising photos he'd snapped after drugging them. Enter a Cro-Magnon ex-cop-turned-sleuth/writer named Ammo, who sort of saves the day. You knew he was the book's hero because he never tied his women up when he mauled them. He even wore cologne.

On a literary scale of Spillane to Mailer, it ranked somewhere slightly above cave drawings. But, what the hell, it had helped Max deal with the anger he felt toward his wife and, back then, women in general.

During a drinking jag he mentioned the tome to an agent friend who, smelling a few exploitation dollars, promptly sold it as the first novel by hard-boiled detective author Jimmy Ammo. What made the book interesting to the public was that Ammo was both the author and the lead character of the tawdry tale.

("She ran her lips across mine as the blood poured from her side. 'Do you think you'll write about me someday?' she wheezed. 'I guess so, babe,' I said. 'I have this *thing* for losers.'"
THE END.)

Assured of anonymity and not minding the cash at all, Max quit his job at the newspaper, using his shattered nerves as a handy excuse, and cranked out a dozen Ammo novels in a period of four years, thus effectively exorcising all the ghosts left over from his personal and professional life.

Jimmy Ammo made Mickey Spillane's Mike Hammer look like a well-behaved schoolboy, but when feminists began making headlines, Ammo began to lose his swagger. In the ERA era Ammo began to look like the dinosaur that he was.

Cady had allowed the series to fade. He took the money and drifted for a while. A couple of Jimmy Ammo movies were made and did so-so. Still, Cady had enough scratch to bum around Europe, grow a nasty beard, and irritate half the population of the Continent with his verbal goulash of English, French, and free-form grunting.

When his money dwindled Cady bought a small home in New Jersey, removed his face fur, and, whipping out his teaching certificate from years before, applied and, much to his amazement, was accepted for a position at Our Lady of Perpetual Hope.

Since then his life had been quiet but rewarding.

When teaching literature he felt that he was learning just as much as his students. He taught them how to open a book and absorb the thoughts of the author. They, in turn, reminded him how fresh and exciting the whole world can be when you gaze at it through the eyes of innocence. But now?

Clint Eastwood pulled a pistol and ventilated the chest of a half-dozen tough hombres.

Now, Cady's innocent days were over. Cady was revealed as the *real* Jimmy Ammo, a guy who would just as soon kill a buxom babe as buss one.

That sort of disclosure would, more than likely, not endear him to the faculty or the PTA at Our Lady of Hope.

He gazed at the photos in the newspaper, not having the energy to focus on the accompanying story. No matter. He had just about memorized it by now. "Cady bears more than a passing resemblance to another time-worn tough guy, big Bob Mitchum. Mitchum was passed over for the role of Jimmy Ammo in the film version of *Murder Me, Murder You* in 1977 when he balked at the sadistic script. At the time he commented, 'I'm no angel, but this Jimmy Ammo is one sick . . .' "

Max slowly eased himself out of the chair, knocking over the remnants of the drink onto the floor. He kicked the newspaper atop the puddle. The article would serve some purpose after all.

He walked slowly into the bathroom and gazed into the mirror. His face was several shades lighter than white. So much for resembling "big Bob Mitchum." A few more drinks and maybe he'd resemble Bigfoot by tomorrow morning. No reporter would have the nerve to stop him then.

The phone in the living room continued to ring. Max heaved a resigned sigh. There was no way he would be able to sleep with the Ma Bell mantra persisting.

He strode over to the offending phone and picked it up. Against his better judgment, he placed the phone to his ear.

"Hello?"

"Is this Max Cady?" a female voice replied.

"Yeah."

"Max Cady who is Jimmy Ammo?"

Heavy sigh. "Yeah."

"You're a real scumbag. You want me to try out on you some of the shit you pulled in your books? Huh? How would you like that?"

Max placed the phone down on the oak desk across from the television. Eastwood was *still* changing the topography of the population of Mexico with hot lead.

Max, remote control unit still cradled in his hand, flicked the TV set off and walked past the phone toward the bedroom.

A lilliputian voice was still sputtering from the receiver. "Answer me, asshole."

Max longed for the 1960s, when strangers would greet you with things like "Have a nice day."

He had been married to Peggy then. Beautiful, innocent Peggy Williams. His first real love and the mother of his daughter. Overworked public defender. Champion of lost causes. Retriever of lost souls. She just didn't have time for a marriage. She had been murdered shortly after their divorce. At a rooftop party held in a tough gang neighborhood. Molotov cocktails were unexpectedly served with the hors d'oeuvres.

" 'They looked like hamburgers' said an eyewitness."

Max collapsed on his unmade bed fully clothed. His head was spinning.

Oh well, he thought. At least tomorrow had to be better than today.

THE CON GAME

Within twelve hours he would find out that, once again, he was wrong.

"Disaster" might not have been a better moniker than Norvell after all.

But it seemed that he was stuck with them both.

CHAPTER TWO

"Ah one, two, three, uhhh. Ah one, two, three."

When Sara was a little girl she used to watch a local dance show that started off with a song, maybe it was Wilson Pickett singing. Yes, it was probably Wilson Pickett. He'd simply yell at the beginning of the song, "One, two, three," and the band would start jumping. One, two, three. And then a whole new song. A whole new melody. A new show.

Tuesday was that kind of day. A whole new song. A whole new melody.

One. Two. Three.

ONE: Sitting across from Sister Mary Paul, Max noticed how much the old woman resembled an anteater. The crone had a nose that just didn't quit, and when she frowned the countless lines in her face sagged toward her chin, accentuating her pronounced proboscis even further. She was frowning demonstratively now. He was waiting for her nose to extend a few feet and grab him around the neck.

Headline: HACK WRITER MEETS DUMBO DEATH.

The ancient nun had never liked Cady, had never really wanted him in her school. Max always had the feeling it had less to do with his teaching abilities than the odd little thing he had between his legs, a loathsome member that Sister Mary Paul seemed to regard as the moral equivalent of a meat cleaver. Max stared into the woman's cold gray eyes and realized that he was in big, big trouble.

As bad off as his situation was, the Pre-Raphaelite principal's condescending attitude made Max want to make it worse. (Headline: AMMO SOCKS SIS—Knocked-Out Nun Sent Into Low Orbit.)

The Dominican dragon was furious, her face covered with red blotches of incipient anger. Her head, which normally shook at

THE CON GAME

a rate of 45 jitters per minute, was up to 78 jpms now easy, giving her the appearance of Katharine Hepburn on speed. A stack of newspapers was before her.

"Have you seen these papers, Mr. . . . *Cady?*" She pronounced his last name as if it were a bizarre social disease.

"I couldn't miss them, Sister."

"I didn't think you could."

"As soon as I walked into your office I said, 'Now there's a woman who is up on her current events. Just look at the stack of papers—' "

"You're not going to make this easy for me are you, Mr. Cady?"

The old woman's voice was terse, brittle. She was breathing through her nose in short, sporadic, teakettle bursts.

"Sister?"

"You have besmirched the reputation of this school, Mr. Cady."

Max couldn't help but grin.

"I fail to see the humor in the situation, Mr. Cady," the elderly nun said, pointing a reedlike forefinger in his direction. "Did you see what's outside the school? The cameras? The reporters?"

"I thought they were here to cover our spelling bee," Max said. "You know, a strong local angle for tonight's *News at Six.*"

"Mr. Cady, look at these stories. 'Jimmy Ammo Loose in Girls' School.' In all my years at this institution I have never been involved in such a horrific scandal. You have compromised the decency of all who work here, of all who study here, of all who send their innocent children to this school to be taught basic Christian values. Under the circumstances I must ask you to submit your resignation, for your own good as well as the good of this institute of higher education."

Max reached into his pocket to pull out a cigarette, remembered that he gave up smoking fifteen years ago, and produced a slightly used toothpick instead. He jammed it into his mouth, giving him just the proper amount of stationary swagger.

"Oh, you'll get your letter, all right, Sister. But I won't be resigning for my own good and certainly not for the good of this antediluvian eyesore you laughingly refer to as an institution of higher education. I'll be doing it for those kids.

"I don't know whether you've noticed it or not, Sister, but for the past five years I've been a good teacher here. No, I take that back. A damn good teacher—"

"MISTER Cady, your books are debased enough. There is no need for profanity—"

"Oh yes there is. The bullshit you're handing me this morning is just as profane as anything I've ever written. I stopped writing that junk years ago. I'm not particularly proud of it. I never put my name on it.

"For the past five years I worked my balls off to try to shape up the English department here. I've tried my damnedest to get these kids interested in reading, in composition, in *thought* and I think I succeeded."

Cady gnawed on the toothpick. "Sure, I'll leave . . . but only because I don't want to see their classroom behavior tarnished by the intrusions of morons, morons like those reporters out there and the self-righteous bigots in this school."

"Mr. Cady, you write pornography. I will not have a pornographer dealing with teenage girls—"

"Well, surprise, your sanctimoniousness. You have allowed just that for the past five years. And guess what? I never slid my hands up one of their dresses. Never copped one feel. Never diddled one solitary damsel."

Sister Mary Paul leapt to her feet, shaking. "Get out of this office, Mr. Cady. Get out now!"

Max slowly arose from his chair, a shambling, unshaven hulk, and stood, towering over the tiny nun. "Anything you say, Sister."

Max exited the office, letting the door slam purposively behind him. He marched down the corridor. The halls were filled with young girls between the ages of thirteen and eighteen preparing for their first class. Several of his students shouted greetings. Most of the girls glanced at him and giggled softly.

Was it his imagination or were they flirting with him?

He flashed a lopsided grin as one or two young students dropped their books in front of him.

Was it his imagination or was he flirting back?

THE CON GAME

TWO: Max Cady didn't *hate* David Maskin, but he didn't enjoy his company either. Maskin was one of those workaholic types in their late thirties who played racketball, wore casual shirts with polo players embroidered on them, drove sporty cars, and had haircuts that resembled the tonsorial splendor established by Ken of the famous Barbie and Ken team.

Maskin was Max's literary agent, a task he had inherited from his older brother, a young man who never evolved into an old man owing to an unfortunate habit of mixing barbiturates and alcohol.

He was waiting in front of Max's home by the time Cady had driven home from the misnamed establishment of Perpetual Hope.

"Top o' the morning, Max." Maskin grinned. Every tooth in his mouth was perfect. Caps, probably.

"Bottom of the barrel, Dave," Max replied, fumbling with his keys. Maskin continued to grin. Christ, didn't this guy ever get depressed?

"In the mood for some company?" Maskin asked.

"No."

Maskin bounded into the house as soon as the door was open. Max tolerated Maskin and, at times, actually admired the guy. Even during an enlightened literary era, Maskin had continued to squeeze money out of the Jimmy Ammo books. When they had fallen out of favor in America and disappeared from the bookstalls, Maskin had begun peddling them overseas, where, to this day, they still sold a fair number of copies. Max had to admit it was a kick to get royalty checks made out for payment in yen.

"I see you haven't changed your decorating style." Maskin smirked, carrying his briefcase into the living room. "Colonial earthquake."

Max grunted and removed a beer from the refrigerator. "I'd offer you a beer but I only have one left and I need it more than you."

Maskin was shuffling file folders. "I'll say you do. I'm here to toast your newfound success."

Max scrunched his face up into a mask of confusion. "What

are you talking about? I just lost my job. My reputation. My identity. Why should I celebrate?"

Maskin held a file folder under Max's nose. "Because today is the first day of the rest of your literary life."

"Have you been adopted by Hallmark cards or something?"

Maskin plopped the file folder down on the coffee table before Max. A dozen paperback book covers fell out. Each one had an action-adventure painting on it with a portrait of craggy-faced Max Cady in the foreground. Max was wearing a trench coat and chewing a cigarette, much in the same fashion that James Coburn had in yesterday's *Post*.

"Neat, huh?" Maskin enthused.

"Uh, Dave. Why don't I want to know what I'm doing on all these book jackets?"

"Today, Max Cady, a.k.a. Jimmy Ammo, you are a very wealthy man."

Max stared hard at Maskin. "I hope your health insurance is paid up."

"Look at these paintings, Max. They're wonderful. We're going to make you a fiction star. The publishing world is dying to produce new heroes, Max. Larger-than-life characters to compete with the movie idols. You know, like Dirty Harry, the Road Warrior, and Indiana Jones. Well, I had an inspiration. I talked to one of the biggest editors in town and—*voila!*—I resold the Ammo books for about fifteen times what you were paid for them in the first place. Plus, I negotiated for a hefty royalty."

Maskin lifted a second file folder. "The publishing company is with you 1000 percent on this too. Look at this! A detailed publicity and promotion tour. TV talk shows. Book signings. The works. These little babies will be hitting the bookstores in a few days and you'll be right on their tail."

"You're going to be on your tail if you've done what I think you've done."

"Now, Max."

"You set me up! The newspapers didn't discover my connection with Ammo accidentally. You tipped them off!"

"It was for your own good, Max. You're dying here. You're losing that old creative urge."

THE CON GAME

"Let me see if I can find something creative to do with my hands and your neck."

The doorbell rang. Max slowly got to his feet, leaving the beer bottle on the coffee table atop one of the new covers.

"Max," Maskin called after him, moving the beer bottle onto a battered copy of *TV Guide* from six months ago. "You might as well do the tour and play along. After all, you're going to need the money. You're out of a job now."

Max grunted and swung open the front door. Reva Brown and Charlotte Valkenburg stood there. They were gorgeous. Reva's black hair cascaded down an off-the-shoulder T-shirt. Charlotte was wearing a jogging outfit that left little to the imagination.

They were both sixteen years old.

"Hi, Mr. Cady."

"We're not bothering you are we, Mr. Cady?"

Max scratched his head, bewildered. "Uh, why aren't you two at school?"

"Well, we just got really mad listening to what Sister Mary Paul was telling the reporters about you and, well, we decided to come over and see if you were all right," Reva said, her hazel eyes meeting his own boldly.

"Yes," Charlotte said, taking a step forward. "We thought we'd come over and console you."

"Yeah, see if you needed anything."

Maskin was on his feet now, peering out at the front door from the living room.

Max chuckled and nodded appreciatively. "Well, thanks, kiddos, but I'm in the middle of a business meeting. I do appreciate you coming over but I'm okay. Now," he added conspiratorially, "I'm depending on you two to keep the class going when I'm gone. Don't let anyone get lazy."

He placed a firm hand on a shoulder of each. "You two were my American lit all-stars. Don't let me down."

"Yes, sir."

"You can depend on us, Mr. Cady."

"Okay. Back to school . . . and don't forget to change into your uniforms, okay? Sister Mary Paul would burst a blood vessel if she saw you like that."

The two girls giggled and trotted back down the walkway.

"Gee," Reva said. "I never noticed it before, but the newspaper was right. He *does* look like Robert Mitchum."

Charlotte glanced at Cady over her shoulder. "Who's Robert Mitchum?"

Maskin stood directly behind Cady. "Max! Why did you let them go?"

"Spare me, David."

"Did you see those little asses? Just look at them!"

"You look at them. You see good times. I see hard time. Fifteen years with good behavior."

"Well, I guess I should get back to the city," Maskin said, looking at his overpriced wristwatch. "I have a four o'clock meeting with a reporter from the *Times.* She'll be out tomorrow to interview you."

"No."

"Instant status, Maxy. Cover story of the Sunday *Times* magazine section."

Max was incredulous. "They're doing a cover story on *me?*"

"Well, sort of. Actually, they're doing a feature on classic mystery writers. They're going to profile you, Spillane, Hammett, Chandler, and a couple of other guys, comparing you with Phillip Carole."

"Who the hell is Phillip Carole?"

"Convicted murderer. Offed his parents at the age of sixteen. Just paroled after doing four years. Wrote a novel. Instant celeb. Writes about crime from the gut."

"I've never heard of him."

"I left a copy of his book on the coffee table."

"Wonderful. I'll read it once I catch up with all those *Harry O* reruns."

"Don't let me down, Max. Talk to the nice lady from the *Times.*"

"You realize that if I killed you right now, no court of law in the nation would convict me."

"Yeah. Yeah. Yeah."

"In fact, I'd probably get a medal from the Environmental Protection Agency."

THE CON GAME

Maskin ran down the front steps toward his Porsche. "Which way did your students go?"

Max stood in the doorway. "Why?"

"Well, maybe they'll need a lift somewhere."

Max flexed his hands, in and out, into fists. "You're skating on thin ice, David."

"Well"—Maskin shrugged—"if I'm skating on thin ice, I might as well dance."

THREE: The image of Sister Mary Paul flickered on the television screen. Max was amazed that she actually looked worse over the airwaves than she did in person. He hadn't believed that was possible.

"And, furthermore," she spat, "it is not the policy of this school to hire emotionally disturbed perverts. We were the victims of a great subterfuge, a type of chicanery—"

The phone rang.

Max lowered the volume on the television set with his remote switch, took a deep breath, and picked up the receiver, expecting the worst.

It was Sara.

"Oh hi, hon," Max began.

Outside his living-room window, hidden by a bougainvillea and the darkness of night, a figure peered in at Cady. The shadow-shape took careful note of every gesture, every movement Max made while on the phone.

"Yeah. I'm watching her now." Max smirked. "You're right. She does look like the Wicked Witch of the West. Yeah. I remember how you hated that movie. How's Peggy? No. How could I forget her birthday? I'll be there."

Max glanced casually at the window behind the desk. Did something just move out there? Probably the neighbors' cat. No big deal.

"Yeah. I know. The phone has been busy a lot. Mostly crank calls. I suppose I'll have to change the number. Yeah. Unlisted. A pain in the ass. Uh-uh. Dorothy hasn't called. She did? What did she say to you? Bullshit. Of course she knew. How else could I give her that amount of alimony?

"Speaking of alimony, is Al late with your check again? No. I'm not making a big deal about it. It's just that . . ."

The figure looked Cady over. Max was big but not muscular. He seemed to have a solid body, but it probably owed more to genetics than exercise. He had a barrel chest and a stomach that was equally fulsome. Not enough a gut to form a paunch, though.

His eyes were heavy-lidded and droopy. His hair was a drab brown streaked with sandy waves of gray. He had the kind of face you'd see a lot at the city desk of a major newspaper or in a squad room at a local precinct or at a hospital at three in the morning. Cady's face betrayed an exhaustion that was as much spiritual as it was physical.

He must have seen a lot in his day.

The figure outside the window wondered just how much of Max Cady figured into Jimmy Ammo and just how much was bullshit.

A cat leapt onto the outside windowsill with a loud hiss.

Cady turned around and faced the window. "Wait a minute, hon. I heard . . . no, never mind. It's just the Lesters' cat. Yeah. I guess I'm a little jumpy. I've had a lot of weird calls. Nah. Just people letting off steam.

"Hey. You know what I found today? Remember when you watched that dance show on TV? The one that . . . Uh-huh. I couldn't remember what the name of that record was for the life of me. Right. Wilson Pickett. *The Land of 1,000 Dances.*"

The figure outside the window waited until Cady had refocused his attention on the phone before snatching the cat off the windowsill. With one swift motion the peeper held the cat up before the bougainvillea with one hand while bringing the knife up with the other. The knife sliced through the neck of the animal effortlessly. The surprised creature didn't have time to cry out. The figure dropped the writhing animal onto the ground and backed away from the window.

Inside the house, Max Cady nodded into the phone. "Right. I'll call you tomorrow afternoon. Right. After my big interview. Good-bye, hon. Kiss Peggy for me."

Cady hung up the phone, walked over to the record player, and placed the needle on side two of *Wilson Pickett's Greatest Hits.* He walked into the kitchen to construct a dinner out of a series of cans when the music began.

"One, two, three uh, one, two threeeeee."

The horn section began pumping furiously as the drummer flailed away. "Na, na, na, na," Pickett wailed.

"Na, na, na," Cady answered back, beginning a whole new song.

Outside his living room, next to the bougainvillea, a small gray cat twitched one last time.

CHAPTER THREE

Max stood uneasily in the doorway gazing into an unbearably bright morning and an equally bright smile.

"I'm Debra Knightly."

"I'm sure you are."

Debra Knightly did not possess the type of looks that men with bad cases of arrested development longed for. She was not the type of woman one would encounter while pawing through the pages of *Playboy*. She was compact and thin, five foot four, and a tad over a hundred pounds. Her skin was alabaster, dusted with freckles. Her hair was a reddish brown. She had bright green eyes, an aggressive jaw, and a no-nonsense attitude.

Cady leaned against the door. He glared at her.

She glared back, her glossy lips forming a professionally tight grin.

She had been warned by Maskin about Cady.

She had expected the worst.

She was not disappointed.

"I believe we have an interview scheduled." She smiled thinly.

"Ah. You must be the reporter from the *Times*." He swung the door open with a professional flourish. "I'll have to see some credentials, miss. I've been deluged by callers all day. Longtime fans. Secret admirers. Groupies."

"Functional illiterates?" the woman said, smiling sweetly and stepping past Max.

Max watched her walk into his living room, swinging her portable tape recorder off her shoulder and onto his coffee table.

She was brash, self-assured, and unimpressed with his literary output.

Within 2.6 seconds he realized he was in love.

Within 2.8 seconds he realized that he had ashtrays older

THE CON GAME

than this woman and his only chance was to maintain a professional coolness.

Max plopped down in the leather chair across from the sofa. The motion caused the chair to emit a rush of air through its many rips. It sounded like a basset hound with gas. "Can we get this over with?"

"No thank you." Debra smiled, setting up the tape recorder. "I never drink coffee. I'm fine."

"Oh, uh," Max demurred. "Would you like something to drink?"

The reporter smiled and said nothing.

Max tightened his jaw as she turned on the tape recorder.

"May I ask you a few questions?" she began.

"I thought that was why you were here."

"For many years you've hidden the fact that you are, in reality, Jimmy Ammo—"

"Not quite. I am, in reality, Maxwell Cady. I am, in fantasy, Jimmy Ammo."

"Why did you never admit to being another person?"

"You get more presents when you have two birthdays."

"Has the merging of your two identities changed your life at all?"

"Oh yes, dramatically."

"How?"

"Well, this morning I was awakened at six A.M. by one of my garbage men. He's been a big Jimmy Ammo fan for years, he said. Ever since he found a copy of my second novel in a trash can. He asked me to autograph a book. That was my big morning. Oh yeah. My neighbor also accused me of killing his cat."

"His cat?"

"Remember the old adage, there's more than one way to skin a cat? Well, apparently, someone found a fairly direct approach last night and left the little critter in the alley. He found his ex-kitty today and, although he knows me to be a stalwart citizen and a real pillar of the community, he accused me of chopping up his feline friend. I'm sure that I will be encountering many more such scintillating experiences in years to come."

Max smiled.

Debra smiled. She shut off the machine. "Let's cut the crap, Mr. Cady. Are you going to be serious or not?"

"As long as we're being honest, Miss . . ."

"Knightly."

"Miss Knightly, I don't want to be here any more than you do. I am doing this story because I have to, not because I want to. You, obviously, are not a big Jimmy Ammo fan and you probably consider this whole assignment something closely akin to covering a cockfight. I don't blame you."

The reporter smiled. This time it was genuine. "You have any beer in your refrigerator?"

"Yeah, I stocked up this morning. I think I'm going to need it."

"Why?"

"Well, no offense, Miss Knightly—"

"Debra—"

"—Debra, but this, how did you put it, merging of my two identities, is probably going to completely destroy what I laughingly refer to as 'my life.' "

Max walked into the kitchen and pulled two Dos X's from the refrigerator. He walked over to the doorway and stuck both bottles into an old-fashioned Coca-Cola bottle opener bolted to the wall. That opener on the wall had actually been the deciding factor in his buying the house. The rest of the place was pretty run-down and nondescript. But having an old-fashioned, soda-fountain-type bottle opener *fastened* to a wall? Well, how could any semi-serious drinker resist?

He returned to the living room and handed the reporter her bottle.

"Here. My glasses have fungus growing in them."

He noticed that she still had the tape recorder off. "I'm not a nasty man, Miss . . . Debra . . . I'm not misanthropic or misogynistic or anything like that. What I am is tired. Very. Very tired.

"I've gone through more careers in the last dozen years than most people do in a lifetime."

"I know. I read your bio."

"It doesn't tell you the good stuff. I learned how to punctuate sentences correctly and write to fit inch space while slogging

THE CON GAME

through blood and bodily debris. I covered my first wife's murder, wanted to murder my second. I pay too much alimony and get too little sleep. My daughter is a single parent and I have nightmares about her living alone in Manhattan. I made a nice sum of money by writing some crap that I never much paid attention to. For the past few years I've found some peace of mind teaching ordinary kids English. And then this mess started. Do you think I'm ever going to be able to go back to teaching now?"

Debra sipped her beer. "I suppose not—"

"You can put money on it, Debra Knightly of the New York *Times*. No more fading into the woodwork for old Max Cady. I'm going to be a celebrity. I'm going to be vilified in the press as the biggest woman-hater in the world—"

"Are you?"

"No. I'm not that tall."

Max took two deep sips of his beer.

Debra reached over and turned on the tape recorder. Max was not supposed to notice the move, but he did. It didn't matter to him. He was now in a talkative mood.

"But you wrote all those books . . ." Debra began.

"Yeah. And then I stopped. Look, those books don't reflect my feelings any more than a Mickey Mouse cartoon reflected the life-style of Disney. I mean, he didn't go around wearing loaf-shaped shoes and four-fingered white gloves, right?

"I'd just as soon forget those books. I'm just not the celebrity type, Debra. I don't fit in with the tragically hip. For me, coke and a straw means a soda at a picnic. I don't like loud music. I'm a rotten dancer. I am not *au courant.*"

"You'd never know it from the way people are clamoring to meet you."

"Like who? My ex-wife's lawyers?"

"Phillip Carole, Eric Paine, just about every literary figure in New York."

"Maybe there's nothing on cable this week."

"Well, they're interested enough to have you share the spotlight with Carole tonight."

Max blinked.

Debra hesitated. "You didn't know?"

"Turn off the tape recorder."

Debra, now unsure of herself, did as she was told.

"Now, what are you talking about?" Max said, not at all sure he wanted to know the answer.

"Well, um, Eric Paine is having a coming-out party for Phillip Carole tonight. When the story on you broke he decided that it would be a good idea to introduce you *both* to the cognoscenti. I thought David Maskin would have filled you in on all this."

Max sat in silence. Headline: AGENT AXED BY RABID WRITER—Bloody Blade Makes Its Point.

He smiled thinly. "I'm sure he was waiting to surprise me."

"Well, that's why he scheduled this interview for today. I'm going to be your escort. I mean, that's why I'm here."

"I thought it was my cologne," Max said, growing angry.

"You might have a good time tonight, you know?"

Max glared at her.

The woman played with the beer bottle, shifting it from one hand to another. "Then again . . ."

"Do you see what I mean about my life getting screwed up? Why the hell would I want to go to this party tonight? I *hate* Eric Paine. I read most of *The Con Game* by that Carole twit last night. As a mystery writer, he's a wonderful convict."

"You didn't like it?" Debra reached for the tape recorder.

"Off the record?"

She slowly withdrew her hand. "Off the record."

"It was awful. It makes Jimmy Ammo's books read like Tolstoy. The guy is a real hack, which is also, I take it, what got him imprisoned."

"He was convicted of murdering his foster family—"

"With kitchen utensils. I'm surprised they didn't try to cop an insanity plea. 'He was exposed to James Beard at an early age.'"

"He always claimed that a long-haired drug addict broke into the house and did it."

"Right. And now he gets off because he's written a book and Eric Paine wants to see him rehabilitated."

"That, plus the fact that he was a juvenile—"

"But tried as an adult," Max added.

"—when his family was killed."

THE CON GAME

"And now little Orphan Philly will become a much-lauded—"

"Well, technically, he's an orphan. But he has a sister. A twin, I think. He went to one foster home, she went to another."

"Great. Maybe she'll show up and start writing gothic romances." Max extended his hands and began cracking his knuckles. "It's just like Paine to pull a stunt like this. Old liberal writers don't die, they just metamorphose into disciples of P. T. Barnum. Watch old Eric's next book get a hefty advance because of this bandwagon he's jumped on. It'll probably be a murder mystery."

Debra watched the burly man before her twitch uncomfortably. The anger showed in his face, yet he kept his voice controlled. The most he would allow himself to lapse into was a slight verbal sneer, a sarcastic slap.

Max Cady didn't strike her as being the lowlife she had expected.

"Why did you do it?" she suddenly asked.

"Do what?"

"Write those books?"

Max slouched in his chair and stared at the ceiling. "Oh, I don't know. I was angry and broke and hurt. The first one was really a safety valve. Once that sold I found a way to make a whole lot of money with very little brainwork. I never had money. Ever. It was a family tradition. All of a sudden I could *buy* things. You know? I never really thought about that stuff as being read by anyone. It was just something you did. You handed in typewritten pages. They handed you a check. It was magical."

He sighed and sank lower into the chair. "I wonder how many minds I poisoned? How many guys screwed up their relationships trying to swagger like Jimmy Ammo?"

He shrugged his shoulders. "I guess I'm going to pay for all that now, though."

The phone rang. "Excuse me."

Debra watched the disheveled man walk to the phone. He picked it up and held it to his ear, not saying a word. "I'll call you back later, pal. I have a few words for you that I'd like to say privately. Short, Anglo-Saxon ones."

He slammed the phone down and returned to his chair. "That was David Maskin . . . who would have been thirty-six on his next birthday."

"How will you pay?" Debra asked, ignoring the interruption.

"Pay?"

"You said now you were going to pay for all that."

Cady pulled out a stack of newspaper clippings from beneath the morning mail on the coffee table. "Look at these. They're all from the last two days' papers. They were hand-delivered this morning in one highly creative package."

Debra leafed through the stories.

Max smiled. "What's wrong with those pictures, boys and girls?"

Each photo of Max had been retouched with a ballpoint pen. His face was transformed into a bizarre death's head.

"Jesus!" Debra exclaimed.

Max reached over and removed the clippings from her hand. "From the marvelous artwork I would venture to guess that someone out there either wants to see me star in the next *Night of the Living Dead* flick or wants to see me very, very retired."

The two sat across from each other in silence.

"Wow," Debra said, feeling stupid as soon as the word hit the air.

"Wow." Max nodded. "I hope you're good at writing obituaries."

The woman stared at Cady. Cady simply smiled and heaved his shoulders up and down. "So . . . what should I wear to the party?"

She blinked.

He chuckled. "Maybe something in a nice basic black?"

CHAPTER FOUR

Max stood next to an immense potted palm in the crowded room and watched Eric Paine, the host of this highly publicized debacle, pump the hands of the invited as they wandered into his expensive Upper East Side brownstone.

"Glad to see you. Glad to see you. *So* glad to see you."

Max raised a forefinger to his lips and frowned. He had never seen a gladder guy in his life. He leaned up against a bookcase. The thin metal structure quivered under his weight. Abruptly he straightened himself, not wanting to knock any valued first editions off the shelf. He turned around. There were no books on the shelf, only boxes filled with video tapes. *Bad Girls, Deep Throat, Pumping Pup.* So, Paine was a real connoisseur of literature, eh?

Max headed for the bar as Paine continued to chant.

"So *very glad* to see you."

Eric Paine fancied himself a man's man, a contemporary Hemingway, full of the right stuff. In reality he was an active bore. His body, muscular during the compact man's thirties, was now, twenty years later, stocky and squat. His short-cropped hair was tinged with gray. His once-square jaw was bookended by jowls and his legendary, penetrating eyes now looked beady, ferretlike.

He was a writer who started off with a bang, literally, writing a novel centered around the bombing of Hiroshima way back when. Instantly lionized, his output slackened. He became a "known" commodity, a recognizable face. And so he did the talk-show circuit, playing the belligerent left-of-center artiste, ready to debate anyone on anything.

Over the years he had honed the role to perfection, sucking up to any cause popular at the time.

During the 1960s he went from pro-Castro to anti-Castro/

pro-JFK, from pro-LBJ to anti-LBJ, to pro-integration/drugs/ black power/free love/hard rock and anti-Vietnam and Nixon. The 1970s found him slacking off on his Black Panther and SDS brunches, catering more toward the needs of the back-to-basics folks. Those who knew that the old values were the best values.

Now, in the 1980s, he was dabbling in daring ideas again. Equal rights for women. Nuclear disarmament. Gay rights. And, of course, justice for all.

Which led him to Phillip Carole, an admittedly out-of-whack young lad from Baton Rouge, Louisiana, who had started corresponding with Paine while serving time for murder. Carole, tired of baring his soul to his lone surviving relative, his sister, Lucinda, began recounting the horrors of prison life to Paine in overtly graphic prose. Paine encouraged the boy to write. The boy took the encouragement and churned out a fairly grotesque exercise in thrillerdom.

The book in itself was no great shakes, but couple the book with the history of its author and you had an instant best-seller.

Paine, speaking eloquently on the boy's behalf, had him paroled at the earliest day possible.

Carole, a thin, wiry man with a pasty white face and a shock of orange-blond hair cut short, punk style, hovered around his mentor in the middle of Paine's crowded living room. The room was appropriately hi-tech. Glass and chrome stood round-shoulder to shoulder with plastic and artificial leather.

Cady stood in as darkened a corner as he could find, Debra at his side. In his hand he held a tumbler full of gin. He gazed at the sawed-off figure of Paine holding court with his guests and at his elongated, elfin protégé.

"Christ," Cady grunted, "look at them. Doesn't it remind you of a Frankenstein film?"

"Max," Debra hissed. "Be civil."

"You're kidding me," Cady replied. "Look at the people here. This gathering proves Darwin had to be wrong."

The room was filled with the trend-setters, the trend-spotters, and the trend-worshipers. The men present probably accounted for 94 percent of the blow-dryer sales in the tri-state area. The women's faces were laminated with makeup. They laughed in monotones and talked through mouths tight with tension. During casual conversations the guests' eyes would constantly dart back and forth in an almost panicky way. Were they missing anyone or anything?

Max, at the party a short twenty minutes, was already half crocked.

He leaned over the *Times* correspondent and whispered in her ear. "If I die, you can have my *National Geographic* collection."

"Are you drunk?"

"Yeah, and it doesn't help. I still feel like Jane Goodall."

"Max! Max Cady?" came a voice from over Max's shoulder.

Debra watched Max stiffen then relax as a short, roly-poly man waddled over. "Kenny," Max exclaimed, "Kenny McArthur. Jesus. How long has it been?"

The rotund man glanced down at his crotch. "Oh, it *has* been longer but, you know, with age . . ."

Max erupted into good-natured laughter.

McArthur, whose face seemed to be perpetually red anyhow, lapsed into a spasm of chuckles which turned it purple. When the two men stopped wheezing Max turned to Debra with a slightly drunken flourish.

"Debra Knightly, this is Kenny McArthur, the best city-desk editor the *Daily News* ever had."

"Pleased to meet you." The man smiled, sending a fine spray of saliva in Debra's direction. "Ooops. Sorry. When you get old your teeth sort of . . ."

"Debra works for the *Times,*" Max stated.

"I envy you your four-syllable words," Kenny said, bowing. "We have to draw the editorial line at three."

"You're lucky," Max said. "The *Post* is allowed only two."

"Yeah," Kenny countered, "but they get to run bigger pictures."

Debra found herself grinning, watching the two old warhorses hoot and holler in the middle of the orthodoxly chic crowd. "Do you still run city-side, Mr. McArthur?"

"Hell, no. I was too good so they decided to put me in charge of entertainment. Now I do movie reviews and the occasional bit of deep-dish gossip."

"I didn't think you knew anything about movies," Max said.

"I don't," the silver-haired man replied with a shrug. "But who's to know?"

Max smirked, nodding toward one of the bookcases. "Our host seems to be a real expert on certain genre films."

McArthur squinted his eyes at the stacks of boxes. "Yeah. He's a video junkie. He has some awful crap here. Legendary stuff. *I Spit On Your Grave, The Texas Chain-Saw Massacre*. Not your basic Disney fare."

McArthur gazed into the crowd. "I wouldn't have come to this shindig if you weren't being honored. Honest to God. I would never have suspected you of being Jimmy Ammo. Man, your wife used to walk all over you, Maxie. And here you are bumping off broads—you should pardon the expression, miss—in your books. Oh Christ, here comes Paine. I gotta mingle. This guy makes me sick. Shit. He has the boy-child with him too. See you later, Maxie. Nice meeting you, Miss Knightly. Slip 'em a five-syllable word next week. Onward and upward."

McArthur spun around and with remarkable dexterity maneuvered his bulbous form into the crowd.

Debra shook her head in amazement. "Was that real?"

"Uh-huh." Max nodded. "But I doubt this is."

"Max Cady, or should I say Jimmy Ammo?" Eric Paine said, extending a sweaty palm. "Delighted. Delighted. And who is this gorgeous creature at your side?"

"Oh, just something I picked up outside. There was a truck full of 'em so—"

"Debra Knightly, New York *Times*," Debra said, cutting Cady off.

Paine smiled the kind of smile used to hide abdominal spasms during a workout. "Delighted."

He nodded to his fair-haired shadow. "And here's someone I'm sure you'll want to chat with, Phillip Carole."

The thin man stepped forward. Close-up, he was even eerier than from afar. His face was waxen, unsullied by line or crevice. His hair was thick and tube-like, his lips translucent, parting only during speech or when he executed a Cheshire-cat grin. His eyes were the lightest blue Max had seen since the days of the drop-dead kids in *Village of the Damned*. He looked like an evil Peter Pan.

THE CON GAME

"Hi," Carole said awkwardly.

Max was startled into the present tense. The voice was amazingly light and upbeat. Of course Carole was still a kid. He had been in the slam since his teenaged years.

"Hi," Max said in a moment of paternalism. "Quite a bash you have going here."

Carole's mouth slid into a near sneer. "Oh. This wasn't *my* idea. It was Eric's. He's used to this shit. Not me. Normally I wouldn't be caught dead in a joint like this. There's no real feeling, you know? No passion. I mean, look at 'em."

"I have seen more animated crowds," Max admitted.

"They're like the living dead, you know? Zombies. They feed on the living, people like you and me, to keep themselves going."

Max found himself smiling in spite of himself.

"How quaint." Paine frowned, leading Debra by the arm. "Let me freshen your drink, my dear. I think these boys have a lot to talk about."

A woman Max had not noticed before calmly walked out of the crowd. Tall and pretty, with short red hair, she glided up to Paine, noted his arm around Debra's waist, and grinned in a very strange manner.

"Asshole," she whispered.

She took the glass Paine was carrying out of his hand and slowly poured the contents on his left shoe. She then handed him the empty glass and blissfully walked away. Paine seemed embarrassed, yet resigned. He glanced at Cady.

Max shrugged. "It's so hard to get good help these days."

Paine chuckled and turned to Debra. "Well, now, it looks like we *both* need a refill, eh?"

Debra allowed herself to be maneuvered out of earshot. Max stood there awkwardly.

Carole whispered conspiratorially toward Max. "I feel like I'm in stir again. I don't know anybody. I thought my sister would be here but she couldn't take the time off from work. I haven't seen her in a while . . . I think she lives nearby . . ." His voice trailed off. "I would have liked to have seen her . . . but she'll show up eventually. She always does."

Max was genuinely touched by the kid's sense of alienation.

"Man," Carole blurted, snapping out of his mood, "am I glad to meet you. When I was in the joint I used to read your stuff all the time. I really got off on it. You know? I mean, your execution scenes, the organized crime stuff? Great shit."

"Uh, thanks."

"I guess you used to see a lot of the stuff when you worked on the newspaper, right?"

"Yeah, I guess."

"Unbelievable. You lived all that stuff in your books, I bet. I mean, I guess a lot of those murders were based on the real thing. I mean, like that firebombing on the roof, where all those people were having a party. Burning bodies raining from the sky. Un-fucking-believable."

"Uh-huh."

"Did you read my book?"

"Uh, yeah. Most of it."

"What did you think?"

Max gazed into his drink for a minute. "You had some really interesting ideas in there, Mr. Carole."

"Yeah. I know. Neat splatter stuff, huh? Of course, I mean, I've never seen most of the stuff in real life. I mean, I'm just a novice compared to you, right? I saw *some* stuff doin' time but not that much. A couple of knifings, you know, with homemade shivs. A shooting. A few beatings, one fatal. We even had one guy get stuffed in a dryer in the prison laundry and that was pretty cool. But most of the stuff in the book I just made up."

"You have an interesting imagination."

"Right. Yeah. Well, I mean that's what we're all about, right?"

"I'm not sure I get you."

"Well, I mean, we take our imagination to the danger point, right? I mean, if we go over the line, that imaginary line, it's full-tilt gonzo time. Insanity. Bye-bye brain cells."

Max blinked at the gnome-faced boy.

Carole smirked and continued. "You know. It's like, the kind of stuff we write about is low-down and dirty, right? It's gross. Women getting carved up. Tortured. Sliced. Diced. But they're not allowed to die until *after* their killers get to have their jollies for a few paragraphs, get their rocks off. It's *totally* nasty. But,

THE CON GAME

man, I mean, we've all thought about doing shit like that, right? I mean, we have that passion inside of us. It's just that we have these brakes that keep us from going over that line."

"What you're saying is that we're all potential homicidal maniacs," Max concluded.

"Don't get pissed off, now. Give me a minute. Some institute in London just did a study, right? They found that the only difference between a paranoid schizophrenic and a writer was that one could use a typewriter. I'm serious. You don't believe me? Look. We all have really base desires, right? Most people bury them. Don't acknowledge them. But us? We're a little more daring. We not only acknowledge them, we spotlight 'em. We drag them out of the shadows for everyone to see. Our readers, siding with our heroes, go 'Yeah, that shit is nasty, let's kill those madmen for doin' that stuff.' I mean, that's what they tell themselves they're saying. But, really, they're getting off on reading about that violence, man. I mean, we all have that passion, man. We'd all like to do it, just once. Our books give people an escape valve. They're a way people can let off that steam so they won't pull that shit for real. But doing it for *real*, man, that's something. I wish I had read your books before . . ."

Max gaped at the boy. "Before . . ."

"Before I went to jail." The boy smiled. "I would have understood what happened to my family better. Coped with the trauma more."

Max looked directly into Carole's transparent orbs. "You're fucking nuts, you know that?"

"Not nuts enough to cop a plea. So, what did you think of the book?"

"It was different."

"And how about that hero, huh? The transsexual cop?"

"An interesting idea."

"And those showgirls getting it like that? In a thresher machine rolling down Broadway?"

"Pretty graphic."

"I read part of an anatomy book to get it right."

"It's always good to research."

"Yeah. Wait until my next book. It'll be a real slice-of-life drama. Hey, that was good, huh? *Slice* of life? It's about this guy who just snaps, man. Bingo. He goes over that line and never comes back."

Max stared at his drink. "I think I'd better get my date and hit the bricks. It's getting late and I'm pretty tired, kid."

Carole's eyes narrowed. "What's this 'kid' shit, Cady?"

"Sorry, I'm feeling very old tonight. Don't let it bother you. Now, if you'll excuse me," Max said, offering his best Brian Keith grimace.

"You can't leave yet. It's too early." Carole began to wiggle his left leg back and forth, like a child with a bladder problem. Max tried to be diplomatic.

"I'm afraid I don't have the stamina I used to. Not all of us are still as energetic as you, Phillip."

"Don't cop a superior attitude on me. You owe me. Man, if it wasn't for me, you wouldn't even have been invited tonight. I'm allowing you to share the spotlight, man."

"Well, thanks. But I'm still tired and I'm still leaving."

Carole leaned his body in toward Max. "So, how about a 'Thank you, Mr. Carole, for having me here' before you split? Didn't anyone ever teach you any manners?"

"I think we had the same teacher. Now get the fuck out of my way before I plant your carrot top into the rug."

Max moved forward, shoving the disgruntled ex-con out of the way. Carole shadowed Max's every move, like a terrier who refuses to leave his master. "What did you really think of the book, Cady? Did it shake you up? Did it make you feel jealous? Are you afraid that you've been outdone? That you're going to seem old-hat?"

Max turned around and faced the boy. "In order, punk. I hated the book. Yes, it shook me up. I thought it was sub-moronic in terms of plot, characterization, and execution. You might want to remember that verbs are action words before you write your next epic. No, I'm not jealous. No, I haven't been outdone, and for the past five years I've been trying to be old-hat. And you know what, punk? I'd rather be regarded as old-hat than *nouveau* frontal lobe."

Carole stood there, shaking, his face growing pink. Cady stared at the wild-eyed author. "Is this an alert or are we really at war?"

THE CON GAME

He left Carole shaking and strode across the room. He found Debra easily. She had watched the entire confrontation from the bar. He pointed her in the direction of the clothes closet en route to the front door.

"I take it we're leaving?"

"We are."

"I take it you didn't like Mr. Carole?"

"I didn't."

Max and Debra snatched their coats out of the closet and made their way to the door, passing Kenny McArthur, now thoroughly looped and fondling a potted palm. "Hey, Maxie, how do you like my date? An anorexic Carmen Miranda."

"Beats your last wife, Kenny. I'll call you during the week."

"I won't hold my breath."

"Good rule to live by," Max grunted.

The pair got to within ten feet of the door when they were confronted by a very concerned Eric Paine and an exceedingly agitated Phillip Carole. Paine was forcing his twitching lips into a smile. Carole simply stood and blinked rapidly at Cady, his nose still making high-pitched sounds.

"Max," Eric pouted, "Phillip tells me you were rude to him. Is that true?"

"What do you think?"

"See?" Carole whined. "He doesn't *respect* me. He doesn't empathize." Paine's protégé seemed under the influence of something stronger than most drugs . . . like maybe mind-control rays from another planet.

Paine attempted to mollify his ward, placing a protective arm around Carole's shoulders. He turned to Max. "Max, Phillip has had a very rough life. As a child he was shuttled from foster home to foster home. His stepparents were cruel to him. Then there were the murders. The notoriety. The trial. The sentence."

"And now the instant fame." Max nodded. "Tough break."

"I've *suffered!*" Carole declared.

"You and 90 percent of the white pages, kid. You want my laundry list? My parents died while I was in service in Korea. Never got to go to their funeral."

"I'm not listening," Carole pouted, placing his hands dramatically over his ears.

"I saw heavy combat. I have more metal in my legs than you'll find in most of today's cars. I've gone through two wives. I've flushed away most of the money I've made in gin mills. You getting all this down?"

"I'm not listening."

"Yeah. Life is tough . . . but always interesting."

Max headed for the door, leaving Carole fuming.

"Why don't you just retire again? I'll be the best, Cady," Carole yelled abruptly. "I'll be better than the best. And you're going to help me! You . . . my teacher!"

"You make friends easily." Debra nodded, putting her hand on the doorknob.

"Yeah. I attract goal-oriented people."

"BUTCHER! BUTCHER!"

"Huh?" Max Cady stared into the angry eyes of fifty pickets outside of Eric Paine's town house as Debra swung the door open wide.

The picketers, mostly women, jeered as the twosome slipped down the front stairs and made their way toward the street.

"INFLICT PAIN ON ERIC PAINE!"

"BETTER DEAD THAN READ!"

"Who are these people?" Max hissed as they double-timed it away from Paine's home.

"Victims' righters. Some of the picketers are relatives of Carole's foster family . . . his victims. The rest are members of support groups. They're furious with Paine for getting Carole out."

"Forget his past crimes. He should be put back in for his personality," Max said, slipping into his overcoat.

Behind them a window shattered.

"END ALL PAINE," the picketers chanted.

"Sounds like Eric is at the top of their hit list." Max smirked.

"They're pretty harmless," Debra said. "Just noisy. Here comes a cab."

A Yellow Checker Cab barreled across East Eighty-ninth Street. Max raised an arm to flag him down. Something fell out of his coat.

"What's this?" Debra said, stooping to pick up the fallen parcel.

"I don't know," Max said. He held the package in his hand. It was a tattered copy of his first book, *Murder Me, Murder You*. "Someone must have slipped it in my coat when it was hung up. I sure didn't bring it with me."

"Maybe it's someone's idea of a joke."

The cab pulled up to the curb. The two examined the book closely. "There's no note. No anything," Max said.

"Hey," the cab driver called. "Are you two gonna read that fuckin' book by the light of the silvery moon or get in the cab?"

Max jammed the book back in his overcoat and held the door open for Debra. He climbed inside the cab. The cab driver was staring at Max hard. He bore a striking resemblance to Mr. Potato Head.

"Something wrong?" Max asked.

"Hey, ain't you that Jimmy Ammo guy?"

"Uh, sort of."

"Sort of my ass! I'm pleased to meet you, Jimmy. I read your stuff when I was in the seminary. Fuckin' great."

"Seminary?"

"Yeah. I dropped out. Saw one of the maids bend over dustin' one day. It was good-bye Jesus and hello Hefner."

Max said nothing, too numb at this point in the evening to be startled by anything. "Hmm."

"Where to, Jimmy? It's on the house." The cabbie pushed the off-duty sign atop his cab.

The cab darted off, Debra chuckling at Max's discomfort, Max staring suspiciously both at the book in his hand and the cabbie singing the praises of the Jimmy Ammo school of literary know-how.

"Hey, remember that time you was cornered by those strippers with switch-blade tassles?"

"Hmm," Max replied, fingering the book uneasily.

As the car sped off toward Midtown, Max no longer heard the chants of the picketers. He regretted the last two drinks at the party. His mind was spinning. It would be a tough drive home. His head was on fire. The cab slowed to a stop on East Thirty-first. Max allowed himself to be kissed on the cheek as his companion darted from the vehicle.

Max watched Debra Knightly trot up the front steps to the

drab building she lived in. After she got safely inside he motioned the cab driver forward. "Let's go to Port Authority."

"Taking a bus home, Jimmy?"

"Uh-uh, my car is parked there."

"Betcha you drive a real sporty model, huh? A real ace's vehicle, Porsche? Mazda? Subaru? Vette?"

"Uh-huh," Max said.

The cab pulled up in front of Port Authority. Max paid the driver and took the escalator to the parking level. Finding his car, he slid into the front seat and rested his head on the steering wheel. His forehead felt like it was burning. He clamped his eyes shut and wished for the pain to go away. He lapsed into unconsciousness.

By sunrise Eric Paine was also battling to stay awake. More precisely, to stay alive.

His brain had been smashed, effectively disconnecting his sense of concentration. He lay twitching in his study, his arms outstretched, his mouth still spurting gibberish as well as pieces of plastic ingested when the computer display terminal had hurtled into his face.

Blood spurted from his neck. He felt himself deflating.

He shuddered and shook on the floor as the figure above him lifted a computer printer high into the air. Taking careful aim, the figure let the printer plummet toward the floor.

Paine's body shuddered one last time as the sound of bone and plastic splintering filled the room.

Max blinked as the sun began filtering through the morning clouds. He squinted through the windshield at the skyline before him. How long had he been out? He started up the car and chugged away from Port Authority, a bad taste in his mouth and a worse feeling in his stomach.

By the time Max got out of his 1963 Chevy Impala (white with a blue fender) in front of his New Jersey abode, the squad cars were already screaming toward the residence of the late Eric Paine.

CHAPTER FIVE

"Hey, you're a star!"

"I don't know about that, but I am hung over."

David Maskin marched into Cady's house carrying three newspapers neatly folded under his arm. He walked into the living room and carefully sat down on the sofa, neatly missing the piles of dirty clothing strewn about the cushions. He then spread the newspapers out on the coffee table, avoiding any stains that looked new and possibly wet.

"Congratulations. You made every newspaper this morning. Two gossip columns and an actual new item in the "Around the City" column in the New York *Times*. You upstaged Paine's little yahoo but good, Max."

Max stumbled into the kitchen, rubbing his eyes in a vain attempt to exorcise his headache. He had already consumed his weight in Tylenol that morning and nothing seemed to be helping. His stomach was behaving like a Cuisinart and he felt like he could mow his mouth. He had to remember never to mix gin with apricot sours. He had lost nearly six hours last night. Passed out like a common drunk.

"What did the newspapers say about me?" Cady asked.

"Oh, the usual stuff. You know, about how this veteran mystery writer totally unnerved this psycho-killer-turned-author-of-the-hour at his own coming-out party. The *Times* was straight news. The *Post* said you were right out of another time period, you know *The Maltese Falcon* era, but the *News* . . . boy, did they go crazy. Listen to this. 'When Max Cady, a.k.a. Jimmy Ammo, entered the room it was all over for the kid as well as the herd of social butterflies that flapped around him. Ammo, who cut his teeth as a crime reporter before the days of personality journalism, was the *real thing*. It showed. It may have been Phillip Carole's party but it was Ammo's showcase. With a few well-placed words and a shrug of the shoulders, the two-fisted Ammo reduced the ex-con to Jell-O. Ammo's lethal verbal delivery plus his resemblance to Robert Mitchum gave the evening a touch of . . .' "

Cady plopped two Alka-Seltzers into a glass of club soda and laughed. "Who wrote that?"

"A guy named McArthur . . ."

"Figures."

Cady sat down in his armchair with a sigh. "That was a pretty sick party, David."

"Run-of-the-mill from what I hear."

"No. I mean it. There was something weird going on there. I'm not sure what but it just wasn't healthy, you know?"

"Doesn't matter. I heard you held your own through some pretty tacky stuff."

"Who told you that, Debra?"

"Oh, it's Debra now, huh? Yeah. She called this morning to apologize for all those nasty things she said about you yesterday. She's quite impressed. . . . So am I."

Max guzzled the drink. "Well, to be honest, I did enjoy myself in a perverse way. I mean, I was acting the voyeur and all but it felt good to go a few rounds with that punk, verbally spar. I've been giving tests so long in school, I've forgotten how it feels to be the victim of a spot quiz. You know, realizing that you're going to have to answer in a minute but not knowing what the question is going to be or . . . worse yet . . . if it's one of the questions you've prepared for? It was an interesting experience."

"They'll be plenty more of those coming up, Max. This is just the beginning."

"Slow down, David. I'm not quite ready to be a literary freak as yet. Let's see what happens after the *Times* story, okay?"

Max reached over to the coffee table and removed a book from beneath the newspapers. "Oh yeah. I've been meaning to ask you. How long has this little gem been out of print?"

He tossed *Murder Me, Murder You* onto Maskin's lap. His agent picked it up. "Geeze. This one has been through the mill. I don't know. This particular edition is about ten years old. See? It has the lower cover price on it. They reissued it one last time with a higher cover price before shredding it three years ago. Where did you get it?"

"Someone palmed it on me last night. Stuck it in my overcoat while I was mingling."

"Mangling from what I heard."

"Well, like I said, spot quizzes can be—"

Cady's phone rang.

Maskin glanced at it, frowning. "You're going to have to get yourself an answering machine, Max. Pretty soon your phone will be ringing off the hook. It'll wreak hell on your concentration."

"No it won't," Max said, picking up the receiver. "I never concentrate anymore."

Cady cradled the phone. His face slowly drained of its color as he listened to what the caller had to say. He responded with a weak "Of course. I understand. I'll be there as soon as I can. Two hours at the outset."

He gently put the phone back in the receiver. "Shit," he hissed.

"What is it?"

Max walked into the kitchen and dumped two more Alka-Seltzers into a glass. "They found Eric Paine an hour ago. Someone decided to rearrange his hairline with his word processor. His head was effectively placed inside his video display terminal."

"Christ."

"The police want me to pay them a visit."

"What for?"

"I was at the party, right? They want to ask me questions."

"About what?"

Max tossed the drink back and belched. "What do you think? About old Eric and his untimely merger with IBM. They say it's just routine . . ."

Max hesitated before entering the bathroom for a shave. "So . . ."

"So?"

"So why do I feel that I'm in deep shit?"

CHAPTER SIX

When Samuel Lehner was a little boy he wanted to become a priest. Since Samuel Lehner's parents were Orthodox Jews, however, that idea did not go over really big in the old homestead. So, after graduating from college with a bachelor's degree in criminology, he decided to become a cop.

Twenty years later, he still wishes he had become a priest.

His precinct was located in a fairly upscale area of Manhattan. This meant he had to deal with a lot of high-rent homicides, murders involving victims who simply didn't associate with the known criminal (low-rent) element—upwardly mobile types who wouldn't know a food stamp from an Express Mail package. He found himself in the unsatisfying position, more often than not, of not sympathizing with the victims at all. Most of them struck him as being priggish human beings who flouted their wealth or their status one time too many in the presence of a psychopathic lout and paid the consequences.

Columbo he was not.

Lehner sat at his desk and gazed at the photos taken at the scene of the Paine murder.

"In glorious color," Lehner muttered, shuffling through the stack. Paine had been struck over the head by a video display terminal, his face smashing through the plastic screen. Shards apparently severed his jugular vein. Making sure that Paine would not escape from the computer crime in merely serious condition, his killer had then picked up the heavy computer printer and dropped it on the head of the dying author.

"Bull's-eye," Lehner grunted, running a hand over his salt-and-pepper beard.

The lieutenant sighed and slumped in his chair. He didn't like this one. He couldn't say why but he didn't like it at all. There was something *more* here than just murder. He could feel it at

THE CON GAME

the base of his spine, an uneasy twinge. Either he was onto something or it was going to rain. Lehner turned his chair toward his office window, looking out onto a ramshackle courtyard. He caught a glimpse of his own reflection. His once-pretty-boy good looks, under the influence of too many years, too little sleep, and a jaundice-tinged fluorescent light bulb overhead, now resembled the portrait of Dorian Gray.

One of these days he had to take up racketball.

He swung his chair back to the glass partition separating his cubicle from the rest of the precinct. He wondered why, even though they were located in a well-to-do area, the precinct house looked like a cesspool. Cracked walls. Peeling ceilings. Piss-yellow paint.

He glanced at the photos on his desk again.

The problem with the Paine case was that Lehner had too many suspects. Nobody really liked the guy, from his wife to the kid who delivered the newspaper.

On the night of the murder there had been at least twenty party guests who had argued with Paine in his own living room while, outside, a group of fifty wild-eyed picketers chanted slogans encouraging Paine to take a one-way trip to Valhalla. Someone smashed a window in Paine's home with a brick. Paine's house guest, a convicted murderer, had almost put out his lights in front of representatives from the New York press, and Paine's wife had compared him with various sections of the male anatomical chart in between pouring drinks on the poor bastard.

Nope, Mr. Paine was not at the top of anyone's popularity poll.

Lehner's men had been taking statements all morning. Most of the party guests were treating Paine's murder as simply an act of bad taste. Something along the lines of, how could Eric have let this happen?

Lehner smirked at the thought. Yeah. Rich people occasionally get offed, too, folks. Not just welfare recipients.

Outside Lehner's office, Max Cady sat alongside Debra Knightly.

"I understand it was pretty gruesome," Debra whispered,

watching an assortment of expensive call girls and perfectly coiffed shoplifters being shuttled from desk to desk.

"Murder is like that," Cady offered. "Very seldom do people clean up afterward. Bad hygiene."

"My, aren't we testy today."

"Hey. I'm becoming a favorite around here," Max groused, looking at his watch. "I've already been interviewed twice. By two detectives who, together, might possess the intelligence of Inspector Clouseau."

"What kinds of questions did they ask?"

"Real thought-provoking ones. You know, like 'Did you notice anything unusual at the party last night?' 'Did you witness Mr. Paine engaging in any unusual activities?' 'Was there a midget in the punch bowl with a snorkel?' "

"What?"

"I made that last one up . . . although I think there might have been. I detected the faint bouquet of Dr. Scholl's foot powder in the glass I had."

"You handle pressure well." Knightly smirked.

A calm and totally in-control woman in her mid-thirties left an adjoining office escorted by a plainclothes detective. Her face was pale and drawn, which served to accent her fiery red hair.

"There's the ice queen from last night," Cady said. "The woman with the leaky drink."

"Mrs. Eric Paine."

"You're kidding. She's a knockout! Is she a model? How did he ever latch on to her?"

"She's not *that* pretty."

Cady grunted as a disheveled Phillip Carole, his eyes moist and puffy, stumbled from another room. A woman detective escorted him to the front door. "Horrible," Carole mumbled to no one in particular. "Horrible."

"He's taking Eric's death pretty hard," Debra noted.

"Not as hard as Eric." Cady shrugged.

Lehner exited his office, pushing his long hair back off his forehead. "Maxwell Cady?"

Cady eased himself out of the bench. "Yes, sir."

"Lieutenant Sam Lehner, Homicide. And you're . . ."

"Debra Knightly, New York *Times.*"

THE CON GAME

Lehner rolled his eyes heavenward. Great. This is just what he needed. A reporter. "You will remember, Miss Knightly, that you are here to voluntarily give a statement and not to get one from anyone in my office?"

"Yes, Lieutenant."

"Fine. Detective Carson will talk with you in her office. Mr. Cady, will you come with me?"

Cady did as he was told, shambling after the diminutive lieutenant. "Close the door, Mr. Cady."

Cady shut the door leading to the squad room and sat down in front of Lehner's desk.

The bearded cop rubbed his bloodshot eyes and sighed. "We'll make this brief, Mr. Cady. We have about four dozen statements describing the party last night."

"I think three dozen of them came from me. I've been here for two hours."

"Sorry for the inconvenience. These investigations are a pain in the ass. But I don't have to tell you about that. You're a veteran of the crime wars, right? Newspaper beat and all? Night-side?"

"I remember, Lieutenant."

"At this point I really don't have to deal with generalities concerning Paine's party. I have a very good idea of what went on. I gather that you didn't enjoy yourself last night."

Cady slumped in his chair and rested his chin on the palm of his left hand. "Oh, in a perverse way, I suppose I did."

"Explain."

"It was like being at a circus, you know? Surrounded by performers and clowns."

"Did you consider Mr. Paine a clown?"

"Top quality."

"Do you know anyone who would want to see him dead?"

"The book review editor of the New York *Times,* for one."

"Murder isn't funny, Mr. Cady."

"Depends on who is killed."

"Eric Paine died last night in a very violent manner."

"Look. Lieutenant. Let me make this simple for you. I didn't know Eric Paine long enough to dislike him. I never enjoyed his writing enough to read it. I never was attracted to his kind of life-style and I'm not crazy about the crowd he ran with. I think his ex-con protégé is a loon and the only reason I was at his party was because of my agent and the fact that there wasn't anything all that good on television. Ms. Knightly was with me because she's putting a story together for her paper concerning mystery writers."

"She was with you the entire time?"

"Uh-huh. I dropped her off at her apartment before I drove home to New Jersey."

Lehner stared at Cady. His face registered no emotion. "Do you know how Paine died?"

"Uh-huh. I read it in the paper on the way over. Became one with his computer console, right?"

"That's right. Pretty nasty. We figure that he knew his assailant. There was no sign of a struggle in his study and, frankly, I can't imagine how he would allow a stranger carrying a computer to get close enough to clobber him."

"I can't imagine letting a *friend* carrying a computer get close enough to clobber me."

"We haven't figured that out yet," Lehner said, waving a hand in the air for emphasis.

Cady glanced at his watch. "It's finding those little details that makes your job so interesting, Lieutenant."

"I find it so, Mr. Cady. Well, I guess that's about it. If we need anything else we'll call you."

Cady got up and shook hands with Lehner . . . and waited. If he knew cops as well as he thought he did, Lehner, now that he had thoroughly baited Max, would let the other shoe drop before Max got to the door. Max didn't even get two feet away from the desk before Lehner launched into his big finale.

"Mr. Cady, did Eric Paine's murder strike a familiar note with you?"

Cady stood, half facing the exit. "No. This is the first murder by computer I've ever encountered, if you don't count the movie *Westworld.*"

"Those were robots."

"Good movie, though," Cady continued.

Lehner casually reached into his drawer and pulled out a copy of *Murder Me, Murder You.* "I was catching up with my

THE CON GAME

reading this morning," he said. "I love the ending to this. The way Jimmy Ammo manages to stop that publisher from murdering his assistant?"

Cady stared at the lieutenant.

"Yeah." Lehner nodded. "Smashing him over the head with his own typewriter. Sort of poetic justice, don't you think?"

Cady nodded dumbly.

"By the way, your neighbor, nice fellow, said that you didn't get home until a little after six A.M. this morning."

"That's right."

"But you left the party a little after eleven P.M."

"I had too much to drink last night. I slept it off in my car. I was parked in the lot at Port Authority. I took a cab. The driver will—"

"The driver has. He dropped you off at approximately eleven-thirty. He may even face a disciplinary charge for taking you off the meter."

"Uh-huh."

Lehner smiled. "We'll call you if we need anything else, Mr. Cady."

Cady left the office numb from the forehead down. No doubt about it. He was definitely in deep shit.

CHAPTER SEVEN

Max pulled his dilapidated Impala into a series of potholes that passed for a parking space on West 103rd Street. Twisting the wheel to get closer to the curb, Max worked some unexpected, macabre mechanical magic that set the car's horn blaring. He sighed and finished maneuvering the car as a crowd of gangly kids gathered around his battered auto.

The unexpected visitations from the Impala's banshee horn were growing more and more frequent. Max didn't know what caused them. He didn't really care. They were simply another pain in the butt to be endured and dealt with.

Max climbed out of the car, walked to a spot directly in front of the hood, raised a titanic right fist, and brought it down heavily on the auto.

Whooommmp.

The horn sputtered to a stop.

Headline: MAN BEATS MACHINE—Chevy Threatens Suit in Battery Case.

The crowd of kids cheered Max. Max smiled smugly and acknowledged their huzzahs. He walked to the front of his daughter's brownstone apartment building. His right hand was exploding inwardly in pain. Heroism was such a nasty business.

Max entered the front hallway and paused before a brown door spattered with white graffiti. He leaned on the buzzer. A tiny blond woman in her mid-twenties opened the door.

"What was the commotion outside?"

Max kissed her on the forehead and walked into the plant-littered duplex. "An Olympian battle, Cady versus cogs, fought to the death in front of a half-dozen kids who probably, at this very instant, are stripping my car of its hubcaps."

"Dad, the neighborhood isn't that bad. It's getting better all the time. Really."

"Yeah. I noticed you're getting a new breed of quiche-eating rat up here these days. You have any ice?"

"You want a drink to go with it?"

"Yeah. A drink. Plus some ice for my hand."

"What did you do? It looks like a balloon."

"I've been like this ever since I saw *The Elephant Man*. The kiddo around?"

"She's at the day-care center."

"Oh." Max pushed and prodded the pillows of the bright yellow sofa into submission and slumped down as far as he could go without burrowing into the basement.

"How's the renovation coming? Have you started working on the back apartment yet?"

"Haven't had the time."

"This will be a nice place someday," Max grunted. "I hope they let me out of the old folk's home to see it when it's finished."

Max's daughter mixed a drink silently. Sara Clerey had inherited her father's personality. She was exasperatingly stubborn. And the two of them together could push taciturn to new and uncharted areas. The best measure of how far they'd gone were the many shades of purple Maxwell Cady's face assumed.

Today, however, Sara decided not to push it.

Something was wrong.

Max sat on the sofa and stared meaningfully at the beige wall in front of him. His face was a twitching mass of nerves.

Sara handed him the drink. "You want to talk about it?"

"Not in depth. I just came from a police station. I was at Eric Paine's last night."

"Whooops. I read about his murder today."

"'Whooops' is right. The lieutenant in charge of the investigation sees a similarity between the way Paine bought the farm and the way Jimmy Ammo sold one to a slime merchant in one of my old novels."

Sara stared at Max. "So?"

"So? So he practically said I was a suspect. That's *so*."

Max began massaging his forehead absentmindedly. "I should have moved to Tahiti or somewhere exotic after the divorce, you know? This Jimmy Ammo stuff is coming back to haunt me in a major way."

"Well, you *did* write those books . . ."

"Yeah, I know. But give a guy credit. Evolution didn't stop when the first fish wiggled onto the beach and discovered tanning butter. I just want people to lay off. I called Maskin today to tell him that I'm an official suspect, that I'm worried about going to jail, and you know what he says? *You know what he says?*"

"No."

"He says, 'What a great publicity angle!' That's what he says."

"You're kidding."

"Do I sound like I'm kidding? Jesus, he's thick. If there's an idea in his head, it's in solitary confinement."

"Don't you think you're overreacting, Dad? This is an isolated incident. The lieutenant was probably only thinking out loud."

Max relaxed his jaw slightly. "You're probably right. But there's something *funny* about all this. I don't trust Paine's little fawn, that Carole guy. I peg him for a nut case."

"Do you think he murdered Paine?"

"I don't know."

"He'd have to be a nut case to kill his one public champion."

"Yeah, I suppose. Do you have everything planned for Peggy's party?"

"To the last detail. The problem is trying to round up all the food and favors. The Toyota is acting up again."

"Acting up how?"

"It just sputters and stalls for no apparent reason."

"Get the damned thing fixed!"

"Who can afford to?"

"Look, Sara. This isn't the neighborhood to be driving around in in the little Toyota that couldn't!"

"I'll have it checked out soon, Dad."

"Deadbeat skip an alimony check again?"

"Uh-huh."

"The prick."

"At least he's consistent."

Max straightened his frame and reached in his back pocket for his wallet. "Look, I'll write you a check to tide you over—"

"I won't take charity, Dad. I'm an independent adult."

"You're barely older than your kid!"

"You can be so charming at times. No money, Dad. I'll make it on my own."

Max sat in the sofa, his mind trying to come up with a compromise. "Tell you what. If you won't take money, take my car."

Sara blinked at her father.

Max smiled, pulling out the keys. "The car looks like hell but it runs fine. The worst thing that happens is the horn gets stuck. Just pull over and pound on the hood. No problem."

He tossed his daughter the keys. "I don't drive all that much, so I can deal with the Toyota until your check arrives. Agreed?"

"Well . . ."

"Fine. Now give me your keys and I'll be off. I have an appointment with a very pretty lady at a very pompous newspaper."

Sara produced a set of multicolored car keys on a rabbit's-foot key chain. "Are you going to be all right, Dad?"

"Of course I am," he said, walking to the door. "I've gotten through some rough times before. You can slow me down but you can't derail me."

Max kissed his daughter and ran out of her building. He trotted up to her tiny green car parked in front of his, stepped inside, and turned the key.

Nothing happened.

He cranked the key again. Silence. He fed the car gas. No dice. He tried putting the car in neutral before turning the key. No response. He pumped the gas pedal until he was sure the engine was flooded. He cursed the man who had invented the auto. He cursed the country of Japan. He cursed himself for writing those idiotic Ammo books when psychotherapy would have caused him far less grief in the long run. He cursed the gaggle of kids who were standing across the street watching the giant red-faced man bellowing in the small, exceedingly stationary green car.

Finally, in an act of desperation, he pulled his aching right fist back and sent it slamming into the dashboard.

The car rumbled and shook ominously.

Cady turned the key.

The car still didn't start but the radio did and he got to spend the next five minutes parked on West 103rd Street listening to Linda Ronstadt singing "Blue Bayou."

As a police car pulled up and two gorilla-faced officers emerged to check out the strange man in the parked car, Max realized that the gods were conspiring against him.

He had never liked Linda Ronstadt either.

CHAPTER EIGHT

"You're late."

"I had to get jump-started by two cops."

"I had you pegged as kinky from the start."

Max slid into a chair in the dimly lit Poor Richard's Pub in Midtown. He had frequented the place years ago when he was still working at the paper. It was on the same block as The Museum of Modern Art so, in those halcyon years, he could get smashed and take in some of the finer works of contemporary painting on the same afternoon. He used to get so looped back then that Picasso's paintings struck him as being slice-of-life.

Amazingly enough, the people who ran Poor Richard's remembered him with fondness.

Funny what time can do to cloud perception.

The whole block had changed drastically in a few years. The museum now had an ugly building attached to its top housing equally obnoxious dwellers, people with money to burn who didn't blink at spending a million or two on a small, one-bedroom apartment. Somewhere along the line the concept of neighborhood had gone down the tubes.

"I traded my car for my daughter's. Mobility isn't one of its strong points," he told Debra Knightly.

The twosome ordered drinks. Debra began talking about her morning. Max mentally left the conversation and scanned the clientele. Young hipster executives hitting on heavily made-up career women. Secretaries from Lonk Island with hairdos emulating Elsa Lanchester's tonsorial splendor in *Bride of Frankenstein*. Receding hairlines with potbellies. Face-lifts and chin-tucks. All highly animated. All as totally removed from reality as one would want to imagine without direct guidance from Fellini.

"Are you listening to me?"

Max blinked twice. "Sorry. I'm still in a daze."

"I didn't know Paine's death shook you so much."

"It didn't. It doesn't. It's just that . . . well, suddenly, I find myself starting from scratch, from square one. I was just a teacher until three days ago. Now I'm something *else*. Jeez. I feel like the oldest adolescent in existence, just sort of gallumphing around, trying to figure out which foot goes before the other. I'm also a little drunk."

"So I figured."

"One drink on an empty stomach will do it every time."

"Feel free to make it two. I'm on an expense account."

"Right. You'd love to see me get really plastered . . . so I could expose my innermost secrets. Tell you about the years I spent with Elizabeth Taylor and her wildebeests."

"What?"

"Okay. I've never met Elizabeth Taylor. But I *have* hung out with wildebeests quite a bit."

"Eric Paine is being buried tomorrow."

Max sat, glumly, as a waitress placed a menu before him. "I suppose I'm supposed to attend the festivities?"

"It would be a nice gesture."

"I suppose you want to escort me?"

"It would be a nice story."

"Right." Max ordered and downed a double shot of tequila.

A small man dressed in coveralls walked over to the table. "Mr. Cady?"

Max stared at the man. "Yes?"

"Mr. Maxwell Cady?"

"Maxwell Norvell if you must know."

"I have a package for you, sir. Will you sign, please?" A pad and a pen were thrust in Max's direction. He signed and was handed a manila envelope.

Max placed the envelope next to his drink. Debra was intrigued. "Aren't you going to open it?"

Max stared at the envelope. "I don't think so."

"Come on, be a sport."

Max picked up the envelope with great trepidation.

Headline: HACK WRITER VICTIM OF LETTER BOMB —Literary Purists Defense Front Claims First Victim.

THE CON GAME

He ripped open the top of the envelope and pulled out a magazine.

Knightly gaped at the parcel. *"Vogue?"*

"And, me, not a subscriber."

"I don't understand."

"Let's see. That is definitely my name on the envelope, so there's no mistake about that. I guess someone really wants me to have this complimentary issue of *Vogue.*"

"But why?"

"If you really want to tax your brain, try to figure out who would know I was meeting you here for lunch."

Debra Knightly frowned.

Max grinned. "Everyone knows what I'm doing except me. Now do you see why I'm so confused?"

Confused and more than a little apprehensive.

Max tossed the magazine onto the table and picked up the menu again. If someone was trying to drive him crazy, they weren't doing too bad a job of it.

CHAPTER NINE

Max didn't like funerals, finding solace only in the fact that he was better off attending one than being the guest of honor. He stood uncomfortably in the old stone structure of St. Andrew's on the Upper East Side as a Catholic priest took possession of the pulpit and began extolling the virtues of Eric Paine. Within a few minutes it was clear that the man was bucking for a Pulitzer in fiction.

Debra Knightly gazed at the large, ornate statues of the saints perched in oval cubbyholes throughout the church. She was more than a little angry with Max. He had been late picking her up for the Mass. Actually, he was lucky to have made it into the city at all.

Halfway through the Lincoln Tunnel, the Toyota had decided that it was allergic to exhaust fumes and would not be able to function in an enclosed environment filled with said fumes.

As Max was towed out of the tunnel he tried to be philosophical about it all. What he would spend on towing charges he would save on gasoline bills.

The Toyota eventually sputtered up to Debra's house forty-five minutes late. Luckily, the hearse carrying the computerized remains of Paine had gotten caught in traffic in the Garment District and, so, the entire circus had begun late.

As the priest rumbled ever onward Max took note of the crowd. Most of the people resembled professional mourners, the types found in small villages throughout Europe who, for a few lira or pounds or marks, would follow the casket to its final resting place and wail at Concorde-jet volume every so often. The louder the sobs, the more numerous the sobbers, the more respected the deceased.

St. Andrew's had more than its share of sobbers this day. Maybe Paine owed a lot of people a lot of money.

THE CON GAME

Leading the hyperventilation crowd was Phillip Carole, whose high-pitched squeaks were loud enough to break the concentration of the priest at the pulpit.

Also wiping tears from their eyes were various editors, beautiful people, and restaurant owners.

About the only person in the crowd showing an appropriate response, in Max's opinion, was the widow, young Mrs. Paine, who stared, stoically, at the King Kong-sized crucifix on the altar.

Max allowed his mind to wander as the priest finished up the eulogy and said a few prayers over the closed coffin. Max wondered if Paine would wind up in heaven or hell. More than likely the son of a bitch would, through some heavenly oversight, elude the flames of eternal perdition and wind up in purgatory.

Ah, purgatory. That wonderful Catholic cop-out. That never-never land somewhere between paradise and eternal damnation. A way station where tarnished souls worked off their lifetimes of sin in some undocumented fashion. Maybe doing menial work for the folks in heaven.

"Oh, Beulah, peel me a grape . . ."

Max remembered the wonderful sense of spookiness he had associated with purgatory when he was a kid. It was sort of an officially sanctioned haunted house, filled with poor souls who yearned to break free.

Once a year, on All Souls' Day, if all good Catholic school children said enough prayers, individual souls would be sprung by the BVM, the Blessed Virgin Mary. Max had always pictured her with a shopping cart, tooling up and down the aisles of purgatory, picking up a half dozen souls here, a half dozen there, and taking them back to heaven with her.

Double-bagged.

Oh well. It beat the hell out of limbo. Limbo was where good little babies who hadn't been baptized went after death. Limbo was a nowhere-land that was permanent. No way they were ever going to get to heaven. They didn't have the credentials. But they weren't heathens, either, so they didn't merit hell. And so those souls just hung out, for all eternity, in a very ordinary, very boring place. The Catholic Church's version of Los Angeles.

Max blinked twice as the ceremony came to an end with a few amens, hallelujahs, and whoop-de-doos. As he shambled out of the church, Debra Knightly on his arm, he wondered if he would go to heaven or hell after his death. He sure wouldn't wind up in purgatory. He was doing time there now.

"Are you up for the cemetery?" Debra asked.

"Nah. I always associate them with those old horror movies, you know? I keep thinking I'll meet Ygor or the Wolfman or Reagan."

"Well, I think I should go along for the story."

"Fine. I'll drive home, Emperor Toho willing." He glanced at his watch. "It's Friday and it's still pretty early. Maybe I can catch *Gumby* or *The Little Rascals* on TV."

"What about our interview?"

"Maybe we can pick it up tomorrow . . . unless you take weekends off."

Knightly walked toward the curb. "I work seven days a week, thanks. You know, if it's easier for you, you can crash at my apartment for the next couple of days. I have a fold-out couch and we could do the interviews casually."

Max crinkled his nose and gazed down at the reporter. "Is that a proposition?"

"Not much of one."

"I take what I can get these days."

"Jimmy Ammo wouldn't approve. This is totally platonic."

Max squinted into the sun as the hearse pulled away. "Naaah. That's okay. I don't think I'd like staying in Manhattan. It's too frantic. People spin around like tops here. No direction."

"I can't believe it. A *snob* from New Jersey!"

Max had the uneasy suspicion he was being watched . . . possibly by Paine's killer. As he maneuvered Knightly toward a cab he casually glanced over his shoulder. He *was* being watched, all right. The problem was that he was being watched by the kind of crowd usually reserved for Superbowl Sunday.

TV reporters aimed their cameras in his direction. Lieutenant Lehner and a few of his flunkies stood in the background trying desperately not to be noticed. Phillip Carole, his bug eyes looking like the hero's from *Return of the Fly,* gaped at Max. Paine's

THE CON GAME

widow gave him a Medusa stare. Even his agent was in the crowd, smirking at the media coverage.

Max watched as the cab carrying Debra to Paine's permanent resting place disappeared down the street. He then slipped behind the church and, with a little bit of coaxing and a lot of prayer, managed to get the Toyota's engine to turn over.

Before entering the Lincoln Tunnel, he made a pit stop at a bar on Tenth Avenue. It was seedy and dark. His head ached and his stomach was tight. He had a tequila sunrise with no ice. The throbbing in his head eased a little. He had another drink. Then another. And another.

He hadn't tossed them back like this in years. He had to watch it. In his last months at the newspaper this kind of drinking had caused Max quite a few problems. Suddenly he felt very old and very tired. He walked to a table next to the jukebox and fell asleep.

Vague, shadowy images invaded his thoughts. Blood was pouring. People were screaming. Hands clutched Jimmy Ammo's trench coat.

The next thing he knew he was behind the wheel of his car. He was heading for the tunnel. Max shook his head from side to side. It was amazing what the human body could do on automatic pilot.

He made the half-hour drive to his New Jersey home in a zippy seventy minutes, stumbled into his living room, and fell asleep on the couch. His sleep was disturbed by a knocking on the door.

Max lurched toward the door and yanked it open. A fresh-faced messenger handed him a package.

"Sign here."

Max did so. The kid took the receipt and stared at it. "Hey, aren't you Robert Mitchum?"

"Nah. Mickey Rooney. I've been taking steroids."

Max shut the door and carried a manila envelope into the living room. It was five o'clock.

He opened the envelope. Inside was a copy of the new edition of Max's second Jimmy Ammo novel, *Better Than the Best.*

Max began thumbing through it.

At 5:25 the phone rang. It was Debra Knightly.

"Turn on the news on channel two. Hurry. There's a bulletin."

Max did so, leaving the phone off the hook. Jamie Soon, New York's leading fashion model, had been found murdered. More details to follow as the channel two news team gathered the story.

Max picked up the phone. "I don't get it."

"That *Vogue* magazine yesterday? That was Jamie on the cover."

Max pondered that. "What do you know about the murder?"

"Nothing. I'm home. I'm on my way to the office, though."

"I'll call you in half an hour."

"Right."

Max sighed and slowly dialed the *Daily News*. "Kenny McArthur, please."

Silence.

McArthur's voice oozed out of the phone in a tone of mock civility. "Drawma—"

"Kenny, it's Max. Are you drunk?"

"Nah. A long lunch."

"How long?"

"Seven shots. Maybe eight. I drink them for the vitamin C. Those lemon slices are very healthful."

"How close are you to city-side?"

"About fourteen feet away."

"What have you heard about this model murder?"

"You want what's going to be in the paper or the gory details?"

"Details."

"Jamie Soon. Age twenty-four. She was found in the basement of a professional building, the one her agency is located in. Stripped. Killed with her own clothing. Garroted with a stocking. Beaten with high-heel shoes."

"Rape?"

"Too early to tell. Pathology just started working. Doesn't look like a sex crime, though. I talked to Mathews. He managed to get there just as the police arrived. He thinks it's your friendly neighborhood sicko."

"Any relatives?"

"Not in the city. Midwest. Classic story. Small-town girl comes to big city and becomes a big star."

"Then becomes a statistic."

"There are ten thousand stories in the Naked City . . ."

"You are drunk . . ."

"Feeling good, that's all. She had a roommate."

"Male or female?"

"Female. Platonic variety. An actress. She's pretty shaken up. She had to identify the body."

"Can you get me a name and an address, Ken?"

"Name, sure. Address, not so sure."

"It's important."

"Give me an hour. I'll have you know that this snooping will probably cause me to bump a review of *Invasion of the Pod People from Mars*. A very relevant film."

"I saw that when I was twelve."

"This one's a remake. Sir Laurence Olivier plays the lead pod."

"As much as I hate to deprive the world of culture . . ."

"Give me an hour. Why the interest?"

"I think we may have a serial killer on our hands, Ken."

"A repeater? Who besides the model—"

"I think, just maybe, Eric Paine and this Jamie person were killed by the same person."

"Proof?"

"A hunch. And I think I may be on his hit list as well."

"Hunch again?"

Max fingered the novel. "Hunch again."

"Well, your professional hunches used to be pretty good. But your personal ones . . ."

"An hour?"

"An hour."

"Thanks, Ken."

"You owe me many lemon slices."

"Straight up. Catch you later."

Max held the book in his hand. There was a painting of tough Max Cady as tight-lipped Jimmy Ammo on the cover. Max turned the book over. On the back of the book a small, thumbnail description of the plot was featured, printed in a pool of blood.

"A TORTURED SOUL PUSHED TO THE BRINK OF SANITY LAUNCHES A MURDEROUS CAMPAIGN TO PROVE HIS OWN WORTH. CAN JIMMY AMMO FIND AND STOP THE PSYCHO BEFORE AMMO, HIMSELF, TOPS THE LIST OF NEWLY DECEASED CELEBRITIES?"

"Shit."

Was there such a thing as a copycat killer who was into pulp fiction?

Max tossed the book onto the couch and dialed The New York *Times*.

"Debra Knightly's line."

Max could feel his heartbeat pounding, both within his constricted chest and above his throbbing eyes. Maybe it was all a coincidence. But if not . . .

"Debra Knightly."

"Debra, it's Max."

"I haven't found out too much yet—"

"Never mind that. Just keep me plugged in to things as they develop. Hey, does your offer still stand?"

"Huh?"

"About the couch in your apartment."

"Sure, but . . ."

"I'll be over in a couple of hours, all right? Keep your night free."

"Sure but . . ."

"I'll explain when I get there. Call me if you hear anything juicy, okay?"

"Max, what's going on?"

"Maybe nothing."

Max hung up the phone and walked into his bedroom. He pulled out and angrily packed a suitcase. Maybe he was crazy. Maybe all this wasn't really happening. But if it was then there was going to be a bloodbath in Manhattan the likes of which hadn't been seen since the Son of Sam killings.

THE CON GAME

And caught in the middle of it all, his hands covered with the blood of the innocent victims, would be Max Cady.

The guy who dreamed up the systematic slaughter in the first place.

Headline: LIFE IMITATES TRASH.

CHAPTER TEN

The Checker Cab sputtered through the streets of Manhattan, avoiding the potholes on Madison Avenue as it made its way uptown.

Max glanced at a piece of paper in his hand. Eighty-fifth off Madison. Very classy address."

"Very rich young ladies," Debra Knightly replied.

Max grunted, watching the office buildings gradually fade into a series of terminally chic boutiques and pricey clothing stores.

"You don't think you're overreacting about all this?"

"You said yourself that this Jamie woman was on the cover of that *Vogue* magazine."

"So?"

"So, why would someone send it to me?"

"Possibly as a means of introduction. For all you know *Vogue* wants to do a profile piece on the mucho macho Jimmy Ammo. Maybe this was a writer's or editor's cute way of saying 'Hello.' Max, I didn't call to tell you about her murder for any real reason. I just thought it was a strange coincidence. That's all."

"I never really put much stock in coincidences."

"You're really serious about this serial killer?"

"Yeah."

"But why?"

"Just a feeling I have."

"But . . . ?"

"But it's too early to tell yet. All I know is that, in the past few days, I've gotten a note and two clues delivered to me. Two murders have been committed that are pretty similar to the ones in my books and if there *is* a nut case out there and he *is* trying to duplicate the killings in my novels then we're going to be in for one hell of a time."

THE CON GAME

"How so?"

"There are six, count 'em, six major murders in *Better Than the Best*."

"Why couldn't you have written romantic farces?"

"Because my life was one." Max pulled out the copy of *Better Than the Best* from his coat pocket. "In this one my psycho killer feels inferior so he decides to strike back by eliminating the ten most glamorous people in New York. He eradicates the leaders in the world of glamour, sports, pop music, theater, TV, and religion. He never gets further than six murders. Jimmy Ammo tracks him down and saves the day."

"Hooray. Do you really think someone will try to duplicate all your key killings?"

"Who knows? The Ammo books are sure on everyone's minds these days."

"If you have six people getting killed in one book and you wrote ten—"

"Twelve—"

"—novels, then . . ."

Max nodded, still staring at the sidewalks of Madison Avenue. "Yup. Manhattan is going to look like a Sam Peckinpah film festival really soon."

"You have no proof of any of this, though, right?"

"Right."

"It's just a theory, right?"

"Right."

"It might not be happening this way at all."

"Right."

"Then why do I feel sick to my stomach?"

The cab pulled up outside a high rise just off Madison. "Because you're a perceptive lass."

Max paid the cabbie. They walked into the front entrance and buzzed the apartment reading Soon/Poston.

"Who is it?"

"Max Cady, Ms. Poston. I have a few questions for you concerning the death of your roommate."

"Are you with the police?"

Max hesitated. "I'm working on the case, yes."

"Come up."

A nasal buzz shook the door leading to the interior of the building. Max pushed the door open and walked to the back ground-floor apartment, 2A.

He was greeted by a gorgeous blonde. Her long hair was disheveled and her eye makeup was badly streaked.

She didn't bother to say hello. "I told the detectives everything this afternoon."

"I know," Max said. "I only have a few brief questions, Miss Post. I'm really sorry to inconvenience you."

The woman glanced at Debra, decided to ignore her totally, and focused her eyes on Max. "She was such a giving person."

"I'm sure she was, Miss Post."

"Bambi."

"Bambi?"

"Bambi Post. I'm an actress."

"Loved your movie." Debra smiled. "The scenes with Thumper were terrific."

Max gave Debra a crooked look. "Now, Bambi. When was the last time you saw Jamie alive?"

"An hour or so before they . . . I . . ."

"Where was that?"

"In the Ascott Building. We have the same agent. Actually, Jamie got me my agent. Jamie was guiding my career, you know? Like a big sister."

Bambi crinkled her nose up in a gesture that was her interpretation of grief. She looked like E.T. sniffing at a bad Reese's Cup. "She was so giving. It will be hard to find another roommate willing to pay this amount of rent."

"I'm sure it will. Tell me, was Jamie alone the last time you saw her?"

"Why, no."

"Was she with a man? A thin, young man?"

"No. Actually, she was with a young girl. Jamie told me that she had met the girl in the lobby of the building. A struggling model she said. They were going to have coffee and discuss the modeling business. She was like that, Jamie. Always so giving."

"You two hadn't gotten any weird letters lately, had you?"

"No. Mostly bills."

"Strange phone calls? Breathers?"

THE CON GAME

"No more than normal. We change our number a lot."

Max frowned. He was stumped. "Well, I suppose that will be it, Miss Post."

"Bambi . . ."

"Bambi. Thanks for your time."

The woman stared at Max for a moment. He waited for the inevitable question.

"Haven't I seen you somewhere?" Bambi asked.

"Maybe."

The woman scrutinized his face. "Didn't you work at the Stage Door Deli?"

Max sighed, shook his head no, and left the building.

He and Debra stood in the crisp spring air under the light of a noonday sun.

"Why did you ask if she was with a young man?" Knightly inquired.

"No reason."

"You suspect Phillip Carole, don't you?"

"The guy is a loon, Debra, a one-man production of *Cuckoo's Nest*."

"No evidence to connect him to this one, though."

"Nope."

"But you still suspect him?"

"Remember the party? He'll be better than the best? The son of a bitch is trying to outdo me."

Debra shook her head sadly. "I think you're really misreading this, Max. I realize that you're obsessed by your books right now but it seems to me that you're throwing coincidence upon coincidence. You don't know for a fact that there's someone out there aping your plot lines. You don't know for sure that there is some*one* out there at all."

Max nodded. "I *do* know, I just can't prove it. The problem is that if *I* make the connection between my books and the murders, someone else will eventually too."

"Who?"

"Police. Press. Mystics. Who the hell knows?"

Out of the corner of his eye Max took note of a crème-colored sedan parked around the corner on Madison. He watched as the car eased its way forward toward the spot where the twosome conferred.

Max refused to react as a man resembling a bulldog climbed out of the passenger's seat.

"Maxwell Cady?"

"That's right."

"Detective Fitzsimmons, Homicide. Lieutenant Lehner would like to have a word with you."

Max smirked at Debra. "Bingo."

CHAPTER ELEVEN

Lieutenant Lehner was not in a mood to receive visitors. It was Friday night. He was supposed to be home. In bed. Or in front of the television. This evening, however, was an extension of his day. He hadn't been home in sixteen hours. He was hungry. His face felt greasy and unwashed, the way skin felt following nine hours in an airplane at the mercy of canned air. He stared at Max Cady and Debra Knightly. They sat before his desk and fidgeted.

"I don't suppose either one of you would like to explain just what you were doing at Ms. Poston's apartment tonight."

"Max had a theory," Debra began.

"Miss Knightly was working on a story," Max said a half-beat behind.

Max glared at Debra. Debra smiled weakly.

Lehner never was a fan of Nick and Nora Charles routines. "Miss Knightly, if you would be so kind as to wait outside my office for a moment. Have a cup of coffee."

"I don't drink coffee."

"Then go outside and don't have a cup of coffee," Lehner snapped. "Sergeant Malloy, escort Miss Knightly out of here."

A beefy man in a blue uniform, possessing a shape that was the result of years of inhaling mashed potatoes, led Debra out of the room.

Max stared glumly at Lehner. The veins in Lehner's forehead were throbbing. "Now, Mr. Cady, exactly what were you doing questioning the victim's roommate?"

"I, uh, wanted to know . . . a few things."

"Are you turning detective now, Mr. Cady? Yet another career move?"

"Not really."

"Miss Knightly mentioned a hunch you had? A theory?"

"Well . . ."

"I'm all ears, Mr. Cady. Like a donkey."

"They're not that *bad,* Lieutenant."

Lehner stared at Cady. Cady said nothing. "Well, Mr. Cady," Lehner sighed. "Since you won't reveal your theory to me concerning the demise of our model friend, let me give you a hint as to mine."

Lehner pulled a small plastic bag out of his desk drawer. "Do you know what this is?"

Max blinked as the lieutenant dangled the plastic before him. "A baggie?"

Lehner smiled thinly. "Yes indeed. A Baggie. And can you see what's inside the Baggie?"

Max squinted his bloodshot eyes. There was a tattered slice of something or other inside the Baggie. "A scrap of paper?"

"Very good, Mr. Cady. You see? We are making progress. Now, can you identify this scrap of paper?"

Max strained his eyes to no avail. "No, sir."

"Yes. It is rather teeny, isn't it? Well, I tell you. When this little piece of paper was given to me a few hours ago, I couldn't identify it either. It's only a half an inch or so long. About just as wide. It has a number on it—45. And a single word on each side—'zone' on the one and 'breast' on the other. I sent it to the lab for a quick once-over. It was pulp paper, they said. Cheap pulp paper. The kind of paper you'd find in a paperback book.

"Ah-ha, thought I, a bit of a paperback novel. Now, here's a slip of paper found at the scene of a crime that is directly linked to a paperback novel. But what novel? What paperback? Surely, thought I, there must be thousands, maybe hundreds of thousands of books published each year. The chances of me linking this scrap with any one particular title are next to nil. Wouldn't you think so, Mr. Cady?"

"Uh, yes. Sure."

"So did I. So did I. But then I thought to myself. Now, wait a minute. Samuel Lehner, you've been a policeman all your adult life. Surely you have some sixth sense, some gut-level feelings that you can trust by now. So, I decided, screw the odds, I'm going to play a hunch. And do you know what I did?"

"Not really."

THE CON GAME

"I went out and bought my second Jimmy Ammo novel in two days. I bought a spanking brand-new edition of your second literary milestone, *Better Than the Best.*"

Max remained silent as Lehner continued his spiel, glaring at Cady.

"An interesting book. Of course, I've only skimmed it. I read it when it was first published. Can't remember a bit of it, though. That either says something about my memory or your writing style. Anyhow, I took note of that flashy painting of you on the cover. Quite nice. Good likeness. The cover is very sturdy too. Nice gloss. But the paper inside? Oh, the paper. Mr. Cady, they did you wrong on the paper. They've printed your opus on very cheap pulp . . . the kind of stuff that yellows within a year or two . . . not the fine stock they printed paperbacks on when I was young."

"I'll complain to my agent."

"Do that, Mr. Cady. Give him hell. Well, now, I have this brand-new paperback in my hand and I'm compelled to open it to page forty-five. Do you know what I find?"

"I have a feeling I do, yes."

"I thought you might intuit what I'm driving at. Yes, indeed. Page forty-five, when torn like our scrap here, has the word 'breast' on one side and 'zone' on the other. Remarkable, isn't it?"

"Remarkable. Lieutenant, just where did you find the scrap?"

"Ah, I was getting to that. It was in the palm of Ms. Soon's right hand. She had clenched it during her death throes and, later, when we pried it open, there was this piece of paper. Do you know what that means, Mr. Cady?"

"She was holding a copy of my book during the time of her death?"

"Either that or her killer was."

"I suppose."

"You wouldn't remember what was on page forty-five of your book, would you, Mr. Cady?"

"Lieutenant, I haven't thought about these books in half a dozen years. I don't even remember half of the plots."

"Let me refresh your memory, then. On page forty-five a fashion model named Zoe Campbell is murdered by a deranged killer. He breaks into a studio she is modeling in, sneaks into her dressing room, and kills her with the props she is using."

"I remember that part of the book, yes."

"Good. Good."

Lehner reached into the same drawer and removed a second Baggie. There was a wad of paper in it. "Guess what?"

"What?"

"We found the rest of page forty-five stuffed down Ms. Soon's throat. Now, what does that tell us, Mr. Cady?"

Max was growing angry.

"No comment? Well, it tells *me* that Ms. Soon's killer is a psycho. It also tells me that someone out there is using your books as an inspiration."

"It *does* seem that way," Max conceded.

"Who do you think that might be, Mr. Cady?"

"I have my suspicions," Cady answered.

"So do I," Lehner said, abruptly switching topics. "You left your job at the newspaper because of nerves, right? Nervous breakdown? Hallucinations? Blackouts? Punch-outs in bars? Visits to the drunk tank?"

"No."

"It's in your file."

"I used all that as an excuse to quit and still get a few months' severance pay. I left to write the Jimmy Ammo books."

"You even have a doctor's certificate on your file."

"I had a friend make it up."

"Would he testify to that?"

"He would if he were still alive."

"Ah, your doctor is no longer with us?"

"Plane crash in Europe."

"Pity."

"Lieutenant Lehner, say what you want to say to me so I can get the fuck out of here. I'm tired and getting pissed off."

Lehner brushed back his mane of hair and screwed his face into a mask of barely controlled rage. His eyes were topped by what seemed to be one continuous eyebrow. "I have nothing to say to you, Mr. Cady, except 'Watch your ass.' I don't like being screwed around. I don't like being lied to. I don't like people getting killed for no good reason.

"I have two people butchered in my precinct in twice as many days. Both of them are somehow connected to you and your work. You put in an appearance around both victims' homes shortly before or after the killings."

"Are you telling me I'm a suspect?"

"I'm telling you to watch your step, Mr. Cady. I'm telling you to remember one thing . . . I'm not one of those curmudgeon cops you have in your novels, lovable louts with hearts of gold. My heart is almost unreachable while I'm on duty, Mr. Cady, and I'm on duty all the time. I'm playing hardball, Mr. Cady. I'm playing for keeps."

"So is the killer, Lieutenant."

"He's pee-wee league, Cady. I'm the pro team. Now, do you have anything to add?"

Max considered confiding in Lehner, telling the lieutenant about the strange packages and about his suspicions concerning Phillip Carole.

Gazing at the lieutenant's crimson eyes, he decided against it.

Max got to his feet. "As much as I enjoy one-man shows, Lieutenant, I think I'll stick to Hal Holbrook's tours for entertainment."

Cady turned and left the office.

Lehner's face assumed a beet-red glow. The lieutenant exhaled suddenly. It sounded like the hiss of a cobra.

Cady heard it as he walked toward Debra Knightly. "By the time this is over, kiddo, you're going to get one hell of a story," he said, taking her by the arm.

CHAPTER TWELVE

The early morning sunlight battled its way through a dozen hanging plants before making its way to Debra Knightly's living-room floor. Magazines were scattered on the rug, dog-eared copies of *Psychology Today, Smithsonian, Film Comment, Mother Jones,* and *World Press Review.* Max had unceremoniously removed them from the coffee table with one sweeping motion of his left arm.

He sat hunched over the table with a dozen paperbacks, a few sheaves of typing paper, and a ballpoint pen.

Debra Knightly stumbled into the living room. "My God!" she yawned. "You're up already?"

"Nope," Max replied. "I haven't gone to bed yet."

"What are you doing?"

Max pointed to his newly purchased complete collection of Jimmy Ammo tomes. "I've been catching up with some of Jimmy's exploits. A real hard-boiled type, this pal of mine."

"You were up the whole night *reading?*"

"And taking notes. Look. You might think I'm exaggerating but let's work on the assumption that there is some sicko out there trying to live up to my novels, okay?"

"Okay."

"And let's say that he or she is doing this for some reason . . . other than sheer lunacy . . . and that reason has something to do with me."

"Aren't we egocentric."

"So, that would make our killer someone who either knows me or has a grudge against me or would benefit in some way from the killings."

"How would someone benefit . . ."

"Well, let's say that there's someone out there who would love

THE CON GAME

to see me behind bars for a murder I didn't commit just because they really don't like me."

"Like Phillip Carole?"

"Yeah."

"How about your ex-wife?"

Cady smirked. "You have a point there. I know this sounds ridiculous, but I swear I'm onto something here."

Max pulled out a sheet of paper. "Look. Here's what I've been doing all night. In *Better Than the Best* our little psycho offs six of the brightest stars in New York."

"Uh-huh."

"But he's trying to wipe out the top ten. In order, we have glamour, sports, journalism, pop music, theater, and religion."

"Those are the victims that he tags."

"Right. But, let's say that our real-life killer is smarter than the killer in the book and he eludes capture. The remaining four were politics, art, big business, and detective fiction."

"This sounds like an episode of *Jeopardy.*"

"Go ahead and laugh, Ms. *Times*. The whole reason for Ammo getting involved in this is that he figures out he's on the hit list and he wants to save his own butt."

"How noble."

"Ammo was never a knight in shining armor but he was pretty effective. Now, look, I've made a series of lists."

Knightly knelt down next to the coffee table and gazed at the sheets of typing paper. On each one a series of names had been scrawled. "I don't know if I'm up for this before my coffee," she muttered.

"Take a look at them. You're probably a lot more aware than I am of who's hot and who's not these days. But if this guy's going by the book these are the likeliest victims I can think of."

"Are the ones on the top of the list the ones you think are the best in their fields?"

"Yeah. I've listed five names in each category, just in case I'm not up on the latest popularity polls."

Debra scanned the litany of possible cadavers. "Max, you get an A in current events."

Max leaned back against a floor pillow and rubbed his eyes.

"Great. Now I'm going to get a few hours' sleep. You go out and track 'em down."

"Uh, Max. I hate to tell you this but I *do* have a day job? A source of income? A real responsibility?"

"You want these people to die needlessly because you were working on a story about potholes making the streets of New York a combat zone?"

"How did you know I was working on that story?"

"Just a guess. Someone writes that story every spring. It's traditional. The winter snows bring heavy salting. The salt ruins the asphalt. Then comes the rains. There goes the macadam. Ad nauseum."

"You know a better angle?"

Max pointed to the handwritten lists. "This could be front-page stuff, my dear."

"Okay. I'll find out their addresses. Then what?"

"Then I will visit each one and warn them."

"Warn them that their lives are being threatened by a killer who may or may not exist?"

"I have a way with words. They'll believe me."

Knightly waddled into the kitchen, her bunny slippers slapping against the floor with a series of "splats." "Some people aren't as gullible as I am, Max."

"If you're making coffee, I'll have a gin and tonic."

"It's a little early to start drinking, isn't it?"

"Not if you haven't been to bed it isn't. I'm going nappies now."

"That's right." Debra reached into the liquor cabinet below the kitchen counter. "Uh, Max, I couldn't help overhear some of the conversation you had with Lehner."

"It wasn't much of a conversation. More of a monologue."

"Did you have a nervous breakdown?"

Max rubbed his eyes with his right thumb and forefinger. "No. Not really. I was drinking pretty heavily following my divorce. I was really worried about my kid. I blacked out a few times. Went to a few parties and wound up places I didn't recognize. That sort of stuff."

"Sounds serious."

"It wasn't fun. But I had to let off steam. I quit that shit as soon as I started writing the books."

"Lehner doesn't like you, does he?"

"No. But, then again, I don't like Lehner either. That seems fair to me. One of the benefits of living in a democracy."

"I worry about you, Max."

"You should."

"You've been through a lot during the past few days."

Debra walked into the living room and handed Max his drink. Max gazed at the concoction. "This is just the start of the ride, kiddo. It's going to get a lot rougher."

"You don't seem too upset."

"I'm not exactly famous for my good luck. I'm the kind of guy who falls backward and breaks his nose."

Knightly walked back into the kitchen. "Let's hope your luck improves by tonight."

Max took a sip of his drink and frowned. "Why?"

"The next category we'll cover is professional athletes. Your King of New York Sports is Terry Scott, Yankee outfielder extraordinaire, right?"

"Right."

"He's one of the biggest assholes ever inflicted on Western civilization . . . and he comes back to the city from a road tour this afternoon. He'll be ready to roll by this evening."

Max finished the drink. "Just find out where he'll be tonight. I'll make nice-nice. Night-night."

Knightly watched Max stagger into her bedroom. She heard him collapse on her bed. She wasn't sure but she had a feeling that Cady was a person who enjoyed being on the edge. She sincerely hoped he wouldn't tumble off.

SNAPS was the kind of bar that, in the early 1970s, was known as a meat market. In this age of enlightenment, however, it was referred to as a trendy kind of place one frequented in the hope of starting a meaningful relationship. Hanging plants were surrounded by Tiffany lights, highly polished wooden floors, and inane conversation.

Orthodox jocks, both professional and painfully amateurish,

matched swaggers, John Wayne-ing it around the bar while heavily made-up women watched from the sidelines.

Max sat at the bar feeling very old. This was the kind of joint he envisioned going to if he died before making a good confession. He drank down his third shooter of tequila and positioned himself at an angle facing the front door.

Debra had told him that Terry Scott spent every night in town in the joint, talking loudly at the bar and picking up the best-looking woman in the place with little or no effort. Max didn't like the guy already.

Max had never been even vaguely interested in sports. While still a teenager he had tried out for the high school football team, made it as a defensive linebacker, but quit soon thereafter. He just couldn't understand what the fuss was about . . . why seemingly sane young men would beat each other's brains out over the possession of a badly stitched ball.

Similarly, he had never shared the nation's enthusiasm for baseball. Boxing was good for a laugh now and then. Wrestling was low comedy. Horse racing bored him. The lure of winter sports eluded him and, to Max, swimming was not a sport . . . it was staying alive in the water.

Yet, people simply assumed that Max was a jock. After all, he was big and possessed a body that resembled a VW van. Max's idea of exercise was running for a bus.

He ordered another shooter and gazed at the faces at the bar. Men in neatly sculpted haircuts, *Magnum, P.I.* mustaches carefully trimmed. Wide necks. Lots of arm punching.

Max sighed and aged visibly as the evening wore on.

At 9:05 a titanic black man strode into the place. Wearing a cowboy hat and form-fitting jeans and trailed by three young, hero-worshiping college kids, Terry Scott marched up to the bar.

"Hiya, Mike," he called to the bartender (whose name was Arnold). "A Wild Turkey for me and beers for my boys."

Max watched as Terry did his number. Much backslapping. Overly loud jock talk. A few minutes of haw-hawing. A small group of women began moving from the tables toward the bar. The young ladies began positioning themselves strategically

THE CON GAME

around Scott. Not near enough to be obvious but close enough to be within reach.

Max decided he should make his move before the women did.

He slid off his bar stool and shuffled over to the Yankee outfielder. "Uh, excuse me," he began.

Scott turned around, irritated at first (another autograph hound?). He stared at Max. Scott's face assumed a puzzled expression. He knew Cady from somewhere.

"Do I know you?" he asked.

"Uh, not personally," Max replied.

"You in the movies, man?"

"No. I'm a writer, actually. Max. Max Cady is my name."

Scott continued to stare. He could go either way now. Would it be hostile or hospitable? "Cady? Cady? I don't know no writer named Cady."

"I wrote under the name of Jimmy Ammo."

Scott's face twisted into a jack-o'-lantern grin. "Jimmy Ammo! My man. My main man."

He pumped Max's hand. "I love your books. Many's the time I use 'em to get me pumped up during spring training. Hey, Bill," he called to the bartender, "get Mr. Ammo here another drink."

The barkeep, whose name was *still* Arnold, slid another shot in front of Max. The women, who had been steadily approaching Scott, froze in their tracks. Perhaps it would be considered rude to intrude on this newly begun conversation.

"Jimmy Ammo. In the flesh. I thought you were a made-up guy."

"I was. I am. It's a long story," Max said. "Can we talk?"

"That's what we're doing, ain't it?" Scott laughed and faced his trio of underlings. They chuckled on command. "What does hard-boiled Jimmy Ammo have to talk with sweet-faced Terry Scott about?"

Max downed his shot. "I think someone wants to kill you."

"They gonna have to stand in line, man. Everyone, from my ex-wife to the commissioner of baseball would like to see my ass in a sling."

"I'm serious, Terry. I think someone wants to see you dead. They're using my—"

"Jimmy, my man. Don't do this to me. This is my *home*, you know? This is where I come to *party.*"

Accenting the word "party," Scott turned to the coven of female admirers a few yards beyond his grasp. They responded visibly. Scott flashed them a glistening smile. The women began their slow forward assault.

"Yeah," Max continued. "I know this is a bad time to catch you but I'm serious, Terry. I have reason to believe that there's a crazy on the loose—"

"Jimmy. Jimmy. Jimmy. I can take care of myself. I'm *young*. I'm in my *prime*." The athlete stared at Max's craggy face. "*I* can take care of myself. Got that?"

"I'm sure you can but we're dealing with—"

"No, *you* are dealing with. And, from the looks of you, you having a hard time of it, man. Somehow I always pictured you as being younger, tougher. You'll excuse me for saying so, but you look beat to shit."

"Yeah, I'm suffering from bottle fatigue but I'm serious about this psycho—"

"And I'm serious about you cramping my style, Jimmy." Scott leaned in toward Max. He smelled of liquor and expensive cologne. "Look, man. Give me a break, here. You're scaring off the local talent. This is my little pond. I choose my catch for the night. People like me 'cause I'm an *up* kind of guy. You're coming in here like Vincent Price rattling chains. Give it a rest, okay?"

Max stared at the baseball great and suddenly saw him in a body bag.

"Look, you asshole," Max said, losing his composure. "I'm not here because I like this place and I'm not here because I give a shit about you. I just resent the fact that you can be turned into a statistic under my nose by some lowlife who is out to make a name for himself as a mass murderer. I'm just doing my job as a citizen, that's all."

Scott narrowed his eyes into slits. "Well, consider your duty done, old man. Now, blow."

"Max didn't move. Scott turned to his three mini-goons. "Mr. Ammo is leaving, boys. Show him the door."

Max found himself lifted off his bar stool and carried toward

THE CON GAME

the front of the bar. Within seconds he was introduced to the pavement.

The three men tossed Max a good ten feet toward the curb. His head hit a parked car and he slumped onto the sidewalk. Struggling to stand, he managed only to get into a kneeling position. His eyes refused to focus. Maybe Scott was right. Maybe he was an old man. He certainly felt that way now. He massaged his head furiously, coaxing his eyes into use.

Headline: AMMO MISFIRES—Man Turned Into Welcome Mat at Local Bar.

After a few minutes of recovery time, he was seeing single pedestrians saunter by instead of groups of three. A few of the strollers gazed at Max and made "tsk-tsk"-ing sounds at the sight of a grown man nearly flattened on an Upper East Side sidewalk.

Max slowly staggered to his feet, using the parked car as a brace. Blinking the haze out of his eyes furiously, he spotted Terry Scott leaving the bar with a tall blonde in tow. He watched them climb into a cab. He had tried to save that arrogant bastard. Whatever happened now wasn't Max's fault.

He took a deep breath and decided to walk back to Debra's apartment. The night air would do his head good, and lord knows he needed the exercise.

One half hour later, across town, on a lower West Side pier, Terry Scott was feeling shards of his skull slice through his brain like a hot knife through butter.

The athlete didn't have time to cry out. The blow had nearly taken the back of his head off. He collapsed facedown on the filthy floor of the warehouse, his eyes opened wide in shock for all eternity. His body made a valiant effort to hang on to consciousness. Nerve endings sputtered and fluttered, causing his arms and legs to twitch helplessly. His mouth flopped open and closed as his lungs pushed a torrent of air forward. The tremors gradually subsided. The eyes remained, unblinking, focused on another dimension. Terry Scott was now an ex-baseball star. He was now an ex-everything.

His killer dropped the weapon next to the body.

A Louisville slugger hit the pier floor with a resounding thud.

The killer smiled as the last vestiges of lifeblood dribbled from the gaping wound. "Going, going . . . gone. Grand slam."

CHAPTER THIRTEEN

Max, still fully dressed, stirred in his sleep. He was curled on Debra's living-room couch, twisted into a fetal position. A blanket was draped over his body. He was having bad dreams again.

Fire rained from heaven. His pregnant daughter cried out to him for help. His second wife, dressed as the Wicked Queen from *Snow White,* galloped through a long hallway upon a red-eyed, black stallion. A woman in white, surrounded by flames, wailed in long, sorrowful tones as she slowly rose into the heavens.

Max blinked himself into a state of half-wakefulness.

No doubt about it. He'd have to stop drinking before he went to bed. Either that or stop going to bed after he drank.

He remained on the couch, straightening his body somewhat. His brain still ached from his head-on collision with the parked car. He gingerly probed the top of his skull for bruises. There was considerable swelling. He'd probably walk around looking like a unicorn for the next two days.

He heard voices in the hallway. He identified Debra's. Two other voices, harsh, grating, and male, overrode her protests.

Max opened his eyes wide as Lieutenant Lehner and the pear-shaped form identified as Sergeant Malloy entered the room. Malloy stood in the alcove. Lehner sat on the couch at Max's feet.

"Good morning, Mr. Cady," he said, flashing a Cheshire-cat smile. "Always sleep with your clothes on?"

"I left my feety pajamas at home."

"You look like hell, Mr. Cady."

"No offense, Lieutenant, but seeing you the first thing in the morning doesn't do a lot for my peace of mind."

Lehner grinned wider. He resembled a wolf in a well-worn suit. "Consider me a wake-up call."

THE CON GAME

"Lieutenant, do you have a specific reason to be here or were you guys looking for a third for breakfast?"

"We came to ask you a few questions. Do you mind?"

"I suppose not."

"Fine. Where were you last night at ten o'clock?"

"Walking."

"Walking where?"

"Walking here."

"Will anyone corroborate your statement?"

"If you mean did anyone see me walking through the streets of Manhattan that would recall me, I doubt it. I didn't wear my chicken suit last night. I pretty much blended in with the crowd."

"What time did you arrive at Ms. Knightly's apartment?"

"I suppose elevenish."

"Elevenish."

"Maybe eleven-thirtyish."

"Where were you walking from?"

"A bar named SNAPS."

"What were you doing there?"

"Drinking."

"And arguing."

Max peered into the lieutenant's eyes. He could see something whirring in the back of the man's mind that resembled a bear trap. He didn't like that. "No. Chatting, actually."

"With Terry Scott."

"Uh-huh. But I'm sure you knew all that, right? You know I was at the bar. You know I talked with Scott. You know I was escorted from the bar by a few of his goons for cramping his style. Now, is there some reason for this bedside chat, Lieutenant?"

"Terry Scott was found early this morning on West Sixteenth Street. His head had been smashed in with a baseball bat."

"Apropos."

"You don't seem surprised."

"Honestly, I'm not. I went to the bar last night to warn the jerk that his life was in danger."

"How did you know that?"

"I didn't know for sure. I was playing a hunch. I believe that some nut case out there is duplicating all the major killings in my books."

"Any nut case I know?"

"Maybe."

"Care to share your thoughts with me, Mr. Cady, or would you like to come downtown with me and I can question you formally?"

"Don't bullshit me, Lehner, you're dancing in the dark right now. Feeling around. You can't connect me with Scott's death even circumstantially. I saw him leave the bar with a blonde in tow. Why don't you find her and question her about his last hour?"

Max rubbed his right hand through his hair. It felt matted and damp. He was in worse shape than he thought. A depressing concept that surprised him.

"We're trying to do just that," Lehner replied, chewing on his beard with his upper teeth.

"I suppose you found pages of my novel at the scene of the crime?" Max began, stifling a yawn.

"You're very perceptive."

"I swear to you, Lehner, I'm just as pissed off about this as you are."

"I doubt that, Cady. But, in time, you will be just as upset."

"Do you really think I could just go out and murder someone for no reason?"

Lehner stood up and headed for the front door. "Everyone has a reason for murder, Mr. Cady. Even the nut cases. People hear voices. People have visions. Men think their wives are having affairs. Women believe their husbands to be cheating on them. Children hate their parents. Parents hate their neighbors. Some killers swear they are controlled by aliens. Others converse with their dogs. There's always a reason, Mr. Cady. I'll be in touch."

Lehner exited the apartment. Malloy followed.

Max sat up in the couch and stared at Debra. "Not the best way to start the day."

Debra carried a manila envelope with her into the room. "Just what happened last night between you and Terry Scott?"

"He thought I was putting a damper on his evening and had

THE CON GAME

me thrown out of the bar. That's all. I didn't try to hit a home run using his head, though, if that's what you're getting at."

"I know that."

"We are an elite group. What's that you're carrying?"

"I don't know. It came for you last night. Messengered over. You must have just missed it."

Max grabbed the envelope and ripped it open. He stuck a hand inside the package and pulled out a Yankee baseball cap. "Son of a bitch," he hissed. "Carole is really yanking my crank."

"Max, maybe you'd better consider other—"

"It *has* to be Carole."

"Why?"

Max was stymied. "Because it *has* to be, that's all."

Debra walked toward the bathroom. "I can't argue logic. What's your next move?"

"I think I'll pay a visit to the *News*."

"Don't you dare give an interview. You're mine."

"It's nice to feel wanted." Max eased himself out of the sofa. "Actually, I'm going to visit Kenny McArthur. Maybe I need a fresh sounding board for all this."

"You nervous?"

"Yes." Max nodded. He was nervous. He was hitting the sauce more than he had in years. He had had too much to drink last night at SNAPS. He was beginning to lapse into his old patterns. He hadn't blacked out, exactly, but he didn't remember the walk home. He didn't remember entering Debra's apartment or falling asleep.

That was a bad sign.

He could've gone anywhere last night. He could have done anything. He *knew* he hadn't followed Terry Scott and beat his brains in but he couldn't prove it . . . either to the police or himself.

He remembered Carole's pasty face contorting into a maniacal mask at the party talking about that fine line that we don't dare cross over. Max wondered, for a moment, just what made ordinary people vault over that barrier, do the unthinkable. And once there, how did ordinary people come back?

Max sank back down onto the sofa and began massaging his

eyes. Maybe, just maybe, if he massaged enough, he could make the day disappear.

Across town, at his desk, Lehner glared at the stacks of papers strewn across his desk. Sergeant Malloy hovered around the lieutenant like some great bear. Lehner tossed a few of the papers onto the floor, revealing a small stack of hardcover books underneath.

"Do you really think Cady is the killer?" Malloy ventured.

"He's our best bet," Lehner said. "He had a nervous breakdown. He's an ex-alchy. He's under pressure. We know he tried to hide his Jimmy Ammo alter ego for years. Now, suddenly, he's exposed. His quiet life is shattered. He has to cope with being a professional tough guy. The pressure is intense. Maybe too intense.

"He says he's not proud of Ammo. Maybe he's not. And if he's gone off the deep end, maybe these killers are his way of getting Ammo out of the picture for good. Maybe he's framing his alter ego."

"You don't like him at all, do you?"

"Personal feelings have nothing to do with this, Sergeant. The man is not tightly wrapped. What really gauls me, though, is that he is no kind of writer."

Lehner fondled the stack of hardcovers on his desk. "Look at this stuff. Hammett. Chandler. Leonard. Now, these are writers. But Max Cady? A hack. An insult to my intelligence. He should be imprisoned for his books. Forget murder!"

CHAPTER FOURTEEN

Boy George was crooning in the background on the jukebox. The bass was turned up so high the song sounded like a tribal war-chant. The lights were low. Shadowy figures hovered over the salad bar like strange creatures huddled over a communal water hole. Waitresses dressed like Tinker Bell. The maitre d' looked like Peter Lorre. There were no peanuts at the bar . . . only cheddar-cheese fish.

At a corner table, under a badly drawn picture of Humphrey Bogart, the two men sat, protecting a bowl of hidden treasure from the rest of the crowd.

Kenny McArthur rubbed the traces of salt from under his bottom lip. "One day someone is going to invent a pretzel that doesn't shed."

He stuck his pudgy paw, once again, into the only bowl not filled with cheddar-cheese fish in the Tide's Inn.

Max ordered another shooter. "Pretzels without salt are like . . . pretzels without salt."

McArthur rested a round chin on his salt-caked hand and gazed at Max. "Maxie. You're rattled."

"How can you tell?"

"Because you're quietly getting soused and talking nonsense, that's why. Remember how things used to be at the paper? Remember toward the end? Ease up, Max. I thought you were on the wagon."

"I was. I'm not anymore."

"Pity."

Max slumped down in his chair and gazed, bleary-eyed, at the bar. "How bad was I, Kenny? Back then, I mean?"

"Pretty bad."

"Was I violent?"

"You honestly don't remember?"

"No."

"You never took it out on people. People you ignored. Inanimate objects? Forget it. Once you threw a phone right through Fletcher's glass wall. The one he gazed out upon the city room through. Amazing. Fletcher just stood there, gaping. You were indignant about something or other. The next day the glass was replaced and you didn't remember a thing.

"Another time the phones weren't working so you hung them out the windows of the drama department until the phone company came and repaired them. It was pouring out that day.

"People you left alone. You were, however, the undefeated champ when it came to *things.*"

"I was a lush, huh?"

"I chalked it up to your marriage. You were going through hell. We all tried to ignore it as much as we could. Fletcher let it go. After all, you were still writing."

"Meeting all my deadlines."

"Meeting all your deadlines."

"No one tried to stop me?"

"No one knew how. Maxie, you were perfectly normal most of the time. I've never seen anyone hold liquor like you did. You'd be fine and then, without any warning, you'd just go off the deep end. It would last an hour, maybe two, and then you'd be in tip-top shape again. Remarkable, it was."

"It's all a blur."

"I know. You'd just blank out. During those times you were really far gone you weren't Max Cady. You were someone else . . . Max Cady plus."

Max buried his face in his hands. "Do you think I could kill anyone, Kenny?"

"Only through bad syntax."

"Someone is trying to make it seem that way."

"So you said on the phone."

Max peered through his fingers. "I don't know what to do."

"You can lay off the sauce for one thing. Some of us, like me, for instance, can safely drink our way through life. I am a bachelor. A fifty-year-old bachelor. The chances of me meeting Miss Right and having children, lawn jockeys, and a dog are pretty slim right now. I can drink my way into happyland every night without doing anyone any harm . . . except myself. You, however, are now in the spotlight. People are watching you, Max. And, if what you say is true, not just your fans. With the cops breathing down your neck, you better stay alert. You have a daughter and a grandkid to worry about, right? Her husband sure isn't going to support the old homestead. Think about them."

"I know. It's just that I hurt less after a few drinks. I can close my eyes and just drift. Feel my head grow heavy. Hear my breathing. *Feel* my breathing. It's just so peaceful. I can actually hear the world drift away, hide in some corner for a time. It gives me room, gives me time to just chill out."

"Not a good plan right now, Maxie."

Max dropped his hands to the tabletop. "I know. This is the time I should be in top form, right? This is when I should be proving to the police that it's Phillip Carole and not Max Cady who is committing those murders."

"Don't get hung up on Carole exclusively, Max. There could be a lot of reasons for these killings."

"Carole has a grudge against me, Kenny."

"Yeah. Well, the way I remember it, so did six out of ten New Yorkers back when you were filing stories daily. In all seriousness, this scumbucket you're after could be someone you pushed out of shape in a story way back when. It's something to think about, anyway."

"It has to be Carole."

"Not necessarily. Let's look at what's going on here. A couple of killings superficially linked to your books. There may be a pattern. There may not be. We can't rule that out right now, Max. It could be a coincidence. You could be letting your sense of melodrama get the best of you."

"What about my little packages? My little clues?"

McArthur nodded affirmatively. "They *do* tend to back up your theory."

"Which brings us back to Carole."

"Which brings *you* back to Carole." McArthur's face, already red and blotchy, grew even more crimson. "I, uh, did a little fact-checking after your call. I tried to come up with people who would benefit from either Paine's death or your incarceration."

Max blinked at his former newspaper crony. "And . . ."

"Well, the funny thing is, you seem to have stepped into a very large pile of cosmic ca-ca by coming out of literary retirement."

"It wasn't my idea."

"So you say . . . which makes things more interesting. For instance, if you go to jail on murder charges, what do you think will happen to your books?"

"They'll be shredded?"

"Hell, no. Their sales will probably skyrocket. Now, who will that benefit?"

"Me?"

"Right. Unfortunately, you'll be serving a life sentence. However, one fellow who will be walking around loose on the outside world and collecting a fee for all those brand-new editions being sucked up is your agent."

"David?"

"Right. And Mr. Maskin engineered your coming-out party, too, didn't he?"

"Yeah."

"Well, now, here's an interesting tidbit for you. David was Eric Paine's agent too."

"You're kidding."

"Nope. And, more than likely, Paine's body of work will sell quite a bit more now that his body of bones is safely interred."

"I don't believe it."

"While you're visiting the wonderful world of incredulity, let me clue you in to one more interesting wrinkle. Gloria Paine, the widow? She hated Eric. He was a bit of a putz when it came to home life. So, she took a lover. Someone she knew. Someone she liked. Someone . . ."

"David?"

"Bingo."

"You think that David and Paine's widow have set me up?"

"I don't think anything. I'm merely suggesting a possibility."

"And Carole?"

"He's in the running too. He's definitely one brick short of a full load."

"And what about me, Kenny?"

THE CON GAME

"I don't know, Max. What about you?" The two men lapsed into an uneasy silence. Finally, McArthur spoke. "If you respect my opinion, you might do two things."

"What?"

"Keep tabs on the whereabouts of Paine's widow, little Davie the wonderboy, and Carole."

"And . . ."

"And knock off the drinking. You're only going to hurt yourself . . . maybe kill yourself."

"Or someone else."

"You're a bad drunk, Maxie. You don't unwind when you drink."

"It's my brain, Kenny. I can't shut off my brain."

"Who can? Just get it to slow down a little bit."

McArthur picked up a pretzel and held it before him. "A wonderful invention, the pretzel. A crisscross of dough. Cooked and glazed. Tough yet tasty. Covered with salt. Perfect bar food. It coats your stomach and allows you to drink without falling over. At the same time it makes you thirsty enough to *want* to drink until you fall over. It's a very Zen concept, this pretzel."

Max ordered another shooter and willed his fast-mounting fear to fade.

"Zen my ass."

CHAPTER FIFTEEN

Max sat, slumped, in Debra's apartment. "He's taunting me," he said, growing angry. An envelope was crumpled on the floor before him. A television guide was perched on his lap.

"That's all that was inside?" Debra asked, sliding onto a sofa.

"Believe me, this is enough. The biggest name in journalism is next, right? Who's big in New York? Jimmy O'Haloran has his column in the *Post*. People adore him. And Roger Gardner is the big man on the boob tube. Since we've just been presented with a free copy of *TV Guide* . . ."

"We can safely assume it's Gardner?" Debra shook her head in amazement. "I still can't believe this is all happening. It's . . ."

"Crazy? No kidding."

"Now what?"

"Now, I try to warn Gardner that he's our killer's next victim . . ."

"If there is *a* killer . . ."

Max stood up and walked across the room. "There has to be a killer. Not only that but it has to be someone who's watching me like a hawk."

"Why's that?"

"I'm getting the packages at your house now and not my own. I've been here only two days." He grabbed his overcoat and slid into it. "I hate the spring."

"Why?"

"It's so upbeat."

"Why don't you call the police? Get them involved?"

Max dismissed the thought immediately. "And then what? What do I tell them? I suspect some loon of offing people because he wants to prove he's a better writer than I am? They already think I'm crazy. That'll cinch it."

THE CON GAME

He grabbed the *TV Guide* and thumbed through it. "Our superstar works at CBS, right? What times does he go on?"

"Five o'clock and eleven o'clock on weekdays. Six and eleven on Sundays."

"If I hurry, I can catch him before the six."

Max shambled toward the door. Debra sighed and watched him go. "Are you going to be all right?"

"Probably not. I despise Roger Gardner. In this case I think the killer might be doing the world of journalism a service."

Cady left Debra's apartment, closing the door behind him. Debra remained on the couch. She reached up and grabbed her television remote and flicked on channel two. *The Rockford Files* had just started. She had been meaning to get the television's color-set button fixed for quite some time. As much as she loved James Garner, it was hard to like a purple hero.

Max made it to the television studio, located in Manhattan's West Fifties, in record time. Of course he had lunged through a lot of red lights. He parked his daughter's sputtering car on the rooftop lot and made his way down to the front entrance. A guard who resembled Joe E. Ross from the old *Car 54, Where Are You?* show sat at a desk, his attention fully devoted to the late afternoon edition of the New York *Post*. Max cleared his throat to get attention. The guard slowly raised his head from behind the tabloid. He gazed at Max, unimpressed. His face had more lumps than a relief map of the Andes.

"Yeah?" he exhaled in Max's direction.

"Loquacious, aren't we?" Max smiled at the guard. The short, squat man did not return the grin.

"Who are you here to see?"

"Roger Gardner. I phoned earlier."

"Name?"

"Cady."

The man scanned a list of neatly typed names mounted on a clipboard. "You're not down here."

He placed the clipboard down and resumed his reading. PREZ TO REDS: DON'T PISS ME OFF.

"Try Ammo, Jimmy." It would be like Gardner to list him like that.

The guard slowly looked up from his paper. "You Jimmy Ammo?"

"Sometimes," Max said, feeling awful.

The pockmarked guard's face slid into smile mode. He wrote out a pass. "Here. He's in studio 2A. Down that puke-green hall and through the orange doors."

"Thanks," Max said, grabbing his kernel of paper.

Max walked for a few moments until he found himself surrounded by pear-shaped men with headsets. A young girl carrying a ledger trotted by. "Excuse me," Max called after her. "Roger Gardner?"

"Dressing room 3C," she said over her shoulder.

Max wandered across the studio. Technicians were scuttling around the wire-strewn floor like ants in search of stray crumbs. One fellow would move a cable one way. Two seconds later a second man would appear and place the cable back in its original position.

Cameras were being maneuvered into position. TelePrompTers were being placed in front of the newscaster's circular desk set. Max was amazed at how small the set looked in real life. On the tube it seemed quite spacious and futuristic, sort of like the deck of the USS *Enterprise*. Close-up, however, it looked closer to a Datsun's dashboard with delusions of grandeur.

A drunken fellow sporting a walrus mustache was being carted past the TelePrompTers by two technicians. A young girl followed behind them, carrying coffee. Max grinned to himself. It was Dr. Wally, the weatherman. Max had always suspected that Dr. Wally gave his weather reports while sloshed. There was no other way to explain why, night after night, his commentary on the weather sounded like a James Joyce novel read aloud in Norwegian. Still, old Wally was real and quite enjoyable . . . which is more than could be said for Roger Gardner, the silver fox of TV journalists.

Boasting a slicked-back mane of steel-gray hair, a dimpled chin, and a voice straight out of a Richard Burton film festival, Gardner, in Max's humble opinion, represented everything that was wrong with television journalism.

A former Grade B movie actor (the only time he ever achieved starring status was in a film called *Invasion of the Pod*

THE CON GAME

People from Mars, an epic wherein he got to intone to his terrified daughter "That may look like your canary, Tweety. That may sound like Tweety. That may even *smell* like Tweety but, honey, in reality, that's a pod person from the planet Mars!"), Gardner turned to television announcing in the mid 1960s.

When TV news started to expand its time slots (most people don't remember that the evening news was a mere fifteen-minute affair until the Kennedy years), Gardner found himself reading wire copy on a local New York station.

Eventually he became a pretty hot local commodity. (Max hated to admit it, but the guy *was* rather dashing.) He had gone network ten years ago and his ratings hadn't flagged since the first night he appeared.

Max chalked that up to the way the man delivered the news. He had the habit, like many TV journalists, of turning every event, either major or minor, into a poignant, slice-of-life short story, complete with O. Henry-esque twist at the end. When the story itself didn't offer a dramatic or ironic fade-out, Gardner would come up with one himself, even if it had nothing to do with the story.

Very often a story that began "What started out as a practical joke ended in tragedy today in the Bronx" would somehow end with Gardner making some inane comment about "something that the ancient Greeks discovered the hard way . . . tragedy is the flip side of laughter." The story itself would concern thirteen people burned to a crisp in a neighborhood bodega as the result of a sparkler setting fire to a pair of curtains. For the record, no one would laugh during the entire story, the victims would be Puerto Rican and not Greek, and the nearest thing to Sophocles seen on camera during the entire coverage would be a charred picture of John Belushi dressed for the toga party scene in *Animal House.*

Still, Gardner managed to finesse his way through his illogical, melodramatic turns and his ratings remained at the top.

Max found the door to 3C. He knocked.

"Enter," came a booming voice from within. Max rolled his eyes, opened the door, and stepped inside.

Gardner was sprawled on a Naugahyde couch reading a copy of *Daily Variety.*

He glanced at Max. "Be with you in a second. They ran an item on me in Army Archard's column. Yesterday. It's impossible to get a copy of *Daily Variety* in New York on the day it's printed. You have to wait twenty-four hours for them to get out here. That's one of the advantages of living in Los Angeles, I suppose. That and the fact that the women out there don't ever wear very much clothing."

He sighed and placed the magazine on the couch beside him. "Can't find it. I'll look later."

Max sat down, uninvited, on a canvas director's chair. Gardner flashed his patented grin. "So you're the great Jimmy Ammo, eh?"

"You ought to know," Max said, fishing in his overcoat pocket for a small package. "You broke the story the other night."

He tossed out a small jar in Gardner's direction. The newsman jerked his hands in front of his chest and caught it instinctively.

"What's this?"

"Mustard," Max said, straight-faced. "It goes good with ham."

Gardner smirked and placed the mustard atop the magazine. "You don't like me much, do you, Cady?"

"Nope."

"I can understand that. A former print journalist having to come face-to-face with one of the men who is responsible for the collapse of newspapers nationwide."

"I'm speechless."

"Our backgrounds may be different, Cady, but aren't we the same breed of man? We each trained to get where we are today. We each studied the little tragic acts that make up this play we call life. While you chased ambulances I chased after audiences. I performed in radio, TV, films, and theater."

"Really?" Max deadpanned.

"Yes. I even played *Macbeth* once."

"Who won?"

Gardner stared at Cady. "What do you want here, Mr. Cady?"

"I came to warn you."

THE CON GAME

Gardner flashed Max an inquisitive look. Max could tell it was meant to be inquisitive because the newsman slanted his left eyebrow higher than normal debonair level.

Max sighed and continued. "I think someone is going to try to kill you."

"Who?"

"I'm not sure."

"Why?"

"I'm not sure."

"Why?"

"I can't tell you. It's just a theory I have. But if you let me stick close to you for a day or so, I think we may be able to catch our killer before he catches you."

Gardner seemed to be impressed by that thought. It certainly would make for a wonderful headline. Excellent publicity across the country. Around the world. The broadcast journalist nodded to himself. Yes, that would definitely put him in the superstar arena, with a salary boost to match.

There was a knock at the door. Gardner called out, "Enter," and the young girl with the ledger peeked in. "Two minutes, Roger."

"Jolly Roger's on his way, dearums." The newsman smiled.

The girl groaned and backed out of the dressing room. "They call me Jolly Roger here because I'm such a happy guy," Gardner said, standing. "Look, Mr. Cady, Max. I'd love to hear more of your exciting theories concerning yours truly but I have a news show to do."

"They're more than mere theories," Max said. "Two people have already died."

"Why haven't I heard about it then?"

"You have. Terry Scott was one of the victims and that model Jamie Soon."

"Jamie Soon. Jamie Soon. I can't say that I remember—"

"Two nights ago? How did you phrase it? 'Pervert claims leggy victim'?"

"Oh. *That* Jamie Soon."

"Yeah. Eric Paine's death may even be connected."

"Are you drunk?"

"No. If I do get plastered, though, I'll come out and do your weather, okay?"

Gardner smirked. "Tell you what. Stay here and we'll talk after the show. Fair enough?"

"Fair enough."

Gardner left Max in the tiny dressing room and walked down the hall to the studio. Max sat down in front of a monitor and watched the newscast.

A thin girl with red hair and large sunglasses stuck her head in the dressing room. "Want some coffee or anything, Mr. Cady?"

Max barely looked up. The newscast was fascinating in its own, mind-numbing way. "A little coffee, please. With cream."

The girl returned a moment later with a Styrofoam cup. She placed it in front of Max as he watched Gardner sail through a puff piece on day-care centers.

"Thanks." Max nodded as the girl turned and left.

Gardner droned on and on. He had a talent for monopologues. When there was nothing left to be said, he continued saying it. Max stifled a yawn.

Uncle Wally appeared in front of the weather map and managed to mistake Virginia for Colorado.

Max leaned forward to laugh and found himself sprawled on the floor. He attempted to climb back into the director's chair, managing to bring it down on top of his chest instead.

His head was swimming. He heard Gardner's voice echo through his mind. He was talking about Terry Scott.

Max sent his left hand spiraling up toward the ceiling. It seemed to detach itself from his arm as it slithered across the Naugahyde couch. Max wriggled across the floor to catch up with his hand. He sent his other hand zipping flat onto the floor's surface . . . just like Spiderman and his webbing. Thwaaap. That's what it sounded like. Thwaaap. Just like in the comic strips.

Max the web-slinger hoisted himself onto the couch. Thwaaap. Christ, that was funny. Max laughed a lot over that one. Whoops. Too much.

Gardner was out of the television now.

He was standing above old Maxie. The redheaded girl was

THE CON GAME

next to old Jolly Roger. Her sunglasses looked like the front end of a Porsche now. Max began to laugh again.

He was giggling. Maybe if he kept it up he could attempt a genuine, by-god guffaw.

Gardner was saying something to Max. Being veddy chipper. Sleep it off, old chum. That sort of thing. Veddy sporty. Understand the stress you've been under.

Max began laughing even more.

Gardner smiled paternally at Max and gave him a casual salute, off the side of the forehead type. John Wayne. Errol Flynn. Gung ho. Pip-pip. Tallyho. God and country. All that. He turned and took the girl by the elbow.

"I haven't seen you around the studio before, have I, child?"

"Tonight's my first night," the woman replied in a whisper.

Max howled with laughter. Her first. Your last. Ahahahahahaha. Old Jolly Roger. Gung ho. Pipdy-pip. Old chappie, you're walking off with the girl who drugged old Maxie-waxie's coffee.

A sudden pain in his stomach caused Max to curl up in fetal position on the sofa. He straightened suddenly. Doubled over again. The pain hit him in waves. He stiffened and curled, stiffened and curled, over and over again, like a snail after being bombarded with salt.

Salt. Pretzel salt. How Zen.

Max's stomach was slowly making its way up to his chin.

Max fought back the pain for a moment.

What would Jimmy Ammo do in a situation like this?

Max Cady threw up.

All over *Daily Variety*.

Headline: SCRIBE RUINS RAG: Barf Blox Pix.

CHAPTER SIXTEEN

Max tried desperately to focus his eyes. He felt as if he had been drinking doubles and now he was seeing the same way.

"Max?"

A female voice cut through the slosh that was hovering above his eyes. "Max? It's Debra, Max."

"And Kenny, Maxie. I'm here too."

Max blinked his eyes slowly. Pain shot through his head like shards of hot glass.

He licked his lips. They were dry and chapped. They tasted vaguely like phlegm. "The doctors told us that if you could walk, we could take you home."

"Easy for them to say," Max said, trying to prop himself up on his elbows. "If I could walk I would have been out of here hours ago . . . wherever here is."

He shook his head clear. He was in a hospital room. A hospital hallway, actually. Or something that looked like it. He seemed to be shuttled against a wall with an all-purpose portable screen set up around him. Outside the screen what sounded like a sneak preview of the new Godzilla versus the world film was taking place. He was amazed he had slept through that din.

"At the risk of sounding like Dick Powell as *The Thin Man*," he muttered, "what happened?"

Before either Debra or McArthur could reply, the portable curtain pulled back and Lieutenant Samuel Lehner and the lump known as Malloy pushed their way in.

"First off, it was William and not Dick Powell who starred in *The Thin Man*. He didn't actually play the title character either. However, he became so closely identified with the term that he starred in a subsequent series of films using *The Thin Man* in the title. All based, of course, on the classic novel by Dashiell Hammett."

THE CON GAME

He smiled at Max. Max felt like he was gazing down the basket of a cobra.

"As to what happened, Mr. Cady, well, we were hoping that *you* could tell *us* that."

"Uh, not at the moment, Lieutenant. I'm still working on easy questions, like . . . Who am I? Where am I? That sort of stuff."

"Fine. Fine. Well, here's what we know officially, Mr. Cady." The lieutenant picked up a small notebook and began thumbing through it.

"At about five-thirty last night you showed up at a television studio on West Fifty-fourth Street demanding to see Roger Gardner. Although you weren't on the official guest list, you bullied your way past the guard."

Max winced, recalling the guard's preoccupation with the *Post* and Jimmy Ammo's less-than-Emily-Post-approved sense of social decorum.

Headline: AMMO CLOBBERS COP: Savage Sap Slices Through Studio.

Lehner continued. "You met with the victim—"

"Victim?"

"Ah yes, more on that later. I'm doing this sequentially, if it's all right with you."

"Fine. I'm a sucker for surprise endings."

"You chatted with Gardner before the newscast in his dressing room. We have a floor girl who saw you—"

"Two floor girls—"

"Two?"

"Yes. A girl with short red hair and large black sunglasses. She was the second one." Lehner gave Max a quizzical look and began gnawing on his beard with his upper lip. Max relaxed slightly. He saw that he had piqued Lehner's interest. He smiled at the lieutenant. "But more of that later."

"Gardner did his newscast and, presumably, returned to his dressing room before leaving for dinner. His nightly routine usually consisted of him leaving the studio at approximately seven-thirty and returning for the eleven o'clock broadcast at approximately ten-thirty P.M."

"Did he usually have dinner dates?"

"I have no idea. Why?"

"Just checking."

"Last night Mr. Gardner did not return for the broadcast. When technicians checked his dressing room they found it a shambles. Searching thoroughly through the hallways, they found an open exit door, a door leading to the rooftop parking garage. You were found on the landing, Mr. Cady . . . passed out cold. They called an ambulance and brought you here."

"What was the verdict?"

"Barbiturate overdose. Quaalude's actually."

"Far-out. I was probably looking for my Blues Magoos records when I collapsed."

"They pumped your stomach out when you got here. You really weren't in all that much danger, Cady. You wouldn't have actually died . . . just suffered a lot."

"You sound disappointed, Lieutenant. I'll try to die for you later on. What happened to Gardner?"

"They found his body about two hours later."

"Where?"

"On the rooftop garage of the studio. He had been strangled with the cord of a studio headset. Been dead for a few hours."

"Did anyone see him leave the studio?"

"We haven't found anyone yet," Lehner said. "The last person seen with Gardner off the set was you, Mr. Cady. What do you think of that?"

"Not too much."

"I have enough now to arrest you for suspicion."

Cady squinted into Lehner's face. "No you don't or you would have already. Even the circumstantial evidence is thin. Would you like to hear what really happened last night?"

Lehner turned to the lump. "Malloy. Take notes."

"During the five o'clock newscast I was offered a coffee by a red-haired young girl. She brought the coffee while I watched the show. During the show I began feeling woozy. By the time Gardner showed up again, I was out on my back in his dressing room."

"Prove it."

"I can't. Interesting thing, though. Gardner *did* have a dinner date last night. At least he was leaving with one."

THE CON GAME

"Your redhead?"

"Uh-huh. She's the one you should be looking for, Lieutenant."

"You think she's our killer?"

"Maybe. Or maybe she just *knows* the killer or maybe even just *saw* him. She's the one who slipped me the Quaaludes and coffee, an interesting concept of cutting down on the caffeine shakes but not one I would recommend for masses."

"You're not funny, Cady."

"But I'm trying awfully hard, Lieutenant. Now the big question is . . . did she drug the coffee herself or was she handed the coffee by someone else at the studio?"

"Why did you show up there, anyhow, Cady?"

"To warn Gardner, Lehner. You know that. You *know* that these killings are being lifted, victim for victim, from my books. You've probably found the appropriate pages stuffed in Gardner's pockets or somewhere by now, right? Anyhow, I tried to keep him alive last night. That's all."

"You didn't do a very good job."

"Neither did you, Lieutenant. And you get paid for that sort of thing. I free-lance."

Lehner motioned for Malloy to close his notebook. "I'm not going to bother to warn you, Cady. You're my celebrity suspect. I don't know *why* you're pulling this shit and I don't care. I never try to psychoanalyze psychos. But I *will* stop these killings, Cady, and I *will* see you behind bars."

"In them, perhaps. Behind them, never."

Lehner's face assumed a Day-Glo red demeanor. He flexed his fists. "Don't push it, Cady."

"I understand your frustrations, Lieutenant. We've all sprung from monkeys . . . you just didn't spring far enough."

The lieutenant and his portly familiar turned and marched away from the bed.

"Maxie, are you crazy?" McArthur said, shaking his head sadly. "That guy is going to be all over you."

"That's fine with me. If his men stick close, then the killer won't be able to get near me."

"You're nuts."

"A distinct possibility but one that I wouldn't want to consider right now. Where are my clothes?"

Debra handed him a clean shirt and pair of slacks. "Here. Your old clothes smelled like a science experiment."

Max sat up in bed and slid the pants under the sheets to put them on. Debra laughed softly. "I have seen that stuff before, you know."

"I rue the day they began teaching sex education in grammar schools," Max muttered, zipping up his fly.

"Watch your ass on this one," Kenny advised, allowing Max to use his shoulder as a support while climbing slowly out of his sickbed. "You may be in over your head here."

"Tell me about it."

"I'm serious. I'm a little bit intrigued about this story—"

"Sorry, Kenny," Debra warned, "this one's an exclusive."

"Not if it goes hard news, honey. Just stick to the features and you'll be fine."

"Children, children," Max intoned, trying to summon up some feeling in his legs. "There's plenty of me to go around."

Max wiggled his toes. He felt his strength returning. The killer had made a mistake last night, a major mistake. All along he had tried to push Max to the limits, make Cady suspect himself in the killings. But last night Max wasn't drunk, he wasn't in an alcoholic stupor during the murder; he was drugged, plain and simple.

Max Cady knew that he was coming apart at the seams but, now, he also knew that he definitely wasn't directly connected with the killings. But this psycho was trying awfully hard to convince everyone, including Max, that he was *more* than just connected. That thought only caused Max to want Carole more. He wouldn't rest until the punk was caught.

"Earth calling Max," Kenny intoned. "Come in, Max."

Cady shook himself out of his mental reverie. "Sorry. Just thinking about our boy."

"Before you get on your Carole crusade again," McArthur cautioned, "shall I play show-and-tell?"

Max shrugged. "What are you talking about?"

"Well, I got curious about some of the supporting players here, Maxie," Kenny said, "so I kept on digging. Your boy Mas-

THE CON GAME

kin? The agent? Well, aside from the fact that the guy's been engineering your career to benefit his own pocketbook, he has a little bit of a police record."

"How little?"

"He did two years for petty larceny ten years ago. His big brother, Peter, managed to smooth things over as much as he could for the kid."

"And when Peter died he left the agency to David, figuring that little brother had straightened out by then."

"Seems that way."

"No big deal. So the guy has a record."

"Now we come to the bereaved widow of Eric Paine."

"Little Gloria, happy at last?"

"Uh-huh. It's Gloria Paine now. Back in 1974 she was known as Lou-Anne Bevens . . . bereaved widow of Clem Bevens. Clem, it seems, was an alleged wife-beater. Lou-Anne, his third wife, was about to get her first whomping when the lovely lass beat him to the punch."

"That pun was beneath you, Kenny."

"Sorry. It's just that I don't get to play detective very often anymore. I'm usually writing about Jacqueline Bisset's wet T-shirts or something. Anyhow, Lou-Anne smashed Clem's head in with an ax handle while he was asleep. Claims that he started torturing her before bedtime but fell asleep before he could really get going.

"The police found some cigarette burns on her body and some small bruises. She made a good impression in court, though. That, coupled with Clem's record as a hell-raiser, softened the jury somewhat. They convicted her of involuntary manslaughter—"

"Involuntary?"

"Don't ask me how. Anyhow, she wound up getting a suspended sentence out of it. The judge figured she had done a year all told during the trial procedure and that was enough for such a sweet young thing."

"Shit," Cady muttered. "I hate it when things get complicated. I can't even get a good vendetta going."

Max staggered into the emergency ward corridor. Kenny and

Debra flanked him, steadying his quivering body. "I need a drink," Max said.

A woman came in holding her young boy in her arms. The boy looked like he was in two pieces. She was screaming in language Max didn't understand as the doctors gingerly lifted the boy and placed him on a gurney.

Max shut his eyes as his friends led him out of the hospital. It didn't help.

The boy's screams triggered a tidal wave of cries from years past: ambulance whining, squad cars shrieking, fire trucks bellowing, victims whimpering.

He saw an avalanche of faces. Some were frozen in one, last silent scream; others continued to bleat as they were placed, battered and bleeding, on stretchers by impassive ambulance attendants. Flashbulbs went off. Relatives moaned. Police waved off bystanders in guttural tones.

The faces continued to come forward. One after another.

Max blinked away tears of surprise.

Those were ghosts he thought he'd exorcised years ago.

CHAPTER SEVENTEEN

Max walked briskly uptown. He had a system he used when he was in Manhattan, a rhythm. If he timed himself correctly, he could average one uptown or downtown block per minute. Crosstown blocks usually took anywhere from a minute and a half to two, lights included. By walking at a brisk march (or slow jog), and adhering to this time schedule, he could accurately estimate his time of arrival at any destination.

He arrived at David Maskin's office precisely on cue. Eleven-thirty a of m. David's secretary was named Candy. She was an attractive woman in her late thirties who wore Kabuki makeup and blouses that didn't seem to possess top buttons. Professionally disinterested in anyone who walked into Maskin's office, she nonetheless chatted with Max.

Max, it seems, was different from most clients.

His Greta Garbo stance and his current involvement in a homicide investigation elevated him to minor legend status.

"Are you going to trap the killer?" Candy asked, intrigued.

"I beg your pardon?"

"Are you going to catch this copycat killer?"

Max just gaped at the woman.

Candy grinned, running a heavily taloned hand through her blow-dried blond mane. "Oh, David's been telling everyone about the murders. He's really excited about all of this. He thinks that the killer will kick your novels up to Sherlock Holmes status in the book-selling community. Really."

"Really."

"Sure. Today most of the best-selling crime books are nonfiction. You know, writers attach themselves to mass murderers, license the rights to the killers' stories, and then just crank 'em out. But your books are fiction, you know? Nobody reads fiction nowadays, unless it's romance. *Lace Honeymoon in Dark Cas-*

tle? Well, David figures that your novels will sell like nonfiction best-sellers if these killings keep up. He sees you as being a real celebrity.

"You know, like Truman Capote? Only you're a lot taller. And you don't strike me as being a sissy, if you know what I mean. But like that. Like a real celebrity.

"Personally, I think that this killer that David is always talking about is a really strange person. I mean to take a book and try to make it real, that's not too sane. You know, it's like, imagine if everyone who read a book did that? You'd have people killing people all the time."

"Either that or hunting great white whales."

"Huh?" Candy stared at Max, her eyes forming one, spiritual inquisition mark.

"Nothing at all. Is David off his other call as yet?"

Candy glanced at the phone lines. "Why, yeah."

She buzzed Maskin.

"Yes?" the phone burped, in a decent imitation of Maskin's voice.

"Max Cady is here. He's been here for fifteen minutes."

"Fine. Send him in."

Max prodded himself out of the canvas chair that sat in Maskin's waiting room and walked into David's office. Maskin's office was suitably high-tech: chrome with glass with more chrome and more glass. A few plants. If you tossed in a strobe light or two, you would have had a mini-disco.

"Max. Max. Isn't this exciting?"

"What?"

Maskin stepped forward and pumped Max's hand as if he expected butter. "The killings. I've been following the stories and putting everything together by myself."

"Wonderful."

"I'll say. Since your involvement in the killings, even in a diluted form, has been made public, book orders are up. Congratulations."

"I would have preferred ordinary autograph parties, actually."

"Let's take what we can get. As long as the murders continue, we're a hot commodity."

"I can see you value human life very dearly, David."

Maskin frowned. It didn't seem sincere. It was more like a childish pout, really. Imagine Charlie Brown trying to essay a decent Hamlet. "Max. Of course, I genuinely mourn for the victims but . . . as long as there is a psycho killer out there willing to give you a lot of free publicity, let's go with the flow."

Max, seated in a chair directly in front of Maskin's desk, placed his large, sausage-shaped fingers on the desk top and sighed. "David, look. Someone is butchering people out there. That's bad. Someone is also dragging me into it. That's very, very bad.

"I am being used. I am being set up. I'm pretty sure I know who's doing it, but I'm not sure why. There are too many variables for my liking. So, just in case you know more than you let on, which is exceedingly doubtful, let me say this.

"I've always had reservations about you. You're the kind of guy who deals in baloney and insists it's food for thought. Okay. That's your business. You're an agent. But, lately, little birdies have been telling me bad things about you. Cheap shots, maybe. But, in all fairness, I have to let you know that I'm aware of your police record. I'm aware of your involvement with the wailing widow Paine. I'm aware that if I'm framed or implicated in any of these killings, you will reap a substantial reward in terms of royalties while I will get nothing but a change of neighborhoods, trading New Jersey suburbs for state pen submorons."

All traces of color drained out of Maskin's face. "Max! You don't actually think that I have had anything to do with these killings? I—I—I'm aghast. I'm appalled. I'm a former altar boy, you know?"

"So was Hitler."

"No shit?"

"Yeah. He was kicked off the squad, though."

"Me too."

"Ever hold down a job as a paperhanger?"

"No."

"Well, you may be redeemable yet."

Max stood up and headed for the door. Maskin scrambled out of the chair and followed his client. "Max, I swear to God, I'm not trying to get you into any trouble. I really don't know anything about this murder stuff. As for Gloria and me, well, I haven't confided in anyone about it in light of Eric's death and all."

"Bad publicity?"

"It just happened, you know? I mean, Eric could be a real shit. He genuinely abused her. She needed someone to turn to and I was there."

"How convenient."

"Max, you might as well know. Gloria and I intend to get married after the estate is settled. For the time being, however, we're being discreet."

"I didn't think you had it in you."

Maskin sighed and shook his head. "You really don't have any respect for me, do you?"

Max smiled. "Not in the least, David. During the past eight days you have successfully destroyed my entire life, fragmented any peace of mind I might have been trying to accumulate, and plunged me headfirst into a murder investigation. Why should I respect you?"

Max walked out the door and past Candy's desk.

Maskin followed close behind. "I made sure they got a good artist for the book covers, didn't I?"

Max kept on walking.

Maskin continued to follow, shouting, "Hey! At least you look like *you* on those book covers and not Spiro Agnew!"

Maskin stood, fuming, at the exit door. Max stood, down the hall, waiting for an elevator.

"You don't look like Broderick Crawford, either," Maskin continued. "That's thanks to me."

The elevator arrived and Max, silently, stepped inside.

Maskin stood in the doorway. "Yeah," he muttered. "Things could be a lot worse. You could've looked like Dagwood Bumstead on those book covers if it wasn't for me."

He allowed the outer door to swing closed before turning and, walking past Candy, heading for his office.

"Mr. Maskin?" Candy asked.

"Yeah?"

"Who's Spiro Agnew? Dagwood I know about. He's in the comic strips, right?"

"Yeah," Maskin said, returning to his office. "So was Agnew."

CHAPTER EIGHTEEN

The inside of the New York *Times* looked like the old city-room set from the *Lou Grant* TV show only tackier. Pressboard dividers separated desks from other desks in a lame attempt to simulate real, architecturally solid office privacy. Wandering through the pressboard corridors, you had the feeling that if you found who you were looking for within fifteen minutes you would be rewarded with a large wad of cheese.

Max loped through a series of zigzagging causeways until he found a wall with the hand-lettered plaque DEBRA KNIGHTLY attached to it. Next to the plaque was a small sticker picturing a clown with a red circle-slash superimposed over his face.

"No bozos," Max chuckled to himself. He wondered if that would exclude him from Debra's cubbyhole. He stuck his head over the wall. "Knock, knock," he said, peering down at Knightly.

"Come on in, Max," Debra said absentmindedly.

Max strolled around the wall and sank into a contoured plastic chair next to Debra's desk. "You look like I feel," he said.

Debra shuffled through a group of papers on her desk. "Autopsy reports on the Ammo book victims. Pretty gruesome, Max. I don't think this person is very stable at all."

"You're kidding me."

Debra shuddered and looked at Max. "Sorry. It's just that this stuff is so gross. It's out of my line, you know?"

"Have you heard from the dear lieutenant?"

"Yes, as a matter of fact. He contacted both Kenny McArthur and myself. It seems that we are the only outsiders, aside from you, of course, who know about the book pages being left at the scene of the crime. He made us swear to continue not to publish that one detail. He thinks that, if the killer turns out to be someone *other* than you—"

"So he does have his doubts after all. How sweet."

"—the pages may be the big clue."

"He watches too many *Kojak* reruns."

"I never liked *Kojak*."

"Me neither. Too brash."

"How was your chat with Maskin?"

"He's either a very good actor or just a very good agent."

"You read him the riot act?"

"Uh-huh. And he seemed quite shocked."

"What now?"

Max pulled out a piece of handwritten paper, the paper bearing the names of the most popular trend-setters in New York. "I guess I go see our next potential victim."

"Who's that?"

"Rudy Randall, pop star extraordinaire."

"Suppose I see him instead?"

"You're a fan?"

Debra flashed a childlike grin. "And how. I have every album he ever recorded."

"That must go back to 1968."

"1967. He was known as 'The Rooster' back then. He was the lead singer of a British blues group known as Chicken Coop. Amazing voice. Simply amazing."

"Yeah. I remember. It always sounded like he had been gargling with razor blades. I saw him a few—"

"Everyone compared him to Ray Charles—"

"He bottomed out very hard for a while, didn't he?"

"Yeah. Early 1970s. His manager killed himself. Rudy took it pretty hard. A second manager swindled him out of nearly a half-million dollars and signed two different contracts with two different labels for him. After the manager split, Rudy was stuck in the middle of a lawsuit. All parties agreed to drop all suits if Rudy upheld both his contracts. As a result he spread himself out pretty thin, doubling his record output. After two years he just packed it in and took a pretty lengthy hiatus. Came back strong in 1976 though with a new image—"

"British fop."

"Sort of. New, very produced sound. He started a whole new career."

"He sounds like a fighter."

"He looks like a lover."

Max stood up and picked up a copy of the *Times* entertainment section. "I'll try not to swoon. He's playing at the Garden tonight?"

"The first of a five-day stint."

"You know what hotel he's staying in?"

"Trade secret."

"Suppose I promise to get an autograph for you."

"Inscribed to Debra? With love?"

"With love and great passion."

"He's at the U.N. Plaza."

Max smiled and headed back toward the maze of plasterboard. Debra yelled over her wall, "You'd better remember that autograph."

"I'll remember."

Max frowned trying to find the door. He hoped the Rooster paid attention to what Max was going to tell him or Debra's autograph might wind up being a collector's item by the time the day was over.

The U.N. Plaza was the kind of hotel that Max scrupulously tried to avoid. It was too slick and too chic for his tastes. The people at the desk acted as if they were doing you a profound favor by glancing in your direction and uniformed security men tried to act casual as they eyeballed every visitor who entered the lobby.

"Rudy Randall, please," Max requested of an ice-blonde sitting behind the front desk.

"Is he expecting you?"

"I doubt it." She gave him a Medusa look. He wondered if she combed the snakes out of her hair in the morning.

Max attempted to screw a smile into place below his nose. "Tell him it's Jimmy Ammo. I'm a fan of his."

The woman gave him a second Gorgon glance but her confidence wavered enough for her to place the call to Randall's

THE CON GAME

room. Even from his side of the desk he could hear Randall yell "No shit!" over the phone.

The woman interpreted Randall's remark as she replaced the phone on the receiver.

"Mr. Randall says he'd be delighted if you visited his suite. 1402."

"Thanks." Max nodded. He waited for a glass-lined elevator to arrive to take him up to the fourteenth floor.

On the other side of Manhattan a thin package was being slipped under Debra Knightly's apartment door by a bored messenger. It was a record album . . . Rudy Randall's latest.

CHAPTER NINETEEN

A black man dressed in a shiny gray suit and looking like a belligerent Buddha swung open the door to room 1402. "Cmonnin."

"Thanks," Max said.

A tall, thin man, in his late thirties, wearing skin-tight jeans, a torn T-shirt top, and a haircut that looked like the active end of a feather duster bounded toward the door. "Max! Or should I say Jimmy now?"

"Max is fine, Rudy. I didn't know if you'd remember me."

Randall's face broke into a lined smile. "How could I forget! It was my first U.S. tour. Filled with screaming crazies and teeny-boppers. Surrounded by hipper-than-thou reporters, all except for one old grouch in the back of the bus who kept on saying, 'Crime is my beat.' Over and over again."

"Well it *was,*" Max said, raising a protesting hand. "Christ, that was a long time ago."

Rudy wrapped a protective arm around Max's stooped shoulders. "We've both held up pretty well, though, I suppose. Want a beer?"

"Sure."

Max walked into the center of the suite's living room. Overstuffed furniture, glass table, thick carpet, the kind of room usually reserved for the cover of *Metropolitan Home* and the habitats of Beverly Hills plastic surgeons. "Your taste in hotels has . . . changed," Max offered.

Randall padded in carrying two lagers. "No more Holiday Inns, if that's what you mean."

"I seem to remember portable TV sets too."

Randall broke into a laugh. "Oh yeah. We made everything portable back then."

"Right through the windows and into the swimming pools."

THE CON GAME

"You were just as guilty as we were. As a matter of fact, I recall you leading Chicken Coop into quite a few rowdy situations. All the other reporters just watched. You were the only one that joined in."

"Nearly cost me my job," Max chuckled.

"How's Peg-o'-my-heart?"

"She died," Max said, staring at his lager. "Quite a few years ago. Sara, the little girl, is a big girl now. Divorced with a girl of her own."

"Wow."

"How about you?"

Rudy rested a pointed chin in his palm. "Single at the moment. Two wives, two divorces, and three palimony suits in a dozen or so years. Not bad but not a record."

Max found himself smiling at Randall. It really *was* good seeing this good-natured goof again. It reminded Max of another time when things were a little less crazy, a little less grim. Randall stared at Max and laughed out loud. "I can't believe you're Jimmy Ammo. You could have knocked me over with a Biafran when I saw your picture in the paper. I mean, really, Max. I read a few of those books when I was on the road. It was like you crossed Sam Spade with Conan."

Max nearly spit up the beer in his mouth. He giggled and a few snorts of beer foamed up through his nose. "It's a long story, Rudy. I stopped writing them a long time ago. I hoped everyone would forget about them. Then this whole mess happened . . ."

"What mess?"

"This publicity. My agent brought the books back and leaked out who Jimmy Ammo was and—"

"Sounds like literary blackmail."

"Not quite literary."

"You're right." Randall grinned. "I was being kind."

The two men drank in silence. The black Buddha prowled around in the kitchen. Finally, Randall spoke. "You didn't come here to talk about old times . . . unless you've changed a lot over the years."

"I didn't." Max began to feel uneasy.

"So, what's the deal?"

"I don't know how to say this."

"Try forming the words with your lips and push out from the diaphragm."

Max exhaled slowly. "Rudy. Someone is going to try to kill you tonight."

Randall didn't seem surprised.

Max continued his spiel. "I'm serious."

Randall sighed and got to his feet. He walked over to a massive window and looked out onto the United Nations Building and the East River. "A lot has changed since the last time we saw each other, Max. I've become a star, then a bum, and, now, a star again. Me. Rudolph Randall. Son of a coal miner and a shoe clerk.

"Remember how things were on that first tour? Crazy but simple? Remember how the music was just blues with a backbeat. I'd get up there and sing 'Squeeze My Lemon' and the crowd would go wild and that would be the end of it. The tour would be over. I could go home and that would be that."

Randall turned slowly from the window and faced Max. His face seemed to have aged a decade. "It's not like that anymore. I can never go home. I'm stuck, Max. I'm stuck in a limbo, in a never-never land I've created for myself. Success today, fame today, means never being able to go out alone without guys like Bluto over there . . ."

The black man grunted.

"It means having seven or eight cars instead of one so fans won't get used to you driving around in a model they can recognize from a distance. It means no more casual lunches, no more backslapping friends, no more strolls in the park . . . no more private life."

Randall offered an ironic smirk as he returned to his chair. "It also means living with fear gnawing at you twenty-four hours a day. Some of my fans, some of my biggest fans, Max, quite frankly are weird. Some people start out liking your music and wind up worshiping you, like a sort of demigod. They invent myths concerning your life-style, interpret your songs in deep and meaningful ways.

"They come up with a set of rules you're supposed to live by, and if you transgress those rules, they feel it is their duty as your

THE CON GAME

devoted followers to punish you for your insensitivity, for your sins."

Max tried to offer a soothing response. All he came up with was, "I—I—"

"Crime was your beat, remember? Well, the fear of crime is my life now. We get crank calls and letters constantly. We get bomb threats. Odd little people showing up at the gates at all hours. I have a security system outside my house that rivals anything you've seen in a James Bond film. We have metal detectors attached to the mailbox.

"All this because I opened my mouth to sing a little blues once upon a time."

Randall slouched in his chair. "I'm not feeling sorry for myself, you understand. I'd never stop singing. It's just that it's all so hard to comprehend. I love music. It's my life. And, damn it, I resent having to live my life like a frightened animal because I choose to continue to love music.

"Look at John Lennon. What harm did he ever do to anybody? The poor bastard. All he wanted to do was make music, to take his ideas and match them with melodies and give those melodies to whoever wanted to listen. Because he chose to do that, he had to cope with a lot of emotional crap. Okay. You're prepared to do that. Handling success can be a big part of this job.

"But what did he ever do, either in his life or in his music, to justify the kind of death they gave him? Gunned down in the streets, for Christ's sake. You don't do that to the worst criminals in this country. And the son of a bitch who did it was a fucking *fan!*"

Randall began massaging his forehead with his palms. "Lennon's death really let the rest of us know that we were wide open. Almost every performer you meet on the road now has a football team of security men in tow. George Harrison hardly leaves his house anymore. Elton John still goes into a trance when he talks about Lennon's murder. He tours maybe once every two or three years. It's nuts. We're all scared, Max. You know why?"

"No."

"Because no matter what we do, it's not going to be enough.

We could hire fifty security men and if one, dedicated crazy wanted to kill us, he could do it. If he's stopped on Monday, maybe he'll come back on Tuesday or Wednesday or a week from Wednesday or a year from Wednesday. But if he wants to do it, he'll come back. He'll be patient. Remember *The Most Dangerous Game?*"

"The book where the crazy guy on the island hunts down people?"

"Yeah. Remember how patient he was? Almost loving. The hunter tenderly stalking and eliminating his prey." Randall shivered. "A lot of us feel really helpless, Max. We *have* to go out on the road and perform. It's part of our business. It's part of our job. But, mostly, it's an essential part of our life. Once we do that, though, we surrender all control of our lives to some psychos out there who want to be recognized as our biggest fans."

"This psycho is a little different, Rudy."

"How?"

"He's a fan of *mine.*"

Randall motioned to Bluto for a second beer. "I don't get it."

"There's someone out there who is imitating all the murders in my books sequentially. He's working on the second novel now. He's matched the first two fictitious victims with two real ones and the next one he's due to off is a rock-and-roll star."

"Me?"

"Sure seems that way."

"Well, his motives may be different but the end result will prove the same, right?"

"Look, Rudy, you're a bright man. Maybe you're too bright for the business you're in—"

"Ah-ha! A professional chauvinist."

"Can't you do something? Cancel the show?"

"Hardly."

"Alert the police?"

"Afraid not, Max. If we increase the presence of the police at the Garden, then the kids will automatically act rowdier. They react badly to uniforms. Can't blame them, really. If we bring in plainclothesmen, the kids *sense* it. Cops have a way about them, you know? A mentality, an us-versus-them aura that the kids can smell. Things can get ugly."

"What about hiring people then who will just stick with you from dressing room to stage?"

"I have Bluto."

"How about seeing if Bluto has a few friends? Will you do that as a personal favor?"

Bluto handed Randall another beer. "How can I resist a personal favor that might save my ass?"

"Great." Max sipped the last frothy bit of lager in his bottle. The phone in the next room rang. Randall excused himself. Bluto followed.

Max found himself nodding off. He blinked and refocused his eyes. Gazing around the room, he noticed a large box under the windows. He walked over and peered inside. Microphones. He picked one up and held it.

"Ah-ha!" Rudy said, reentering the room. "You've found my private stash."

Max replaced the mike. "Do you always carry these around?"

"Uh-uh. These were just ordered to replace the ones we mashed last week. They wound up here instead of the Garden. They'll be in place before tonight."

"Well," Max said. "I guess I'll hit the road. Can you do two more favors for me?"

Randall gave him a fishy look. "What am I letting myself in for? Well, I suppose."

"Let me be there tonight with you."

"I didn't know you liked rock and roll, Max."

"I don't. Crime is my beat, remember? But I might be able to spot this lunatic in a crowd."

Randall considered that. "Fine. Meet me here at six-thirty, we can go over together. I'll tell the groupies you're my father."

"Thanks."

"Second favor?"

Max motioned to a pile of eight-by-ten glossies of Randall perched on the glass coffee table. "Can you sign one of those for me?"

"You want an autograph? I'm touched."

"It's not for me. It's for—"

"—a friend. Yeah I know. How should I sign it?" Randall waved a hand in the air. Bluto produced a pen.

" 'To Debra . . .' "

" '. . . with love'?"

"How about 'with love and great affection'?"

Randall began scrawling on the photo. "You're just like your books, you know? Very, very verbose."

Max placed the beer bottle on the glass table. Randall absentmindedly snapped his fingers. Bluto produced a coaster and slid it under the bottle. Max glanced at Randall and then at the television set perched in the middle of the living room.

Max wondered if the television set realized how safe it was.

CHAPTER TWENTY

Max stared at the Rudy Randall album on the kitchen table. "No note came with it?"

Debra shook her head, admiring the autographed eight-by-ten in her hands. "Nope. Gee. He really is cute. How did you manage this?"

"He respects his elders."

"Would you like me to bring in the wheelchair now or later?"

Max pounded his fist on the table. "Damn it! Carole is a real maniac, you know that? He doesn't give a shit that he's killing innocent people just to make a point. He's gloating over it. He's enjoying taunting me."

Debra remained silent. Max went to the refrigerator, flung the door open with a snap, and pulled out a bottle of beer. "Well, tonight, I'm going to stop him cold."

Debra sighed, knowing that she wasn't going to like the direction the conversation was heading toward. "How are you going to do that?"

"You mean, how are *we* going to do that."

"That's what I was afraid of."

Max sat across from Debra. "Look. All we have to do to get Lieutenant Twirp off my back is *prove* that Carole is in the same vicinity as one of the murder attempts."

Max made a conscientious effort not to say "murders." After all, Rudy was a survivor. . . .

"I'll go with Rudy to the Garden tonight and you, my dear, will do your first stint at police stakeout work."

Debra blinked. "Which means?"

"I'll loan you the Toyota. You simply pull up across from the Paine brownstone—Carole's still living there, right?"

"Yes."

"And watch the son of a bitch. If he leaves the building follow him. If he heads for the Garden, call Inspector Clouseau."

"And while I'm playing like I'm part of the architectural splendor of Ninety-first Street?"

"I will be accompanying Rudy Randall to Madison Square Garden."

"I don't suppose we could switch assignments?" Debra asked hopefully.

Max pursed his lips and raised the beer bottle. "Not on your life."

Or, more to the point, Randall's.

After much coaxing Debra got the battered Toyota to start. She sputtered up to Ninety-first Street and pulled into an empty parking space a half block away from the Paine brownstone.

She took a paperback book out of her purse and prepared to devour it while she waited for Carole to do something . . . anything. Since a psychiatrist also had an apartment in the Paine building, there was a steady stream of people entering and leaving the structure.

A businessman.

A young mother.

A woman in a business suit.

As darkness approached Debra found herself staring at the second floor of the brownstone. She couldn't swear to it, but she thought she saw Carole near a window. The figure was thin enough, almost emaciated.

She put the paperback down on the seat beside her and squinted her eyes. Yes. It was Carole. The young man walked over to the window and pulled a pair of flimsy lace curtains closed. He then walked away from the window. A light flickered on, illuminating the room in an eerie glow. It must be a fluorescent bulb to get that kind of strobe effect, Debra reasoned.

Through the curtains, she watched Carole move across the room and sit in a chair in front of a flickering television set. He sat and watched the television, bending over occasionally to reach into a bag of potato chips.

Debra yawned.

THE CON GAME

It was not exactly prime-time fare . . . even by contemporary television standards.

As the sun disappeared behind New Jersey, Debra continued her vigil. Carole continued his viewing.

Max sat, or rather twisted his body into an upright fetal position, in the back of Rudy Randall's limousine. The limo had tinted windows, allowing its occupants to gaze out upon the streets of Midtown Manhattan at dusk but shielding the riders from the stares of the curious outside.

Randall was clothed in what looked to be an Earl Shibe paint job. Mylar and leather covered with strips of gaily colored silk. Max couldn't help but stare and Randall couldn't help but notice.

"Consider it a uniform, Max," Randall said.

Max sighed and shook his head. "It's nice to know the collegiate look isn't dead."

Randall smiled to himself and scrutinized the streets outside. "Now, prepare for your descent into the inferno."

The limo headed west on Thirty-fourth Street, angling itself for the backstage entrance of Madison Square Garden on Thirty-second off Seventh. Approaching the Garden from the East Side, Max could see the mobs of kids on queue outside.

His jaw dropped at the sight. Young girls with bare midriffs, half-bared bosoms, and sprayed-on slacks leaned against pink mohawked, war-painted, pimply faced boys so grotesque they would have made James Fenimore Cooper turn to knitting as a means of artistic expression. Leather-jacketed greasers bumped elbows with clean-cut preppies. Torn T-shirts were worn proudly alongside British mod outfits.

"Quite an eclectic crowd you draw," Max said.

"Yeah. If you look hard enough you'll spot people our age in there," Randall said. "Flotsam left over from the old Chicken Coop days."

The limo pulled into Thirty-second Street and a group of *Clockwork Orange-* meets *Night of the Living Dead*-inspired music lovers began to tag along. By the time the auto pulled up to the backstage entrance at least two hundred kids clung to the car. A dozen policemen, two on horseback, charged into the crowd, delicately beating them back with drawn billy clubs.

Max made a move to open the door. Randall gripped his hand and pulled it away from the handle. "Not yet, Max. You'll get us killed. There's a science to this. Watch."

The two men sat in the back of the car with an anxious Bluto. They waited until the metal backstage door was swung open by a bouncer who looked like a personal friend of Fay Wray. Two cops tossed two wooden horses up next to the doors, opening a causeway between teenage bodies.

"Now," Randall yelled.

Bluto practically kicked open the door. Grabbing both Max and Randall by the shoulders, he ran toward the doorway, pushing his charges forward.

"Roo-dee, roo-dee, roo-dee," the crowd cheered.

Rudy waved lamely to his fans.

Max gasped for air.

Bluto growled.

The massive black man tossed the pair through the doors as the security simian made a move to pull them shut.

Max stood inside the Garden gasping for breath as the doors clanged behind him.

Rudy stared at the large man and grinned. "Glamorous, huh?"

A representative from Rudy's record company trotted up to Randall. "Rudy? Hi. Chip Spectrum. Zephyr Artist Relations. Remember? We met at the Lolly Folder funeral?"

Rudy smiled vacantly. "Oh yeah. Hi. I thought Mike Dysan would be here tonight."

"Called away on urgent business. We heard a rumor that Dylan wanted to change labels and Mike wanted to talk to him personally."

"Does Dylan still make records?" Max asked.

The shaggy-haired, perfectly coiffed record executive looked at Max for the first time, slapping a cloth patch on Max's blazer. The patch read RUDY RANDALL NEW AMERICA TOUR: GUEST PASS.

"That'll let you come and go without getting hassled, Mr.

THE CON GAME

Mitchum." He smiled. "Chip Spectrum. Glad to meet you. I've seen all your movies."

"That shouldn't have taken you too long," Max said.

Randall wrapped an arm around Max. "C'mon, Big Bob, let me show you the wonderful world of backstage."

"It's this way," Chip babbled, leading the men toward an elevator. He patted Max affectionately on the back. "I loved you in *The Treasure of Sierra Madre*."

"That was Bogart."

"I loved him in that too."

Bluto trailed after the men sullenly.

Debra Knightly was cold. She couldn't get the Toyota's engine to turn over and she was afraid of simply turning the battery on to activate the car's heater. That's all she'd need. A dead battery. She glanced at the house. Carole was still sitting in front of a flickering television munching away on an occasional potato chip. The whole room was bathed by the television's kinetic glow.

By the time Rudy and Max got themselves situated in the backstage dressing room, the opening act was onstage and belting away. Five guys from Texas who knew three chords among them. They called themselves "The Lowest." Max agreed.

The members of Rudy's outfit were a boisterous lot, a mixture of British musicians from the 1960s and the 1980s. Of the eight musicians present, four seemed New Wave oriented, with haircuts inspired by your Marine local drill instructor, three resembled Woodstock Nation refugees with shoulder-length tresses, and the band's lone female member, the keyboard player, was bald.

"That takes a lot of guts," Max said to Randall, nodding in the girl's direction.

"I'll say," Rudy acknowledged. "That chemotherapy is tough shit."

Max lapsed into silence, not knowing whether he was being made sport of or not.

Two long-legged lovelies in black fishnet stockings and very little else walked into the room.

"Ah, the happy hookers," crowed one of the New Wavers. "See much action today?"

"A lot more than I've seen from your section of the stage lately, doll," sneered the blond half of the tag-team duo.

"Ooooh," the New Waver replied. "I've been humbled by sarcasm."

Randall leaned toward Max. "Wilma Darling and Candice Hilgoes. Two of the best backup singers in rock and roll today."

"Do they really hate that guy?" Max whispered.

"Naaah. It's all part of the give and take we get going before a show. Builds up adrenaline."

The opening band was winding down their set. Max could tell because they were playing their three chords slower now.

He pulled Randall aside for a moment. "Rudy, please. Do me a favor and watch your ass out there tonight. If anything, *anything*, seems wrong, get off the stage."

"You're going to make someone a wonderful wife someday, Max."

Max smirked as the musicians left the dressing room. The guitars, the bass, and the keyboards were already in place onstage. Only the horn players brought their instruments out with them.

Randall was the last man to jog toward the massive stage of Madison Square Garden.

Bluto jogged after him. Max jogged alongside.

"Bluto," Max hissed as the crowd began its "hot-rod" chant, "I don't like this at all."

"Me neither," Bluto growled. "Personally, this music offends me."

The patrolman bent over the tiny green car parked at the curb. Inside, a woman dozed.

"Any trouble, miss?"

Debra awoke with a start. "Uh, no. No, Officer. Not really. The car won't start. I've called my . . . husband. He's on his way."

The cop smiled and nodded. The light of a nearby streetlamp bathed his face in an eerie, dead yellow hue. "Well, roll up your window, then. It's not exactly safe to take a catnap in a car at this time of night."

"Yes, sir," Debra replied. Had she let Max down? Had she let Carole escape the house?

The policeman walked back to Madison Avenue and continued his beat.

Debra cast a furtive glance at the window in the Paine house. Carole was still in front of the television.

Debra sighed in relief and settled down into the seat. She'd call it quits in another hour or so.

Max stood on the sidelines as Rudy Randall performed his last big number of the set. Rudy had explained the routine on the way over.

He'd do one gigantic, final production number and then trot offstage while the band chugged along solo for the last few verses. The band would stop. The crowd would go wild. The band would stand there, facing the crowd, hesitate, and then run offstage.

The crowd would cheer and stomp. They'd light matches and flick their Bics. After a few moments of foot stomping, Rudy would allow a roadie to go out and adjust a mike. The crowd would go wild.

Another minute would go by and then Rudy and the band would come out and do another song as carefully nurtured pandemonium rocked the hall.

This sort of behavior would go on for three encores. Everyone would go home happy: the crowd, which would think it had gotten more than its money's worth; the agent, who would know that this show would be a cinch to book back into the hall at any given time after this sort of audience reaction, and the promoter, who would gleefully note that the planned encores would still end the show before the eleven o'clock curfew . . . after which he would have to pay his union members time and a half.

Max stood next to Bluto, watching Rudy lapse into a bump-and-grind routine as smoke billowed across the stage and strobe lights flickered spastically. Laser beams cut through the smoke and hit a glistening ball hanging, suspended, from the center ceiling of the Garden. Shards of light littered the air like fireflies.

Rudy moved away from the microphone and did a few dance steps with his backup singers. One of the girls tossed him a microphone. Rudy caught it and stood erect, shaking his body in sharp, convulsive motions.

The band continued to play.

The lights continued to strobe.

Max sensed trouble.

Randall continued to convulse, standing amid the swirling clouds of man-made smoke.

"Shit," Max bellowed. He ran across the stage, narrowly missing one of the New Wave guitarists. He hit Randall with a flying body block. He had to break contact. He felt the electricity slice through his legs like hot pinpricks. Rudy was still holding the microphone. Max continued to roll across the stage, his momentum propelling both himself and Randall toward the far side of the stage.

Randall clutched the microphone. Blood was trickling from his mouth. He had bitten deep into his tongue.

Max was vaguely aware of the smell of charred flesh as he came to a stop next to the screaming backup singers. He no longer felt the pinpricks in his legs. The microphone cord had snapped. Contact had been broken.

Max tried to stand up. His legs refused to obey his mental commands. He found himself crawling on all fours to Randall's side. His head was swimming.

He caught a glimpse of a terrified Bluto careening across the stage.

Police were running onto the stage.

The houselights were being turned on.

The spell was being broken.

Max's eyeballs tilted backward into his head. He vaguely made out the backup singers standing above him, screaming.

There were two now.

Just before the accident, there had been three.

"Sorry, Rudy," Max sighed before passing out.

CHAPTER TWENTY-ONE

Max found himself being wheeled down a hospital corridor. A vaguely familiar face gazed down at him. "Maxie? Is that you?"

Max squinted at the gray-haired man above him. "Jerry? Jerry Peters?"

"Yeah. How ya doin'? Geez. It's been years. You look pretty good for someone who is pretty bad."

Max's eyeballs began to tilt upward again. "Easy does it, Maxie," Peters said. "Diane, get an IV set up. Yeah. I run this little emergency outfit. Pretty neat, huh? Come on, Max, talk to me."

Max pulled himself back into consciousness. "I need a phone, Jerry. Can you get me a room with a phone?"

"This is a hospital, Max, not a hotel."

"I need a *phone!*" Max bellowed. Catching himself, he added, "If I don't get one, I'll take my business somewhere else in the future."

Jerry grunted. "You'll get your phone."

By the time Debra arrived Max was already holding court in his room. A spiral notebook and pencils were on his bed and he was carefully maneuvering a phone around a dripping IV bottle.

"What kept you?" Max said.

"Glad to see you're still your old cheerful self. I came as soon as I got your message."

"You weren't home when I called."

"No kidding. I was playing Sherlock Holmes with Carole, remember?"

Max replaced the phone on the receiver. "And . . . ?"

"And he didn't leave the house all night. He watched TV, Max. In the front room. I saw him the whole time."

"Could you have dozed off?"

"Not long enough for him to make it down to the Garden and

back. I heard what happened on the radio coming home. I'm sorry, Max. I know you and Randall had some history—"

"Carole is going to pay for this, I swear."

Debra regarded Cady with a vague sense of dread. "But, Max . . ."

"Yeah. I know what you saw. But I know what I *feel*. I was a good reporter, Debra. One of the best street guys the *News* ever had. It got so I could smell a suspect before the cops ever showed up at the scene. I swear to you, Carole is responsible. If he's not doing the actual killing, then he's putting someone up to it."

"Just to embarrass you? Isn't that a little bit much?"

"You don't deal with logic when you deal with psychos. Look at the Son of Sam killer, Berkowitz? He said he was ordered to kill people by a neighbor's dog. Gary Gilmore? Starkweather thought killing was fun. The guy who butchered those people in that Big Mac attack? He calmly announced that he was going to 'hunt humans' before he waltzed out the door.

"When you talk cold-blooded killing, you don't talk logic."

"You don't talk premonitions either."

"You'd be surprised how many cops rely on gut feelings."

Debra pulled up a chair to the side of Max's bed. "I have a feeling I should stick closer to you during this."

"Why?"

"One way or the other, I'm going to get a great book out of this. It's either going to come off like *Cady the Conqueror* or *Mad Max III*."

Max picked up the phone. "I've been trying to get to Kenny McArthur. I want to see if he knows who was covering that concert tonight with a camera crew. If an MTV or any of the networks were there and they caught that last song, then *maybe* they got a picture of Rudy's killer."

"You *saw* the killer?"

"Sort of. I'm sure it had to be one of the backup singers."

"Can't you just get the police to question them?"

"That won't work. Rudy used two backup singers. When he was electrocuted, there were three onstage. One of the girls handed him the hot mike. If she was wearing insulated gloves, she could have handled that with no problem.

"But, Rudy . . ."

Max closed his eyes and grimaced, recalling the expression of shock and pain on Randall's face as he grasped the mike. The amazing thing about the scene was that, as Max lunged for Rudy and their eyes met, Randall almost looked resigned to his fate. He was almost peaceful. "Awww, Christ," was all Max could say.

The gray-haired man from the hallway entered the room with a sheaf of X rays. Max waved by way of greeting. "Thanks for the phone, Jerry."

"Anything else you'd like?"

"Can I make some substitutions on your room-service menu?"

"Go to hell."

Max nodded toward Debra. "Dr. Jerome Peters, this is Debra Knightly, my biographer."

Peters patted the X rays under his arm. "You almost lost your subject tonight, miss." He glanced at the chart above Max's bed. "You want to see the X rays or have me describe them to you."

Max shrugged.

"Bottom line, Max. You have to take it easy. You nearly got deep-fried tonight. No real damage. God knows why. Your friend's heart was . . . But you? No big deal.

"However. My little portraits here reveal quite a few funny details about your physical condition. One of your lungs is scarred. It looks like it was perforated and healed badly. You have a slight concussion, which, I assume, was the result of tonight's acrobatic display.

"Your lower back seems weak. You're forming a nice dowager's hump behind the neck from your lousy posture, and your feet are flat as hell."

"In other words"—Max beamed—"I can go home tomorrow morning."

"With my blessing."

Peters grimaced and left the room. Debra smirked at Max. "Dowager's hump?"

"Not for publication. All great men have it. Look at Lyndon Johnson. Walter Matthau. Gentle Ben."

"Knock. Knock."

Cady looked up to see the familiar, ever-weary, ever-leering face of Lieutenant Samuel Lehner in the doorway, shadowed by the ever-present hulk Malloy. Max offered him a bright smile. "Lieutenant. Something is different. Let me guess. You've had your beard done."

"Mind answering a few minor questions, Mr. Cady?"

"Yes I do. I gave the police my statement hours ago and I don't feel like going through it again unless . . ."

"Unless . . ." Lehner echoed.

Max grinned earnestly. "Unless you brought me flowers."

Lehner's face took on the expression usually reserved for gargoyles. "Cady. You're in big trouble."

"Tell me something I don't know."

Lehner snapped his fingers. Malloy handed him a notebook. "I found your statements concerning the third woman singer very interesting."

"Thank you."

"It reads as better fiction than anything you've ever put your name to previously."

"She was there, Lieutenant. Ask anyone on that stage."

"We have." Lehner smiled, obviously relishing the conversation. "No one seems to remember a third girl."

Max stared at the wall beyond Lehner. "There were strobe lights going. Lasers. The stage lights were off. The area was filled with fog. Yeah. I suppose they might have missed her."

Lehner would not be deterred. "Not even the two girl singers on the stage—"

"Yeah. They might have missed her too. She appeared right before the last song."

Max took his notebook and drew two zeros. Slightly behind the zeros, to their right, he drew an X. "The O's are our real singers," he said, showing Lehner the drawings. "The X is our ringer. See? She was standing near the fog machine back here, slightly to the right of and behind our girls. They could easily have missed her.

"When Rudy trotted toward the girls, though, our ringer was the closest to him. Why didn't he stop and think? Why didn't he notice the difference in the routine tonight? Why did he grab the fucking microphone from one of the girls?"

"He could have just gotten into the performance," Debra interjected. "I imagine when you're 'on,' the adrenaline takes over and you just run on . . . gut feelings."

Max smiled. "Yeah. That sounds right."

"I hate to interrupt this brilliant reconstruction, Mr. and Mrs. Charles, but the fact is that *no* one but you, Cady, saw this phantom woman. All we have in terms of deviation from the norm is that—one—Rudy Randall was electrocuted onstage tonight by a piece of equipment that was tampered with and—two—the only person near that stage who wasn't a part of the regular tour group was one Maxwell Norville Cady."

"Norvell." Max was growing impatient with the lieutenant. "You know what's wrong with you, Lehner? You have no imagination. Why the hell do you always go after the obvious?"

"Because the obvious is often what's ignored."

"I tried saving Randall's life tonight."

"Could have been a ruse. Something to take the heat off yourself."

"Oh come off it, Lehner."

"Look. All I know is that these killings are all based on *your* books, *you're* always at the scene of the crime shortly before or after or, now, God forbid, during the killing, and you have a history of ding-dong behavior.

"On a slightly more crass note, if I actually came out and stated, in print, that I connected these murders with either you or your books, you'd be the recipient of one helluva publicity windfall, right? Sales would skyrocket and you, Mr. Ammo-recently-fired-from-your-job, would make a small fortune. So, tell me, Max, why shouldn't I suspect you of engineering these disasters!"

Max sat up in bed, almost pulling his IV unit out of his arm. "Only a madman would try to do something like that."

Lehner flipped his notebook closed and handed it to the mountain Malloy. "No offense, Cady, but emotionally you don't strike me as being the rock of Gibraltar. We'll be in touch."

Lehner and Malloy left the room.

Max sat in the hospital bed and fumed. "The man is crazy! He's fucking obsessed!"

Debra said nothing. She merely nodded in agreement. Inwardly, however, she realized that, when it came to obsessive behavior, Lehner and Cady were a lot alike.

CHAPTER TWENTY-TWO

As a rule Max didn't drink before noon. Today, however, with the birds perched, singing in the trees behind the Museum of Natural History, the sun looking deceptively bright, and the sky appearing hopelessly blue, he felt he could break with tradition.

What an awful day.

He sat in a small cafe on Columbus Avenue and had his third gin and tonic.

Before leaving the hospital, he had been taken aside by Jerry. Jerry was very discreet, very kind. Max, you're in pretty bad shape. Do you drink much? As a friend, Max. Slow down. Your motor responses are a little flaky. Do you hallucinate? Black out? Hear voices?

Of course not. Max smirked. That's comic-book stuff. Jerry nodded sadly. Right. Comic book. Still, Max, it's something to think about, eh? Yeah. It was something to think about. That's all he was thinking about. He was losing control. He had to rein himself in until after this was over.

Still, Jerry had scared him. Suppose Max really was having trouble separating fantasy from reality.

Maybe he *was* going crazy. That was a real possibility. He vaguely remembered the story of a French mystery writer who went into states of catatonia late at night and, sleepwalking, became a notorious burglar. Maybe Max had really snapped and become a murderer.

He smirked at the glass in his hand. Funny, right about now that thought didn't strike him as being as farfetched as it did a few days ago. After all, he had blacked out during the time period when three of the murders happened. And no one but Max had seen the third girl singer. Maybe Max had rigged the microphone that had killed Rudy. No, he wouldn't have had access. Ah, but he did. In the hotel room. Max blinked. His eyes were brimming with tears. Was he far gone enough to have faked being drugged at the TV studio? Sure. Why not? Insane people were diabolically clever when they wanted to taunt the police.

He gazed across the street at the back entrance to the museum. A few millennia ago, when he had been an unhappily married man and his second wife was seeing half of the Manhattan Yellow Pages on the sly, Max, not knowing how to cope with the situation, used to slog his way uptown to the museum and sit in the dinosaur room.

Like a lump.

Clad in an accordion-wrinkled suit, wearing a stubble and a damaged sense of self-esteem, he would march into the vast wing of the museum housing the bones of the brontosaurus, the tyrannosaurus, and various other long-dead thingies, and plop himself down on a bench. He would stare at the revered remains and, he felt, they would stare back.

There was a certain kinship he felt in that room, a sense of fraternal bonding. Big, burly mammals. All doomed to extinction. Some had already managed to wipe themselves out, others had that fate yet to look forward to.

Max sipped his drink and smiled.

What the hell was going on? How had he lost control of his life? There was a psycho loose in New York and Maxwell Norvell Cady seemed the only one to be aware of that fact.

He placed the glass on the tablecloth. The tablecloth was made of white paper. In the center of the table was a glass filled with crayons. This was the kind of terminally artistic joint that encouraged its diners (or drinkers) to exhibit their creative tendencies while awaiting the arrival of their doomed-to-be-tardy waiters or waitresses.

Max grabbed a blood-red crayon and casually sketched the body of what seemed to be Godzilla. The head of the lumbering reptile, however, bore more than a casual resemblance to Max.

"I wonder if that's how Walt Disney started?" a female voice said, invading the area.

Max shook his head clear and gazed up at the face of Debra Knightly. "I was looking all over town for you," she said, tossing an envelope down on the table. "Kenny McArthur said I might find you around here. This is the eighth place I've tried."

Max nodded, staring at the envelope. "Did that come by messenger?"

Debra nodded. She sat down across from Max, leaning back in her chair and surveying him with a strange look. "You are determined to paint yourself as a victim, aren't you?"

Max blinked his eyes. The effects of the gin were beginning to hammer their way into his brain. "I don't understand."

"Look at you. You're a successful writer. Half the people in this town would kill their next of kin to be in your shoes. Yet you persist in making yourself out to be some great and grand martyr."

"These killings . . ."

"Fine. Okay. There is someone out there, some crazy, who is killing people based on books you wrote. Random chance. Nothing more. If it wasn't your books it would be someone else's. Max, you should know this sort of thing can't be predicted and it can't be helped."

Max allowed the woman's voice to fade into the back of his mind. He couldn't deflect the feeling that this sort of thing could have been predicted and it could have been helped. He felt responsible for it all. If he had only gone easy on Carole. If he hadn't antagonized him at the party.

And, once he had realized what was coming off, if he had only been more persuasive with the victims. If he had only been on the scene earlier.

He needed coffee.

Max opened his eyes and stared at Debra Knightly. No, he needed a lot more than coffee. He needed direction. He needed commitment. He needed things he couldn't describe.

He wanted to be able to sit back in a small jazz club and listen to Sonny Rollins play while tapping his foot atop sawdust-laden floors. He wanted to hear Duke Ellington's big band play at Carnegie Hall and squeeze the hand of that freckle-faced woman who seemed to know what he was thinking before he even thought it.

He wanted to get up in the morning and walk into the newspaper aiming for the Pulitzer Prize in journalism with that day's story. He wanted to hear his little girl yell "extree extree, reeedallabouddit" when he came home with the late edition in his hand.

But the little girl was grown now. The freckle-faced woman was dead. He no longer worked at a newspaper, and Pulitzer prizes were being handed out for forged stories these days. Jazz was passé. Duke Ellington played no more. Very few clubs had sawdust on the floor.

Max smiled to himself, remembering the dinosaurs across the street.

He stared at Knightly. "What the fuck do you want out of me, Debra?"

Knightly stared at him, unflinching. "A story, Max."

Max smirked. "That's what I thought."

"And what's wrong with that?" she asked. "You had your chance. You worked at a newspaper and you quit when things got rough. You wrote books, Max, and made a bundle. Fine. You made your fortune. You made your reputation. Now it's my turn. I didn't ask for this assignment. I wasn't even much interested in taking it after it was forced on me. But now I've got it and it's mutating into something that could be big, Max. This is the kind of story that makes careers."

"And ends lives . . ."

"Don't turn sanctimonious on me, Max Cady. You covered crimes at the *News* that were a lot worse than the stuff you've been seeing this week. Hell, you even wrote up your own wife's . . ."

Max's eyes suddenly focused. His head became clear. He stared at Debra Knightly as a dog whipped once too often warns off its master. He began to tell her off. All that came out of his throat was a low, guttural noise.

Debra suddenly found the tablecloth interesting. "I'm sorry."

"No," Max said. "You're right. There's a story in this for you. My job is to perform."

He ripped open the envelope. There were two tickets inside for the Broadway show *What a Woman* starring old-time Hollywood star Charlotte Griffiths. Max just shook his head.

"Here I go again."

He felt the hair on the back of his neck rise, strangely. He

THE CON GAME

turned around in his seat and glanced across the restaurant. Settling into a table near the window were Phillip Carole, the widowed Mrs. Paine, and his agent, David Maskin.

Max took the tickets and stuffed them inside his sportscoat pocket. "Let's get out of here, Lois Lane," he muttered. "I am beginning to feel the presence of the old cosmic eight ball rolling in my direction."

CHAPTER TWENTY-THREE

The theater district was changing too quickly for Max's tastes. Some of the old theaters, the really ornate structures that housed some of the greatest plays ever conceived, had been torn down, replaced by a god-awful mall complex that was rising slowly out of the mud and debris with the same finesse displayed by *The Beast From 20,000 Fathoms* in Hollywood's idea of Antarctica back in 1954.

Ironically, the most reassuring aspect of the area was the presence of the street people, the homeless and the thugs, the purse snatchers and the bag ladies, the monte specialists shuffling their decks of cards out on a collection of packing crates, the gaudily dressed con men standing in the doorways of the peep-show houses inviting unwary visitors to "c'monan take alook" while Iranian girls sat in the ticket booths reading paperback novels and looking very bored.

They were a constant.

They would never be torn down. Rousted out of the area, maybe, but even the most optimistic cop knew that their exile would last a week at best.

Max couldn't get the Toyota to start so he had decided to walk to Times Square from Debra's apartment.

He was glad he did. Each successive step managed to exorcise a nagging thought or two, reenergize his sagging spirits.

Today was Wednesday and he knew that *What a Woman* would be holding a matinee performance. Broadway matinees were a unique phenomenon in New York. New Yorkers, more than any other people in America, seemed to thrive on theater—no matter what obstacles were tossed in their way.

Raise the price of tickets and, somehow, avid theatergoers would find the newest discount house to get the best deal. Toss a blizzard over the city, and local drama buffs would somehow make it out of their homes and to the theaters where, they knew, there would be plenty of seats from out-of-town cancellations. Entwine the limbs of theater lovers in old age, frighten them with stories of crime-ridden neighborhoods at night, and they bus their way to Wednesday afternoon matinees.

Max walked into the lobby of the Music Box Theater on West Forty-fifth and flashed his press card, long out of date but still looking quite impressive with a thumb stuck over a few vital numbers.

The young man in the box office regarded the card impassively. "Uh-huh."

"Max Cady. I'd like to see Ms. Griffiths after the performance."

"You and half of the city."

Max twisted his face into a portrait of severity. While it didn't exactly cause the box-office denizen to cower, it did convey a certain sense of ominous urgency. "I'll see what I can do. Wait here until the final curtain call, and then I'll buzz Ralph, backstage."

"Thanks."

Max jammed his hands into his pockets and prowled around the lobby. In spite of the reason he was in attendance, the feel of the place was putting him at ease. The lobby of the Music Box, rightly or wrongly, felt like it hadn't changed one iota since it housed such classic productions as *Of Thee I Sing* and *Of Mice and Men* back in the 1930s.

He stepped outside into the crisp New York air and perused the eight-by-tens from the show displayed on the walls outside. There was Charlotte Griffiths, looking as glamorous as ever, sporting long slinky gowns and kicking up her heels with a troupe of barely postpubescent chorus boys.

Max smirked. Charlotte had aged well. Tough old bird. She was a movie star in the grandest sense of the word back in the late 1940s and early 1950s. Her luminous green eyes and her shock of blond hair, coupled with prominent cheekbones, sent a nation of pinup-crazed males ga-ga for nearly a decade.

She dropped out of sight for a while to marry a movie director, Frederick Remington, Max recalled. That didn't end too well, with Remington's body being found at the sight of a devil-worshiping cult in Culver City, California, in 1964. Today the place was a used-car lot. Datsuns, if Max remembered correctly.

Pushing forty, Charlotte embarked on a torturous comeback, doing guest stints on television shows and a few character roles in films. A series of TV commercials for coffee led her to the Broadway stage in the early 1970s. She was, using a *Variety* term, "boffo" and, since that time, had been a hot box-office commodity both on stage and on the screen.

Yeah, Max mused, she was a tough old bird.

The doors to the theater opened and an army of blue-haired ladies emerged. Buses began pulling up outside the theater. The elderly patrons, buzzing about how "good she looked for her age" and "wasn't the boy who played Feldon a real hunk?" swarmed around the waiting transport.

Max began to wade his way upstream through the torrent of exiting people.

He made eye contact with a few of the women, breaking it before they had a chance to ask "Aren't you . . . ?"

He reached the box office in one piece. The young boy behind the cage gave him a cranky look. "Oh, *there* you are. Ralph is waiting for you. Go up the aisle on the far right and knock on the steel door. Ralph will let you in."

Max nodded. "Thanks, again."

"Uh-huh."

Max waited for the theater to disgorge a few hundred more patrons before he attempted to make his way up the aisle. An empty theater is a very eerie place, sort of like a church late at night. It's devoid of physical life, yet brimming with energy lingering from actors and audiences long gone. It reminded Max of those old films like *The Phantom of the Opera*. He expected anyone and everyone to swing down from the ceiling or come bounding out from behind a curtain.

Max knocked on a metal door and a fellow whose face was a mass of lines and patches of stubble grunted and allowed him to enter a small corridor. He ignored Max and pointed to a door at the end of the hall.

Max grunted back and walked down the corridor, hesitating before the door. He cleared his throat before knocking gently.

"Yes?" came a voice from within. Max blinked in shock. God.

He'd forgotten how many times he had encountered that voice from the other side of a box of popcorn. He couldn't form a word.

"Yes?" the voice repeated a second time.

Max stood there, paralyzed.

Headline: IDIOT STRUCK DUMB—Broadway Star Saved From Inanity.

Finally, the door opened. Charlotte Griffiths, clad only in a robe, stood in the threshold. Max remained fixed in place, much to the amusement of the actress.

"I take it you are either Max Cady or an oak someone has brought for me as a gift."

Max pumped his jaw up and down. "I'm Max Cady."

"Come in, Mr. Cady . . . or do you prefer Mr. Ammo these days?"

Max shambled into the room, almost crushing a petite black woman in her early twenties who was picking up Griffiths's discarded costume. "Sorry," he muttered.

"That will be all, Ramona," Charlotte told the girl.

"Yes, ma'am. And thank you for the time off, ma'am."

"Don't worry about it. I hope your mother feels better."

The girl left, shutting the door behind her. "Sweet girl. Comes from a poor family near Buffalo. Her mother had a stroke. Tsk. The mother is younger than I am. Makes you count your blessings."

She rapped a table with her knuckles. "Knock Formica."

Griffiths sat down before a makeup mirror and began covering her face with cold cream. "Have yourself a seat, Mr. Cady. You're about to see a horrifying spectacle unfold. The removal of the makeup and the arrival of age. It reminds me of the final chapter in *She*. Did you ever read that?"

"Uh . . ."

"Quite a talker, aren't you? In *She*, Asheya, the ageless queen, tries to leave her kingdom with her mortal lover. She doesn't get too far, I'm afraid, before she loses her magic touch and ages, turns to dust, actually.

"The theater is my magic kingdom, Mr. Cady. It is where I can remain young forever. Take off the makeup, though, and I'm just another old broad."

She began wiping the cold cream from her face with a Kleenex. "On the plus side, I'm no longer accosted by mashers on the street when I leave the theater without makeup. On the down side, I'm no longer accosted by mashers on the street when I leave the theater without makeup."

Max managed a smile. "I'm a big fan of yours."

"Figuratively or literally? Maybe both? You're a nice man, Mr. Cady, you have the decency to act awestruck in front of a fossil. Now, what can I do for you?"

"I was wondering if you'd let me escort you to and from the theater tonight?"

The actress briefly stopped daubing at the cold cream. "My, aren't we forward? I'm a little old for you, aren't I . . . although I have dated younger."

"I know you have and no you're not. But that has nothing to do with it."

"Hmm. If it's not chivalry or unrequited love, what can your reasons be?"

"I suspect that someone will try to *hurt* you tonight."

"Aside from the critics?"

Although he felt foolish doing so, Max took a deep breath and blurted his *Reader's Digest* version of his theory. "There is someone out on the streets, Ms. Griffiths, who is determined to wipe out the best and the brightest talents in New York City. He's using my books as a blueprint and, so far, he's been very effective."

Griffiths tossed a handful of Kleenex into a tin trash can. It had a picture of Dumbo on the side. "Did this killer have anything to do with that rock-and-roll fellow's death last night?"

"Yes, ma'am."

"I seem to recall reading that you witnessed his death. That you actually managed to be onstage as it happened."

Max rested his elbows on his knees and stared into his massive hands. "Yes, ma'am, I was."

Griffiths sighed and folded her hands on the makeup table before her. "Well, I'll have you know right now, Mr. Cady, that you won't be allowed on the stage with *me* tonight. The unions would give me hell for it."

THE CON GAME

Max stared at the woman, not quite comprehending. "Then you'll let me escort you?"

"Certainly. If you toss in dinner afterward."

"I'd be honored."

"And I'll be famished. None of this Joe Allen's stuff, let's go some place snazzy. You look like an old-fashioned guy, Max. You dance?"

"A little."

"Big bands?"

"Love them."

"Great." She took an eyebrow pencil and a piece of paper and scrawled out a few words. "Here's my address. Be there at six forty-five. It takes quite a while to put this goop on and then I have to be shoehorned into my sequined gown for the first act. Giving me an extra five minutes for hyperventilation, that should get me onstage in plenty of time."

Max, still feeling very much the fan, stared at the woman. "Aren't you nervous about all this?"

"About this killer?" Griffiths shrugged. "Sure I am. But what can I do? I'll alert the guards backstage to be on the lookout. I'll have you hanging around. And after that? It's out of my hands."

The woman spun around in her chair and flashed a bemused grin at Max. "Look, honey. You're talking to a broad whose one true love was cheating on her with a satanic cult. He broke my heart. They ate his."

She returned her attention to the makeup mirror. "Things don't get much worse than that."

CHAPTER TWENTY-FOUR

Kenny McArthur crouched behind his desk staring at the computer terminal in front of him. Max Cady sat, slumped, in a chair at his side.

"Did you find out about the concert footage on Randall?" Max asked.

"Nothing. No film crews, no TV crews. Nada. Seems that Rudy allowed a few cameras in at rehearsal but forbade them to photograph his visage during an actual performance."

"Shit."

"Depends on your musical tastes."

"Still photographers?"

"Maybe some of the fans caught something, but you'd have to make a public plea for assistance. None of the newspaper people caught anything except for the aftermath. Have you seen this afternoon's papers?"

"No."

McArthur tossed a newspaper under his nose. The New York *Post*. There, on the cover, was Max Cady, entwined with the body of Rudy Randall. McArthur kept his eye on the computer terminal. "UPI caught the moment. We used another photo from the series. The *Post* has the whole series in the centerfold. Want to see?"

Max shook his head slowly from side to side. He knew he'd wake up and this would all be the result of one too many shots on an empty stomach. In case he didn't, though, he'd have to come up with a way to end this nightmare himself.

"Kenny," he said, "what kind of crowd did Carole hang around with when he was away?"

"Cons, mostly. Maybe a guard or two."

"I'm serious."

"So am I. What the hell kind of question is that anyway?"

THE CON GAME

"Could you find out who he was closest to in his cell block? Any contract killers? People with big connections?"

"You still on the Carole kick?"

"Yup."

"Read a lot of Melville when you were a kid?"

"Not funny, Kenny."

"Nope. Melville wasn't known for his sense of humor. Now, if you wouldn't mind leaving me alone . . . I'm doing a think piece for the Sunday color section."

"What on?"

"Rock videos and their effects on cinema."

"What's the angle?"

"I don't have one yet. Movies are mostly shitty. Rock videos are mostly shitty. The question is . . . have movies gotten shittier since rock videos appeared? Will Prince become the new Sir Laurence Olivier? Will Sir Larry cameo in the next Michael Jackson video?"

"How do you justify writing stuff like that?"

"I don't. My landlord does."

"Will you find out about Carole for me?"

"Right after I've finished this graph on Timothy Hutton directing a Cars video." Kenny looked up at Max. "He was the kid who tried to kill himself in *Ordinary People*."

"I missed that one."

"Mary Tyler Moore was his mother. She was a real bitch. Hutton should have opted for matricide."

Cady eased himself out of his chair. "See if you can find out where Carole's sister is too. He told me he used to write to her from prison. I think her name's Lucille . . . no, Lucinda. Maybe there's something in one of his letters to her . . ."

"Another job for Kenneth McArthur, tracer of lost persons."

Max nodded and walked away from Kenny's cubicle. He made his way through the maze of desks until he reached the elevator. A young man with a hound-dog look waddled up to Max. "Excuse me," he said in a raspy voice. "I couldn't help but notice you were Max Cady."

Max smiled. "I probably still am."

"I've been reading about these murders that have been taking place . . . I'm a researcher here . . . and I was wondering

". . . Roger Hebbert is the name . . . if you would mind commenting on the fact that you've been present at three really big killings in the last week."

The elevator door opened and Max stepped inside. "I would . . ."

The researcher's face broke into a smile.

". . . mind commenting," Max finished as the elevator doors slowly closed.

The man's face fell. "You're not so hot, you know," he stated firmly.

Max nodded. Yeah, he knew.

Max stepped out of the *Daily News* building and stood for a moment in the middle of the sidewalk while passersby cursed and gave him dirty looks as they careened around him. (Rule number one: While walking in Manhattan never, repeat *never*, stop in the middle of a sidewalk. If your mother has a stroke while walking with you, drag her into a hallway, but don't stop in the middle of the sidewalk to administer first aid. You will either be trampled or instigate a chain reaction crash that will rival anything ever witnessed on a Los Angeles freeway system.)

Max blinked, bleary-eyed, into the sea of onrushing pedestrians.

He wanted to visit her grave, for some odd reason. Bring some flowers, maybe. Pull up a bench and talk to her. The way he used to. He'd been bad about that. He hadn't been to the cemetery for years now. For all he knew, her grave was covered with weeds, badly tended. He had paid the fee for the upkeep but he hadn't had the nerve to actually go up there and check on things since he started the Ammo books.

Funny though, all those years he wrote at home, although he never paid it much mind, he always had her picture up on the wall. It wasn't framed. It wasn't tacked. It wasn't taped. It was jammed into the frame of a Folon painting he had bought during a rare artistic spree. There she was. Freckle-faced and smiling. Sitting on a Central Park bench. Squinting into the sun.

Forever.

Christ. He laughed to himself. How he dwelled in the past. He was so hollow he heard his chuckle echo.

THE CON GAME

He shook himself free of history and plowed into the army of the marching minions of Manhattan.

If he got out of this mess in one piece, he'd visit the grave. He'd smile at children and pet small animals. Amen.

By the time Debra Knightly returned home, Max was already dressed in a semirumpled suit.

"Off to a reunion of the Bowery Boys' Appreciation Society?" she asked.

Max glanced at himself in a full-length mirror. "What's the matter? Is something crooked?"

"The Republican Party," Debra replied, tossing her handbag onto a chair. "Take off the jacket. I'll press it for you."

Max slid out of the sportscoat. "Thanks. I don't think about those things, I guess."

"It's obvious," she said, walking into the kitchen and plugging an iron into an outlet next to a well-worn toaster. "Big date tonight?"

"Uh-huh." He nodded. "For both of us."

Debra licked her right index finger and touched the underside of the yellow iron. It was almost hot enough. "What are we up to now?"

"Well, I promised Charlotte Griffiths that I'd escort her to the theater."

"Pretty smooth talker, aren't we?"

"It helped when I told her that someone was out to kill her."

"You do know how to woo a girl," Debra said, running the seemingly corrugated suit coat under the iron. "I suppose I'm supposed to stand guard again tonight in front of some other exotic address?"

"Nope."

"Thank God."

"The same address."

"Oh, come on now, Max! Carole stayed inside all night last night. He couldn't have had anything to do with Rudy Randall!"

Max didn't reply. He merely walked over to the kitchen table and yanked his coat out of Debra's hand. He slowly put the jacket on. Debra stood next to him, iron still in hand, fuming.

"And don't think that giving me the silent treatment is going to force me into it again.

"Carole is *not* your boy. You're getting really monomaniacal about this, Max. Borderline crazy. You know that? You're letting your feeling get in the way of the facts.

"And that car of yours stinks. It doesn't start up half the time. It stalls. You can't run the radio without turning the motor over."

Max continued to dress. He walked toward the front door. Debra followed him, iron still poised. She came to a halt in the middle of the living room, yanking the iron's plug out of the kitchen outlet.

"Give me one good reason why I should play policewoman again tonight."

Max shrugged and pulled the door open. "Because if you don't and Carole *is* 'our boy,' an innocent person will be killed tonight and her killer will go scot-free."

He closed the door gently behind him and headed for the elevator. He could hear Knightly swearing at him as the elevator car arrived.

She flung the door to her apartment open. "You're not being fair. You're not making sense."

"Remind me to tell you, someday, about the connection between obsession and good reporting," he said with a smile.

The limousine rented by Max pulled up to the great iron gates of the Dakota on West Seventy-second Street precisely at six forty-five. The guard slowly approached the limo driver.

"We're here for Miss Griffiths," the driver announced.

The doorman walked over to his booth, a little hutch resembling something seen on a Changing of the Guards postcard, and phoned upstairs. While he awaited approval Max glanced out the rear window of the limo.

A few tourists wandered up to the gates, armed with cameras. They snapped photos of each other standing at the gateway, the limo behind them.

Max watched their faces. They wore expressions of excitement mixed, in some strange way, with solemnity. It was here that John Lennon was hit. Max shut his eyes tightly. Lennon staggered into the entranceway, mortally wounded, muttering in shock after Mark David Chapman had opened fire.

The limo was probably perched on the spot where he stumbled and fell.

A chill shot through Max, causing him to shiver. A kid walking through a graveyard . . . that's what he felt like.

The guard and the driver exchanged a few words and the limo slowly pulled into the courtyard.

By the time the driver opened the door for Max to make an exit, Charlotte Griffiths was already double-timing it toward the car to make an entrance.

"I'd ask you up but the place looks like hell," she said. "And, after doing the matinee this afternoon, I *feel* like hell. Move over."

Max slid back into the limo. Charlotte climbed in and sat by his side.

"So," she asked. "How's the murder business?"

"Bad, I hope," he managed to mumble. The limo pulled out of the courtyard and back onto the street. Max felt very uncomfortable talking about the subject of possible death with a woman so full of life. He glanced out at the sidewalk where a group of kids were trotting past the building. They carried baseball bats and mitts and had, apparently, just finished a vigorous game across the street in Central Park. Somehow, the sight was reassuring. There were *some* things that were immune to cultural erosion.

"Look at that," Max said, motioning to the boisterous bunch yammering under the doorman's nose.

"Yeah," Charlotte said. "Lennon got whacked there."

Max lapsed back into silence.

The limousine headed West on Seventy-second Street. The sun slowly made its way down past the ugly high rises on the Jersey side of the Hudson, bestowing a crimson halo on Charlotte Griffiths.

Debra Knightly cursed the green Toyota as it sputtered up Madison Avenue. The car looked and sounded like an environmental hazard. She attracted the stares and smirks of pedestrians and drivers alike as she headed for Ninety-first Street.

If she could have stenciled a sign to hang on the car reading "This is not my car. I am a victim of circumstances," she would have.

Instead, she hid behind a pair of owlish sunglasses, gritted her teeth, and lurched uptown.

Max refused Charlotte's offer of press seats to watch the entire play from the front row. Instead, he opted for a wall near the stage-left exit.

What a Woman wasn't so much a traditional Broadway musical as it was a vehicle. It was written with Charlotte Griffiths in mind and, logically enough, played off her well-known mannerisms, history, and sayings.

It was the story of a movie star who loses a fortune because of a crooked manager and becomes a nanny to a spoiled little rich kid. Eventually she manages to set the kid and the kid's parents straight, get a lead in a Broadway production, then a film, and, finally, regain her rightful status, both artistically and monetarily.

Fluff, to be sure, but entertaining fluff.

At the end of the first act Charlotte marched past a grinning Max and rolled her eyes heavenward. "Tonight's audience seems to be left over from *The Dead Zone.*"

Max shook his head and watched with admiration as she walked toward her dressing room, where a young blond woman waited for the change of wardrobe.

As the actress marched inside Max reflected that the play had been well-named.

Debra sat in the Toyota, parked illegally next to a fire hydrant. She silently ate a greaseburger while mentally cursing Max Cady. On the windshield of the car she had stuck a hastily scrawled sign stating "DISABLED, WAITING FOR TOW TRUCK."

In case any ticket-happy cop approached her, she could point to the sign with some sense of self-righteousness. If he asked her to turn over the engine, she could pretty much guarantee that the car would live up to its windshield billing.

She stared at the brownstone. The emaciated Carole had al-

THE CON GAME

ready entered the front room, had pulled the curtains closed, and had, once again, turned on the television. He was still seated in front of the flickering television screen. It was obvious that the ex-convict had settled down for a long evening of TV viewing.

Debra slid down in her seat and settled in for an evening of angina.

By the end of the third act Charlotte Griffiths had won over the sluggish audience.

She marched backstage and stood next to Max as the crowd erupted with applause.

"Aren't you going out to take a bow?" Max asked as the curtain came down.

"Let 'em get off their asses, first," she said. "I worked my buns off for the past three hours. Let them work up a sweat for a while."

She glanced at Ralph, the stage-door vizier. He pulled the curtain back a crack. He turned and faced Griffiths, grinning.

"Okay, boys," she crowed. "Let 'er rip."

The curtain was pulled upward and Charlotte and her cast marched out to take a curtain call before a standing, cheering audience.

Max laughed out loud as Charlotte cast him a sly "See?" look and winked.

After three more curtain calls she decided that she had given her fans more than their money's worth.

She took Max by the arm. "Now, my dear, get your dancing shoes on because we are painting the town red this evening."

She walked him to her dressing-room door. "Wait here just for one minute while I jump into the shower. I'll have . . ."

She glanced at the blond girl inside the dressing room, carefully folding Charlotte's clothes from the second act. "Freda," the girl replied.

". . . Freda let you in when I come out."

Max's face took on a look of concern. "Well . . ."

"Come on, Max. You don't want me to spread the word that you're a Peeping Tom, do you?"

Max relaxed. "Okay. I'll be right here, though."

"My protector," Charlotte laughed, kissing Max lightly on the cheek. She entered her dressing room, closing the door behind her.

Max pulled up a chair and sat outside the dressing room, attempting to ignore the looks he was receiving from the smirking stagehands.

He sat in the straight-backed chair nervously glancing at his watch from time to time.

After five minutes he began to feel uneasy.

After ten he felt panic slowly invade his body.

He knocked on the dressing-room door. "Charlotte?"

He was greeted by silence.

He knocked on the door again. "Charlotte?"

No reply.

He tried the doorknob.

The dressing room had been locked from the inside. "Freda?"

He glanced down the hall toward the stage. No one was there. The stagehands had disappeared from sight.

He tried shoving the door in.

No luck.

He ran his hand along the door. It didn't seem all that solid. Tossing the chair out of the way, he backed up to the opposite side of the hall, lowered his right shoulder somewhat, and charged into the door.

As he suspected, the door was hollow. While the lock held, the door didn't, splintering inward.

Max slipped on the wet surface of the floor and tumbled to his knees. The room was filled with steam. "Charlotte?" he called weakly.

He crawled toward the shower stall, barely being able to see. His hands were cut by slivers of glass. His lungs were filled with hot clouds of unrelenting steam. He felt like he was sliding down into an inferno.

He crawled up to the shower stall.

Inside, scalded beyond recognition, was a human heap. A low moan erupted from the pit of Max's stomach. He climbed slowly to his feet and reached inside to turn off the hot-water spigot. There was no handle on the spigot. It had been removed. Max

THE CON GAME

bent over and began to pull the body out of the shower when his head exploded in pain.

The shock emanated from a point on his skull near the nape of his neck and spread forward.

The swirling steam rose up before his eyes and he toppled backward.

He heard a thunderclap envelope the room. It was his head hitting the floor. As he drifted off into unconsciousness he heard the roar of Niagara Falls and the sound of high heels retreating.

Debra Knightly awoke with a start. A tow truck was purring next to the Toyota.

"Having trouble, miss?" the driver asked.

Debra glanced past his head. Carole was still in his room, the captive audience of a brightly lit television.

"I'm not sure," she answered.

"I was passing by and I saw your note. Did you call AAA?"

"No," she stammered. "I called a friend. He—he never showed up."

"Well, why don't you see if you can start the car? Pump the gas pedal a few times. Not too much or you'll flood the engine."

Debra did as she was told.

"There," the driver said. "Now try turning her over."

Debra rolled her eyes and turned the key in the ignition. Miraculously the car started. She now had no choice. She had to pull away.

The driver watched the Toyota slowly chug away from the curb.

"Do you want me to follow you home?" the driver asked with a smile on his face that could pass for a leer.

"No. No," Debra said weakly. "I'll be fine."

The Toyota made it to Park Avenue and hung a left. She hoped Max was fine as well.

CHAPTER TWENTY-FIVE

"How does it feel to be mysterious?"

"Awful!" Max said, holding his head in his sweaty hands. He lay, fully clothed, across Debra Knightly's bed. He had spent half the night in the hospital and half the night in the police station. He hadn't been able to sleep and doubted that he could nap now. Every time he closed his eyes he saw Charlotte Griffiths's bright red body, huddled in the corner of the shower stall, trying, even in death, to escape the stream of scalding water.

She had attempted to break her way out of the glass-doored shower, slicing her right hand and wrist. She bled to death as she was being boiled.

Max had a lump on the back of his head that qualified him for unicorn status.

Someone had sapped him from behind. Someone who knew he was outside just waiting to get in.

He had told the police about the wardrobe girl who was there subbing for the vacationing Ramona. They had said they'd look into it.

Lehner was obviously convinced that Max was the psycho killer to end all psycho killers.

Max was simply stuck. He wanted to shut himself up in a dark room and never again emerge into what was passing for reality these days. The police had issued a statement to the press about a male visitor backstage. The media had initially dubbed the caller a "mystery man." Max almost laughed. That was a moniker he could live without.

"My mind is turning into fudge," he muttered.

Knightly offered him a sunny grin. "Your fame, however, is growing."

She held up a copy of that morning's edition of the New York *Post*. "TOO LATE THE HERO, JIMMY AMMO MISSES

PSYCHO. Not too bad," Debra said. "Page one coverage with pictures on page three."

She then moved on to the *Daily News*. "STAR SCALDED AS BOYFRIEND WATCHES. I thought it was very tasteful of them to play down the Ammo angle. Lots of photos of you being carried into the ambulance. Apparently you were a figure out of Charlotte's shrouded past."

She picked up a copy of the New York *Times*. "CHARLOTTE GRIFFITHS DIES IN MISHAP. Trust the *Times* to put it all in its proper perspective. You don't make an entrance until the third paragraph and then as 'former crime reporter and author.' "

Max struggled to sit up in her bed, coming to rest on his elbows. "What's the point, Debra? I don't need this."

Debra tossed the papers onto the floor. "I think you do. You've been playing private detective for a whole goddamn week and you're not doing a very good job of it. I think it's time that you sat down with Lieutenant Lehner and confided in him. Tell him everything you've told me. Tell him about the clues. Tell him about your suspicions."

"I have. Sort of. He doesn't believe me."

"What about me? I've seen those messengers arrive."

"I'm sure he thinks I'm sending them myself."

Debra frowned. "I hadn't thought of that."

Max eased himself back onto the bed and, flat on his back, gazed at the ceiling above him. "And Carole?"

"A homebody as usual. The guy is a real couch potato. All he does is watch television."

The phone in the living room rang. Debra left Max pondering the cracks in the ceiling and answered it. She reentered the room seconds later. "It's for you. It's your agent."

Max attempted to blink his eyes into focus. He slowly got out of the bed and headed toward the living room. The back of his head felt like an Iron Butterfly drum solo.

He picked up the phone. "Yeah?"

"Turn on channel two news. Now. I'll hold."

Max walked over to the small black-and-white Panasonic in Knightly's apartment and flicked it on. A woman reporter was in the middle of a report on the Charlotte Griffiths murder.

". . . an anonymous caller referred to Griffiths's death as the latest in a series of Jimmy Ammo murders. Apparently all the victims have been killed based on plot developments in paperback novels penned by Maxwell Cady, also known as Jimmy Ammo. And, according to an anonymous tipster, all the victims have been found with appropriate pages from Ammo's novels scattered about the scene of the crime."

Max groaned as the camera cut to a picture of a very angry, very haggard Lieutenant Samuel Lehner marching out of his precinct house muttering "Ridiculous. Ridiculous" to every question put his way.

The reporter continued. "Despite the police's insistence that there is no connection between these random superstar killings and the Ammo novels, author Maxwell Cady has been present for at least two of the killings, maybe more. Police say that Cady is not a suspect and the anonymous phone caller has alluded to the fact that Cady, like his fictitious counterpart, is acting the part of detective, attempting to track down the killer before the police.

"Cady's whereabouts is not known at this time."

Max turned off the television and careened toward the phone. "Maskin," he bellowed, while still picking up the receiver, "are you crazy?"

"Crazy like a fox, Max," the agent chuckled. "As long as this killer is out there, we might as well take advantage of it, right? Sales are up, Max. In another week you're going to be *the* name needed to sell magazines or TV talk shows. We're talking *Today*. We're talking *People*. We're talking *The Tonight Show*."

"We're talking murder, David. Real murders, not fictitious ones. We're talking innocent people being killed, and if you don't knock it off with your anonymous phone calls, we're talking me sneaking up on you when you least expect it and turning you into a half a pound of ground round."

"Max," Maskin stammered, "what are you so angry about? I didn't tell them where you were staying, did I? Hell. All those reporters know is that you live in New Jersey and that you haven't been home in a week."

Max had a sudden vision of what he'd be doing in three hours. "David. At noon today I'm going to my granddaughter's

THE CON GAME

birthday party. If you've fucked my daughter and her kid up with this, I swear to Christ I'm going to slap you senseless. You got that, scumbag?"

"I never thought about that, Max."

"You never think, period."

"Max, what can I say? I would have discussed this with you yesterday at that restaurant if you hadn't run off in a huff."

"You were sitting with that nut case!"

"But, Max, he's my client too. I have to—"

"You represent Carole?"

"I thought you knew. Yes, and his book is doing—"

Max slammed the phone down. He leaned against a wall and began coughing.

"Are you all right?" Debra asked.

Max nodded and, still coughing, walked into the kitchen for a glass of water. He could almost feel the noose tightening.

"What are you going to do now?" Debra asked. "Your boy has pretty much set you up, hasn't he?"

Max nodded. Maskin had done just that. He had effectively tossed Max into the center ring. People were going to expect a showdown now. Jimmy Ammo versus the great New York psycho killer. A duel to the death. High noon in Manhattan. Maybe Maskin was just acting like a good, obnoxious agent. Or maybe he had other reasons. Well, it was done now. There was no use crying about it.

"Maybe it will all work out for the best," Max said halfheartedly. "Maybe all this publicity will force the killer into a more outrageous act to try to steal the thunder back from me. Maybe he'll slip up. Maybe he'll tip his hand."

"Or maybe he'll do something really awful, Max. Maybe he'll decide he wants to go out in a blaze of glory."

Max slid into a kitchen chair. "Yeah. Maybe."

He began rubbing his eyes furiously with his left hand. He knew exactly the way the news media would handle the new Ammo versus the world angle. The entire series of killings would somehow be turned into a sporting event. Veteran detective writer versus new killer in town. Maybe they'd even get Howard Cosell to offer commentary. Frank Gifford for color.

Debra was right. Since they were dealing with someone who

was a real Almond Joy, half nuts, they couldn't depend on the guy reacting to any of this new publicity in a logical way. The guy could change his MO and wind up doing a lot of damage to a lot of people.

Max got to his feet and headed toward the bathroom for a quick shave and a shower. "I think it's about time I got some professional help on this. Maybe talk to a shrink about doing up a psychological profile on this asshole."

"You know a lot of folks who are into criminal psychology?"

"No. But I bet Lehner does. I guess it's time I go to the police."

Debra watched Max disappear into the bathroom. She smiled to herself. Cady was tougher than she thought but only half as stubborn.

She liked that.

CHAPTER TWENTY-SIX

"You have no idea how much I admire a man who sleeps in his clothes."

Max flopped down in a seat before a sneering Lieutenant Lehner. "I haven't slept," he muttered, running a hand across his freshly shaven chin. "And besides, these are *new* clothes. I just *look* rumpled."

The hulk named Malloy waddled into the room. "Well, if it isn't Sheriff Dillon. Out to rid the town of crooks before sundown?"

Lehner expressed a modicum of surprise at, what from Malloy, would be considered an outburst. Malloy, his mottled face growing redder, his bulb-shaped nose staying one shade ahead of the rest, sat down on the edge of Lehner's desk and stared directly at Max. "Come to tell us that this town isn't big enough for both of us? Or should we smile when we say that? Or . . ."

"All right, Sergeant," Lehner said calmly, sitting back in his chair.

"I wasn't responsible for that shit," Cady said. "What do you think I am, nuts?"

Lehner grinned. No reply was necessary.

Max sighed. "Look. It was my agent who made that phone call. If it makes you feel any better, I don't like him any more than you do at this point. Feel free to pick him up."

"I might do that," Lehner said, "just to put the fear of God into him."

"I know he made you guys look like assholes this morning," Max continued as Malloy compressed his hands into fists, "but he's set me up pretty good as well. I'm now expected to go one on one with a loon who's been doing just fine in the killing department all week. With the whole world watching and expecting a tag-team match over the next corpse, the guy just might make a grandiose gesture and deviate from his pattern."

Lehner began to show a little interest. "What do you mean?"

"You've read those books. There are some real bloodbath scenes. In *Prelude to Terror* a gang of terrorists blows up everything from school buses to jet planes."

Lehner eyed the ceiling, hissing between his teeth. "Shit."

Malloy, obvious disdain in his eyes, still stared at Max. "How do we know that you're not the loon we're looking for?"

Max said, "You don't. But, tell you what. If this guy sticks to his pattern, the next on his hit list will be Archbishop William Rowland—"

"Bullshit," Malloy spat.

"You're a good Catholic, Malloy," Max guessed. "You know that, as the head of the Archdiocese of New York, he's the most renowned religious leader around."

"I thought he was touring some third world countries," Lehner said.

"He is," Max said. "Until four o'clock Saturday afternoon. He then arrives at JFK. He'll be saying Mass at St. Patrick's on Sunday at ten. It will be sort of a 'welcome home' deal, filled with press and well-wishers. A High Mass too. Very ornate. Very ceremonial. I'd have cops there if I were you."

"We'd have cops there anyway," Lehner replied.

"I'm not talking about men in blues keeping the crowds back, I'm talking plainclothes detectives who know that the archbishop's life is in danger and will keep his holy ass alive."

Lehner picked up a ballpoint pen and began tapping its tip against his already pockmarked desk blotter. "And what exactly will we be looking for on Sunday?"

"I'm not sure."

"Yes you are," Lehner said. "I've been talking to some of your friends lately. People like Kenneth McArthur. He says that you're obsessed with Phillip Carole still. Is that a fact?"

Max remained silent.

"A cop on the beat also took down the license plate of a suspicious car parked on East Ninety-first Street the night before last and ran a check. It belongs to your daughter. It was parked across the street from where Carole is staying, a woman behind the wheel. Got your kid playing stakeout?"

"It wasn't my kid, it was Miss Knightly."

"Ah-ha. The features gal from the *Times*. You tutoring her on crime reporting?"

Max said nothing.

Lehner spun his swivel chair around and faced a window. "You're wasting my time, Cady."

Max quickly stood up and walked out of the room. Malloy watched him leave. "What a whacko," the mountainous man rumbled.

Lehner continued to stare into space. "Put in a written request for a dozen plainclothesmen for Sunday morning . . ."

"You don't actually believe him, do you?" Malloy said. "I think he's our man."

"He just might be. I haven't dismissed that thought. But if he isn't and there *is* a kink case out there who wants to take a crack at the archbishop on Sunday morning, I want to be prepared."

Malloy glowered and made a note in his ever-present pad.

Lehner swiveled the chair around. "Whether he's our boy or just a hapless victim, Cady is close to breaking, Malloy. That worries me. He's being pushed around by everyone in all directions. He says there's a killer taunting him. I'm not sure about that. But he does have us breathing down his neck, an agent who's turning his life into a circus sideshow, and a reporter bird-dogging him for the first decent story of her career."

Lehner returned his attention to the window. "If he wasn't such an annoying son of a bitch, I'd feel sorry for him."

Malloy snorted at the pad. "Well, if you're so concerned about him, why don't you just assign a guy to protect him?"

Lehner folded his hands behind his head and gazed at the tree limb outside his window. It was covered by a half-melted, plastic dry-cleaning bag. Ah, seasonal change in Manhattan. "That's not a bad idea, Malloy."

"You're kidding!"

"Nope. Maybe we should have a man keep an eye on Cady. If

he's a victim, we can keep him out of trouble, and if he's our killer, maybe we can stop him before he hits again."

"I don't like it," Malloy sniffed.

"You don't have to," Lehner said, facing the sergeant, his eyes resembling ice, "I do."

CHAPTER TWENTY-SEVEN

Max pushed the tortured Toyota toward the Upper West Side and his daughter's apartment. The car was in worse shape than Cady, stammering at every light. In order to keep the little automatic from conking out completely, Max would have to shift the car into park and press down on the accelerator.

Cursing louder than his radio was playing music, Max made his way up to West 103rd Street.

His eyes almost left his head when he saw his daughter's brownstone. A steady stream of parents and children were wading through a small but persistent group of reporters.

TV crews sat, leisurely, on the curb, shooing the neighborhood kids away from their dormant equipment.

Max punched the dashboard once.

The radio suddenly picked up a Spanish-language station.

Max sighed and turned the car into a private parking lot behind a Food Mart. With a little luck maybe someone would show up and tow the contraption to the Used Car Graveyard.

He lifted his granddaughter's present out of the backseat and surveyed the scene from a distance. He knew there had to be a way to get into the building without actually running headfirst through the press. He just had to figure it out.

Tucking the present under his arm (an overpriced doll that cried and burped and bitched when you tilted it a certain way and now was mewing like a dying animal from inside the box—he knew he shouldn't have inserted the batteries before he gave the kid the present), he loped around the block and tried to figure out where the back of Sara's home would be, staring only at the fronts of the next street's brownstones.

When he felt he had a pretty good idea, he walked up to the appropriate building and rang the buzzer of the ground-floor apartment.

A suspicious elderly woman opened the door. "Yeah?"

"Uh, excuse me," Max began. "My granddaughter—"

She turned her head sideways. "WHAT?"

"I SAID . . . MY GRANDDAUGHTER IS HAVING A PARTY."

"So?"

"Well, she lives right behind your building."

"So?"

"Well, I was wondering if you could help me surprise her."

"WHAT?"

"I WANT TO SURPRISE HER!"

"So?"

Max heaved a titanic sigh. "Well, I was wondering if you'd let me use your yard. I'll climb over the back fence and walk in through their yard." He held up the present before him like a magic talisman. "You know, surr-prise!"

The woman stared at Max as if he was part of an Alfred Hitchcock film festival. Gradually her face softened. "Aren't you what's-his-face the actor?"

Max decided it wouldn't hurt just this once to go along. "That's right."

"You really as bad as people say you are?"

"Nope."

The woman shrugged. "Pity. You were one of the few that sounded interesting."

She stared at the present and then at Max. "Well, okay. Come on in. Try any funny business and I'll scream my head off."

"Thanks."

The woman led Max through an apartment that was knee deep in fur balls. "Mind the cats," the woman said. "They don't like strangers."

Max sniffed the air. Apparently they didn't like using kitty litter either.

Max walked into the backyard. It was an overgrown patch about twenty feet by twenty feet filled with cats. He could hear his daughter's stereo playing and the sound of children giggling. The noise wasn't coming from the yard directly behind the old woman's, however, but the yard next to it. Max had misjudged by one house.

THE CON GAME

Well, he figured, he probably should make the best of it and hop, first, into the yard behind this one and then into his daughter's.

"Thanks again." He nodded to the old woman as he slowly climbed over a six-foot, rickety wooden fence.

"Say hello to Hank Fonda for me. He's a little too goody-goody for my taste but he has nice eyes. Blue, right?"

"Right."

"WHAT?"

"Yeah. They were blue!"

"Well, what are they now?"

Max sighed. "They're still blue."

"Thought so. Those things don't change."

The climb wasn't going to be easy. Max grunted. The doll began to whine. Max got one foot over the fence when he heard a low rumbling emanating neither from his throat nor the doll's.

A large Doberman was sitting, patiently, on the other side of the fence.

Max grinned at the Doberman. "Hiya, fella."

The dog barked once. A wad of saliva the size of a Rand-McNally globe rolled out of its mouth onto the ground.

Max slowly raised his leg out of the Doberman's range. The fence was beginning to sway ever so slightly.

On both sides of the fence, about four inches from the top, was a thin wooden lip jutting out an inch. Max gingerly placed his feet on the tiny ledges and pulled himself along the length of the fence, the fence top digging into the seat of his pants with remarkable accuracy.

The dog, now growling with the intensity of a kamikaze flight, patiently followed Max's progress, slowly padding along the length of the fence below.

"Mama," the doll whimpered.

"You said it, kid," Max grunted.

The fence began to totter.

The old lady with the cats shook her head, watching Max's perilous stunt. "You never were no Douglas Fairbanks," she called. "More of a Victor McLaglen."

Cady, experiencing a great wave of sympathy for King Kong in his final reel, felt a sliver of fence penetrate his pants. He tried lifting himself off the fence top slightly. His left foot broke through the wooden lip and plunged downward toward the salivating dog. Within an instant the dog was hurtling up through the air toward Max's dangling shoe. Max withdrew his foot quickly, almost toppling back down into the woman's jungle.

"Goddamn it," Max shouted at the dog, "get off my case."

The dog jumped up toward Max a second time. Max, although he was a big fan of the old Lassie series, slammed his foot down toward the oncoming beast in a most uncharitable manner. He caught the dog squarely on the nose with the flat of his heel.

The dog squeaked in both surprise and pain and tumbled back down to the ground.

Max stopped in his tracks.

The dog sat down on its backside with a thump. It sneezed three times in rapid succession, testing its proboscis for possible alterations. Finding none, it stood, sniffed at Max, sneezed once more, and, turning its back, trotted away sullenly.

Max patted the doll. "I've always had a way with animals," he noted and continued on his way.

He reached the end of the fence and gazed down into his daughter's yard. A group of children were playing some sort of board game on a picnic table. Max slowly maneuvered his body from the straight length of wobbly fence onto the corner of his daughter's.

Expecting to find a similar lip on the opposite side of the new expanse of wood to support his weight, Max was somewhat surprised to find his extended foot plunging down through thin air when he reached for it.

No lip.

No ledge.

No balance.

No way he was going to remain upright.

Max found himself tumbling over his daughter's fence and crashing down into a rosebush.

The children shrieked, first in surprise and then in delight as Max rolled, present still in hand, toward the picnic table.

Sara ran out of the house to see what the commotion was. Not

THE CON GAME

saying a word, she extended a helping hand in her father's direction.

Max stared at his daughter sheepishly. A gaggle of parents watched his every move from the living room inside. He grasped his daughter's hand and slowly raised himself to his feet.

"I was in the neighborhood, so I thought I'd drop in," he muttered.

"Mama!" said the box under his arm.

CHAPTER TWENTY-EIGHT

Max sipped a cup of coffee in his daughter's parlor, watching Peggy play with her new doll.

It was night.

The other children had gone home.

Their parents had disappeared into the safer sections of town.

The reporters on the front lawn, tired of playing *Waiting for Godot, Pictures at Eleven,* marched back off into the diorama of New York life in search of muggers, perverts, and TV starlets.

Max stretched his legs in front of him. It was then he noticed his socks. He had one blue one on and one brown one. He smiled to himself. Sara's mother had always said that, no matter how she tried to change Max's appearance, he had an uncanny ability to take any set of clothing and wear it in a manner that suggested Ellis Island.

"How's the coffee?" Sara asked.

"Fine."

"Is it strong enough?"

"If you mean 'Is it sobering you up, Dad?' yes, it is. Besides, I didn't have that much to drink."

"Uh-huh."

"Hey, lots of grown men argue with children."

"Over cheating on a game of pin the tail on the donkey?"

Max frowned. "Well, that Oswald kid was peeking through his blindfold. I had him beat hands down until he cheated."

"Dad, Tommy Oswald is six years old."

"Well, he should learn to play fair *now* before he gets older. Besides, he should respect his elders."

"Right. I'm sure he was really impressed by you challenging him to a round of Indian wrestling to settle it all."

"I offered him two out of three falls."

"I'm worried about you, Dad," Sara said, folding a paper Flintstones tablecloth.

"You should be. The only people who believe me about these murders are McArthur and the *Times* reporter and, for all I know, they may just be humoring me."

Sara smiled. "Reminds me of that song we used to sing. Remember? The B.B. King tune?"

Max laughed and began singing, " 'Nobody loves me but my mother, and she may be jivin' me too . . .' "

"The police are no help?"

"Nope. The only time I'm going to get the police interested in me is when that damned car of yours decides to stall out in the middle of Madison Avenue during rush hour."

Sara nodded. "It has already. In the bus lane, yet."

"Piece of shit. Revenge for Hiroshima. I'm sure of it. How's the tank?"

"Runs okay," Sara answered, sticking the tablecloth into a drawer. "No one can figure out how to fix the horn, though. The mechanic on Ninety-sixth Street said it was an act of God. He said the only way I could stop it from going off whenever it felt like it would be disconnecting it altogether. I feel safer with a horn, though."

"Yeah. No sense driving a mute car. Have you heard from Zorba the Thief?"

Sara shook her head no.

"I don't suppose he's sent his check . . ."

"I'd rather not talk about it, Dad."

"Yeah, well. If he gets too far behind, I'd sic a lawyer on him."

Sara passed by one of the three windows in the front of her apartment. "One of your fans is still outside."

"I thought you said the reporters had gone."

"They have . . . except for this bird."

She squinted through the venetian blind. "He's been out there all day, worshiping you from afar, I guess."

"What do you mean?"

"Well, he wasn't with the rest of the reporters today. He stood down toward the corner, toward Amsterdam more. He was trying desperately to look incognito but, to anyone who knows this block, he stood out like a sore thumb. Skinny twit."

She let the venetian blind shut and walked out into the kitchen. "I don't know what kind of story he expects to get at this hour."

Max put the coffee cup down in its saucer. "Skinny?"

He silently walked to the window and peered through the blind. Across the street, some two house-lengths away, a pale, skinny man stood under a streetlight staring intently at Sara's apartment.

"Carole!" Max exclaimed.

He trotted to the front door and flung it open, dashing out into the damp New York night.

"Dad?" Sara called from the kitchen. "Are you okay?"

By the time Max lumbered across the street to the lamppost, Carole had disappeared.

"Carole!" Max bellowed. "Show your face, you piece of shit!"

Max was greeted by catcalls in Spanish yelled from half a dozen open windows.

Max strained his eyes and caught a glimpse of a reedlike figure darting into an old parking garage half a block away. Cady charged up the street, his flat feet slapping the pavement with an eerie, echoing beat.

He stopped at the entranceway to the parking garage.

"How does it feel to be watched, Max?" a voice whispered from inside. "How does it feel to have someone spying on *you*, the way you've been spying on *me?*"

Max clenched his jaw and ran into the garage. It was small. Maybe three stories with a basement and an elevator for loading and unloading cars.

The place smelled like urine and stale cigarettes. It was badly lit and, at first glance, it seemed like a portal leading to a low-class black hole, the never-ending darkness punctuated by an occasional overhead bulb. Gradually, Max was able to make out cracked walls and a paint-stained ceiling.

Max walked across the street-level floor. The only sounds he heard were his own footsteps and heavy breathing.

He stood motionless for a moment.

High-pitched, maniacal laughter seemed to swirl around him. "How does it feel to be hunted, Cady?"

Max said nothing.

The laughter continued. Then, abruptly, stopped. Silence. Click. Max cocked his head. A familiar sound, yet alien. Creak. Slam. Thump. Max stood his ground, trying to assimilate and interpret what he was hearing. By the time he figured it out, he heard a motor roar to life and the squeal of rubber on concrete.

Max turned and ran toward the exit, his back illuminated by bouncing high beams.

The car was less than ten feet away from mowing him down when he dove down the exit ramp, plunging through a retaining wall of garbage cans and down four small steps leading to the basement.

The car fishtailed out of the garage and zoomed away.

Max lay, sprawled in garbage, attempting to catch his breath. A chorus of angry voices, some in English, some in Spanish, pointed out to Cady, none too delicately, that knocking over garbage cans at ten o'clock at night was considered bad taste and could, indeed, earn him a communal beating.

Max slowly climbed up the stairway and, saying nothing, limped back to his daughter's apartment house.

Sara was waiting in the doorway. Seeing her father, she ran from her home into the street. "Dad. What happened?"

"Never mind that. Just let me get cleaned up. Can I have a drink?"

"Haven't you had—"

"I'll get one if you won't."

He marched inside the apartment. Sara darted into the kitchen and the liquor cabinet.

Max grabbed the phone and dialed Debra Knightly's apartment. He got her answering service. "No message," he told the nasal-toned operator. "No message."

He then dialed Lehner. "The lieutenant isn't in right now," the desk sergeant informed Cady. "He'll be in tomorrow. You want to leave a message?"

"Yeah," Cady said. "Tell him Max Cady called and that Phillip Carole just tried to kill me."

"Is there an 'e' in Carole?"

"Yeah," Max said. "He knows my number."

Max hung up the phone. Sara appeared by his side and handed him a drink. Max looked at the drink suspiciously. "What is this?"

"Kahlua and ice coffee."

"Great."

"Well, you do have to drive home."

"If your car decides to give me a break and start."

His granddaughter, Peggy, trotted into the room. "Pee-yooo," she chirped. "Grandpa, you smell like the park."

"Grandpa doesn't feel well, honey, go to bed," Sara said.

"Grandpa feels fine, honey. He just fell down and go boom."

"Pee-yoo," Peggy repeated for emphasis. "Did you fall down where the dogs go?"

"Where elephants go!" Max said. "And dinosaurs!"

"Wow!" Peggy exclaimed. "Can I watch next time?"

"I don't see why not," Max said. He turned to his daughter. "The rest of the neighborhood seemed to be entertained by this go-round."

Sara smirked. "You're incorrigible, you know that?"

"I practice."

Max put the drink down. "Well, I guess I should go home. Are you okay, money-wise and otherwise?"

"Yup."

"Okay. I'll call you if anything earth-shattering happens with this mess."

"Like tonight's jogging was run-of-the-mill stuff, right?"

Max shrugged. He kissed his daughter. "Good night, hon." He bent down over his granddaughter. "Give Grandpa a kiss, love, I gotta go."

The little girl scrunched her face up into a frown. "Uh-uh. Peee-yooo."

Max attempted to sound hurt. "Is that any way to treat your favorite Grandpa?"

The girl considered this a moment. She picked up her new doll from the floor and held it in front of Cady. "You can kiss Matilly."

Max rolled his eyes and puckered up for the doll. "Good night, Matilly."

THE CON GAME

The doll fixed its plastic eyes on Max. "Euuurrrrrp," it belched.

"Great. I even get the brush-off from inanimate objects."

Max left the apartment.

He found the Toyota, unfortunately intact. Uttering a prayer to Mr. Christopher, defrocked saint of travelers, he placed the key in the ignition and turned it quickly. Miraculously, the car started.

He managed to make it back to Debra Knightly's apartment with little or no aggravation.

By the time he arrived upstairs, using his own key to let himself in, Knightly was seated in the living room prying the shoes from her feet.

She looked up at the thoroughly disheveled writer as he shambled into the apartment. "You look like shit," she said, sniffing the air, "and may I add that—"

"You may not," Max said. "I need a shower."

"I'm not sure I want to ask what happened."

"Don't," Max said, beginning to peel his clothes off en route to the bathroom.

"Lieutenant Lehner called," Debra called. "He wants you to call back."

"I bet he does."

Max walked out of the bathroom wearing one of Knightly's kimonos.

Debra stared at the specter before her. "Feel free to use my robe. What's going on?"

"Carole tried to kill me tonight."

Debra eyed Max with a mixture of surprise and dread. "He couldn't have."

"Why not?" Max said, irritated.

"I was going to tell you," Debra said. "You were so adamant about Carole that I decided to spend my big night off watching his apartment. I borrowed one of the city guy's cars from the paper and, for the last three hours, I have been dining alfresco on East Ninety-first Street watching Phillip Carole settle in for a night of TV."

"Are you sure?"

Debra nodded sadly. "Max, I swear to you, I've been watching Carole all night. He didn't leave his apartment."

Max slowly eased himself into a chair. He seemed to lose his spine as he did so, his body overwhelmed by gravity. Every angle in his massive frame appeared to point down.

Debra gazed at the crestfallen heap before her. "Would you like a drink?"

Max shook his head slowly from side to side. "No, I've probably had too many already."

He closed his eyes tightly and gripped the armrests on the chair. "Sweet Jesus, am I losing my mind?"

CHAPTER TWENTY-NINE

He couldn't shut the faces out of his head. All those faces he thought he had forgotten years ago were back, released by some emotional floodgate that had just been ruptured. They swirled before him now, howling and screaming in rage and pain or, worse yet, twisted and gnarled, frozen forever in violent death.

The mugging victims who put up a fight only to be surprised by a second thug wielding a knife.

The store owners who reached for their guns while the guy in the ski mask opened up with a 12-gauge.

The little girl picked up by a stranger in a van as she headed home from school, discarded like a used rag doll in a vacant lot in Queens.

Twisted faces, twisted limbs, twisted stories.

He had hardened himself to all that in order to get through his job every day, six days a week for nearly a decade. Now, though, now his mind seemed to be crumbling. His strength was being sapped. His thoughts were becoming scrambled. Reality and fantasy were leapfrogging through his life, taunting him by exchanging places when he least expected it.

If it hadn't been Carole last night, who had he seen?

Just a curiosity seeker? A reporter? Suppose no one had tried to kill him at all last night? Suppose all that occurred was a drunk running headfirst into a parking garage when a car was pulling out? And the voice? Suppose he had imagined it all?

He took another sip from the glass before him. His stomach felt like it was lined with worms crawling their way slowly to the surface. Up his throat. Around his tongue.

He heaved a sigh, allowing his breath to blow the ashes off the table.

The jukebox was playing something that reminded him of an old Johnny Weissmuller film. A Jungle Jim ceremonial sacrifice.

A frowsy blonde was dancing next to the bar. Interesting, the crowd that frequented bars at 11:30 in the morning. Not exactly *A-Team* material.

The bartender looked a little like Mr. Toad. Large-lipped and pop-eyed, he muttered under his breath a lot and seemed to have a bad left leg, which caused him to waddle behind the counter.

Max closed his eyes. This was getting to resemble a *Muppets* on mescaline special.

When he opened his eyes Lehner sat before him. Max squinted through his alcoholic haze. He wasn't sure if he was hallucinating or not until Lehner spoke.

"I don't appreciate people who cry wolf."

Max nodded glumly. Next to the bar, where the aging go-go girl bumped and grinded away, the mammoth Malloy stood, glaring at Max. Mr. Toad, made nervous by the colossal cop's presence, was dancing back and forth behind the bar.

The sight caused Max to laugh.

Lehner narrowed his eyes. "What's so funny?"

"Everythin'." Max smirked. "Everythin' is funny. You think I'm crazy. *I* think I'm crazy. Yet, I'm perfecly fine. I'm jus' havin' a run of bad luck."

"Bad luck, eh?" the cop echoed.

"Very bad. Ya see, this guy is killin' all these perfecly swell people and I can't catch him. It's like tryin' to catch a phantom. He's everywhere, Lieutennen, like a bad dream. Everywhere. And everyone he touches gets cold. Dies. Terrible. But *I* know what he's up to and I'll catch him. I'll catch the phantom. He's everywhere, you know."

"Yeah." Lehner nodded. "Like a bad dream."

"Did you know I was a good reporter?"

"No."

"One of the bes. One of the fucking bes. You know what made me so good? I'll tell you what made me so good. I used to report *every*thing. I looked at everything. Some of the cops on the scenes, the younger guys, would be pukin' or pissin' in their pants at what they were seein' but I'd be there, boy oh boy. I'd be there. Did you know a guy named Hanmad, Hanrat, Hanraddy?"

"No."

THE CON GAME

"Before your time. He was a very good frien of mine. A lieutennen. Jus like you. Homicide. We use to go oud and have a few drinks together. Wash the blood off, he used to say. Whadda great cop. Had his head blown off. Before your time. Hostage sidgeration. Near Times Square. We're goin' back a few years here. We both were there talkin'. It was one of those things, you know. Guy inside a coffee shop. Hadda dozen people. Killed three. Waiting game. They had the sergeant shrink on the phone with the guy. Expert at hostage negotiations. The guy asked that he wife be brought to the scene. Fine. Hostage negotiator says awwll right. So, they bring the wife there and it turns out that this guy *hates* his wife, not just dislikes her, but *hates* her. He wants her brought there so he can get a clean hit.

"Sonofabish opens fire. Nails the little missus through the neck. She's dead as can be. Me and Tommy, Tommy was Hanraddy's name, was in the middle of talkin' when we heard the gunfire. We both turned around to see what was goin' on. I hear this whiiizzzz noises. You know? Like boddle rockets goin' off. A whiiizzz. Then a plop. A splat. Like when you drop a melon? I turn aroun' and there isn't Tommy anymore. There's like a jaw and some stuff.

"Five slugs. Whizzz whizzz whizzz whizzz whizzz. Jeezus. I reported that one too. I was good."

Lehner sighed and stared at Cady. "You're sick, Max."

"Don I know it."

"You ever think of taking the cure?"

"Detox? I did that, Lieutennen. I cleaned up real fine. Eighteen months. Then, a week ago. It all sorda fell apart. You know? It all sorda fell apart."

Lehner stood and offered Max a hand. "C'mon. We'll take you home."

"Don' you worry, Lieutennen, I'll pull myself together. I'm gonna nail this sonofabish. I'm tired of bein' made feel like a fool."

"Up and at them, Max."

Max nodded. Lehner motioned for Malloy to help support the staggering man.

Malloy was muttering under his breath. "I don't know why

we just don't lock him up now and prevent another killing, Lieutenant."

Lehner remained silent.

"Instead of mollycoddling him."

The two cops dragged Max toward the door.

Malloy kicked the bar door open. Max winced as the sunlight hit his face.

The two policemen laid Max in the backseat of their unmarked car.

"You drive," Lehner said, sliding into the passenger's seat.

"I don't understand all this, Lieutenant. You hate this guy. You told me so. Why are we being so nice to him? We could hold him for a day without charging him with anything. Get him off the streets for a while."

Lehner stared at the hood of the car. "Ever hear of a cop name Hanraddy?"

"Nope."

"Before your time."

Malloy started the car. Lehner continued to gaze at the hood. "But he was a hell of a teacher."

CHAPTER THIRTY

He awoke on a couch. His street clothes had been removed. A kimono had been wrapped tightly around him. He was covered with sweat, alternately experiencing waves of hot throbbing above his eyelids and shivering bolts of cold throughout his body.

"Are you there?" he asked.

"Uh-huh," Debra replied.

"How long have I been out?"

"Long."

"Did I"—Max didn't know how to phrase this next one—"*do* anything?"

"If you mean did you perform any repulsive bodily functions, no," Debra said, getting up from her chair and moving toward the kitchen and a whistling teakettle. "If you mean did you scare the hell out of me, yeah."

Max remained silent.

Debra continued, pouring herself a cup of tea. "I've never seen anything like it, Max. You were doubled over and moaning most of the night, like you were keeping your internal organs internal by sheer willpower."

"All night?"

"It's Saturday afternoon now."

"Christ," Max muttered, attempting to calculate how long he'd been out of it. It figured up to just about a day.

"It's scary, Max. It's like watching an addict or someone go cold turkey."

Max struggled into a sitting position. "That's all over with," he said with halfhearted conviction. "I've seen the handwriting on the floor."

Debra returned with a cup of tea. "Want any?"

"No."

"Why do you do it, Max? It's dehumanizing."

Max rubbed his face with his hands. He felt greasy. Unclean. "I don't know. Pleasure has nothing to do with it. I've always had problems along these lines."

He offered her a small smile. "When I was first married I had a kid right away, you know? Here I was, a struggling writer and all of a sudden I had these *responsibilities*. I'd be good for months at a time and then I'd just disappear for a day or two. My wife knew me well enough not to worry.

"Her euphemism for it all was 'Max is doing his magic act again.'"

"Magic act?"

"Yeah. I'd walk up a street and turn into a saloon."

"She sounds special."

Max nodded slowly. "She was. I need a shower."

Max lurched to his feet and walked toward the bathroom. He was suddenly filled with anger, directly, mostly at himself. He was being made a fool of. Worse yet, he was actually helping in the process. He was being set up. He was being put down. He was being publicly praised and humiliated at the same time.

And if he kept falling off the wagon, he was accelerating the speed of his frame.

He'd have to keep himself stone-cold sober to match wits with this son of a bitch.

The maniac knew Cady's background. He'd studied him. He knew Max's weaknesses as well as his strong points. Carole was playing Max the way a seasoned musician plays a piano, pounding on all the right keys.

Max knew the tune now, however, and was going to do his best to change it.

Max stepped into the bathroom. "Would it be too much to ask for a pot of coffee?"

Debra blinked. "A pot?"

"Yeah," Max said. "Somebody has lost me a day. I'm going to make it up. Tomorrow the archbishop is going to make a grand appearance. Our boy is determined to make it his last. I have twenty-four hours to change all that."

"What are you going to do?"

"Jam Carole like he's never been jammed before."

Debra rolled her eyes. "You have no proof, Max."

"Goddamn it," Max roared, "I don't *need* proof."

"Whatever you say."

"Did Kenny call? He was tracking down some of Carole's old cronies, checking out the jerk's sister too."

"He called. Nothing so far."

Max went into the bathroom. Debra walked over to the phone. She dialed a number. A phone on the other end of the line rang four times. "Hello?" a male voice answered.

"Lieutenant Lehner?"

"Yes."

"It's Debra Knightly. Max is awake."

"How is he?"

"Not too good. He's still got this fixation about Phillip Carole. I'm afraid he's going to try to do something crazy."

"I'll have a man down there in ten minutes. Can you keep him there for that long?"

"I think so. He's in the shower. He's not dressed."

"Don't worry, Miss Knightly, we'll keep an eye on Mr. Cady. He'll never notice our man."

"Just don't hurt him, Lieutenant, he's really messed up."

"Our job is to keep him from being hurt, Miss Knightly, and keep him from hurting other people."

"Thanks, Lieutenant."

"Good-bye, Miss Knightly."

Debra hung up the phone. She stared at the coffeepot on the stove. It was beginning to perk. She hoped she was doing the right thing. No. She saw the condition Max was in when Lehner brought him home last night. She *knew* she was doing the right thing.

Still, if Max ever found out she was working with the police, he'd kill her.

A sudden shiver shook her small frame.

She didn't mean that literally . . . she hoped.

CHAPTER THIRTY-ONE

Saturday night was shaping up to be starless. Spring was caught between a frigid winter and what promised to be a hot, humid summer and was vacillating, offering a procession of threatening purple clouds and a stinging, moist wind.

The TV weatherman had promised a severe thunderstorm. The problem was, nobody knew quite when. It could be tonight. Tomorrow morning. Even tomorrow night. Until the storm hit the city head-on, however, occasional drizzle and gale-force winds would buffet the area.

Since Max had brought only a suitcase or two to Knightly's apartment, he had to stop in a tourist-oriented clothing store to be overcharged for a raincoat. He didn't mind. This was the kind of weather he enjoyed the most. It was volatile. Unpredictable.

As he marched up Madison Avenue he caught a glimpse of himself in a high-priced leather store's window. Collar pulled up around his neck to protect him from the howling wind, he looked every inch the stereotypical detective.

As he passed the diabolically chic shops on the streets in the Sixties, it began to drizzle. He pulled out an old rain cap ("one size fits all") and continued his slog uptown. A thunderclap echoed in the distance.

The Madison Avenue shops gradually gave way to the more neighborhoody coffee stops and delis in the Seventies. A church. A school.

The street was nearly deserted. It was after seven and anyone who was heading to the theater or a first-run film was already en route downtown via subway or bus or, considering this was the affluent East Side, most likely, cab.

A small white car, a Datsun, puttered by Max and turned a corner directly in front of him, heading east toward Park Avenue. The silhouette of a fat, owlish man could be seen behind the wheel.

Something about the car made Max uneasy. He felt he had seen it before. He couldn't remember where.

Crossing Seventy-ninth Street, Max became aware of the avenue's art galleries, where artistic achievements of debatable quality could be purchased for even more debatable prices.

At Eighty-sixth Street the avenue seemed to calm down a bit. A diner on one corner. A clothes shop on another. The galleries got less strident in their artifacts. The place took on a more folksy feel. As he crossed Eighty-sixth, Max watched a white Datsun round the corner and head up Madison.

At Eighty-ninth, Max passed by a titanic apartment complex, out of place in this residential district. It formed a colossal wind tunnel. Swirling masses of leaves and debris twirled in mini-funnels around the sidewalk. Max held on to his hat for dear life.

Max made it to the corner of Ninety-first and Madison just before eight o'clock. He stood, under a streetlamp, attempting to look like he was indigenous to the area. Fat chance. Even with his book sales, Max couldn't afford to buy a closet on this block, let alone a place to live.

He stood next to a storefront and gazed at the brownstone once owned by Eric Paine. Debra had told him that Carole's quarters were on the second floor. He gazed upward through the drizzle. Yeah. There Carole was, seated before a flickering television screen.

Max heard voices and stepped back into the shadows. A young couple passing by gave him a strange look and then hurried across the street to a Citibank. The boy stood guard, nervously glancing at Max, as his date used her bankcard to gain access to the walk-up window inside.

Max chuckled to himself. He must look like a reject from a film *noir* reunion. So what? If he had unnerved those two, maybe he'd do the same to Carole.

He stepped back into the light and glared at the window. Go ahead, he mused, look out the window, creep. Get a good look at me. I'll be dogging you from now until doomsday if I have to.

There's nowhere you will be able to go that I won't be there with you.

I have the money to do it, I sure have the time, and, boy, do I have the motivation.

The white Datsun tried pulling into a parking space down the block, near Park Avenue. An elderly man emerged from a building next to the space and informed the owner of the car in fairly ungenteel terms that the space he was using was, indeed, a driveway and unless he wanted his vehicle towed he would move it posthaste.

The car pulled away.

Max smiled. A driveway. Imagine a home having a private driveway in Manhattan. That was something you read about in stories by guys like the Brothers Grimm or saw on TV shows like *Ripley's Believe It or Not.*

Max stood on the corner in the drizzle

The minutes seemed to crawl by.

Carole remained, entranced, in front of the television. Max wondered just what it was that held Carole's attention so intently. He allowed himself a smirk. Maybe there was a rerun of *Psycho* on.

The combination of the drizzle and the wind was beginning to numb Max's feet. Although he had remembered his rain hat and had bought a new trench coat, he had overlooked rubbers and, as a result, his feet were wet enough to spawn marsh life.

He decided to take a cautious walk down the block. It was after nine now, and the place was deserted. Most of the block was made up of privately owned brownstones. There was an expensive private school mid-block on the north side and a church on the northwest corner. The prerecorded bells in the steeple were chiming the half-past-the-hour mark when Max became aware that he had acquired a second shadow on the block.

A round man had emerged from a basement-level flight of stairs behind Max and was cautiously making his way to the sidewalk.

Max recognized him as the driver of the white Datsun.

Cady glanced over his shoulder. The round man retreated. Carole still seemed to be entranced by the television. Max de-

THE CON GAME

cided to take a chance and double-time it around the block. He strode up to Park Avenue and hung a quick left, heading up toward Ninety-second Street.

Park Avenue was solidly one-dimensional. Both sides of the street were lined with large, flat apartment buildings having little or no ornamentation or character. Max's tail would have a hard time blending in with this area . . . if he was indeed a tail.

Max marched up to Ninety-second. As he spun around the corner, heading across Ninety-second back toward Madison, he caught sight of the fat man huffing and puffing after him.

Max grinned. All right. Let's just see who you are and what you want. Max broke into a run and galloped down the block, skidding to a halt on Madison and Ninety-second Street.

The little man was carefully charging after Max, trying dutifully to stay in the shadows. Max wondered if the fat man was armed. Probably. If someone is assigned to shadow you, he's either a cop or a crud and, either way, he's not doing the job for an altruistic reason.

Max jogged along Madison, coming to a stop in front of the well-lit Citibank. The fat man slowly walked around the corner of Madison and Ninety-second Street. He marched down the street directly at Max.

An elderly man and his granddaughter gave Max a fishy look as they stepped around him to walk into the bank.

Max watched the owlish man plod down the street. His steps seemed to grow more and more leaden as he grew nearer. His face was white and wore an expression of shock. More than shock. Grief.

Max saw that the man's glasses were halfway off his nose. Something was definitely wrong here.

Max ran from in front of the bank toward the man. The round figure was now staggering. He stopped, leaning next to a storefront three buildings down from the bank. He was wheezing, gasping for air, as if he was recovering from a marathon.

Max grabbed him under the left armpit as the owlish fellow began to slide down the store's window. "Steady, there," Max grunted. "What's the matter?"

The man opened his mouth and a burst of blood bubbled out.

Max instinctively pulled away and the little man pitched forward, an army knife protruding from his back.

"Jesus," Max whispered as the man hit the ground.

Max gazed at his hands. They were covered with blood. The drizzle caused the blood to run down onto his trench coat.

The owlish man hit the pavement and made gurgling sounds. His body jerked into a fetal pose and began to quiver. The blood was now pouring from his wound, forming tiny rivulets. The crimson streams were diluted by the fine mist and sent dribbling into the gutter as tiny blotches of festive pink.

Max opened the man's coat. "Steady," he said. "I'm going to pull you into the doorway here. Can you understand me? I'm going to pull you into the doorway and go and call an ambulance. You'll be okay."

The man shuddered once. He would never be okay again, at least not in this world.

A high-pitched laugh pierced the air. Max spun around. No one was on the street.

He reached inside the man's overcoat and into the pocket of a sports jacket underneath. Max pulled out a folder, the type usually filled with credit cards. He flipped it open. A shield. New York Police Department.

Max fingered the shield in his left hand and whistled to himself. Great. Just great.

"Help! Police! Murder!"

Max stiffened. Other people had astrological signs. He had one that read: CAUTION: DIP.

He slowly turned around and saw the old man clutching his granddaughter in the entranceway of the bank. "Help! Help!" the man screeched.

Max got up and walked toward the pair, his arms outstretched. "Look, I can—"

"Don't come near us!" the old man yelled, retreating into the bank. "Help!"

Windows began to open. Max, his hands outstretched still, suddenly felt very much like the Frankenstein monster on a quick trip through a quiet little town in Bavaria.

"What's going on down there?"

"Hey! You! What are you doing?"

THE CON GAME

"I've called the police."

Max, reviewing all his options, decided to do the intelligent thing. He fled. Running around the corner, he almost mowed down the young couple who had eyed him suspiciously at the bank nearly two hours ago.

The girl screamed.

The young man pulled her out of the way, as if Max were a rabid animal.

The high-pitched laughter filled the air again.

Max had been followed by, not one, but two shadows. And one of them was a crazy son of a bitch who thought murder was a fun thing to pull on a Saturday night.

Max glanced up at Paine's brownstone as he galloped by. Carole was still seated in front of the television screen. Max's mind went blank.

For a minute he toyed with the concept of astral projection.

Thirty seconds later, when a police car's whine cut the air, he toyed with the concept of doing hard time for the killing of a cop.

CHAPTER THIRTY-TWO

Kenny McArthur's apartment reflected the best aspects of the man himself. It was disheveled but sturdy, built in the days before paper-thin walls and cookie-cutter predictability were the rule.

It wasn't much to look at, a small slice of plaster and brick located on the second floor of a nondescript area lying between Soho and Chinatown, a neighborhood where kids still had the name Chico and descriptive words like "Dago, Chink, Mick, Polack, and Jew" were still acceptable terms of endearment.

When Max showed up at McArthur's door the rotund newsman was not so much surprised as he was annoyed. His living room had, over the years, settled on a near forty-five-degree angle and the puddles dripping off Max were slowly accumulating on the side of the room where he kept his battered stereo.

"If you short that out, Max," he warned, "I'll forever despise you."

Max stumbled into the room and, without taking off his coat, sat down on McArthur's prized rocking chair.

"Just passing through or are you here to bring down the property value?" McArthur inquired, easing the door shut behind him.

"I'm in trouble, Kenny."

"That's news?"

"Big trouble."

"How big?"

"First-degree murder? Cop killing? Shall I go on?"

McArthur eased himself down into a chair across from Max. "Shit, Maxie. This is fucked, even for you."

"Tell me about it." Max slumped in the rocker, massaging his eyelids rapidly with his left hand. As briefly as possible he told McArthur about Carole's viewing habits, the owl-like shadow,

THE CON GAME

his murder, and the appearance of one half of the Upper East Side of Manhattan at a particularly inopportune moment.

"Christ," McArthur moaned, *"every*one saw you standing over the body and you *ran?"*

"It seemed like a good idea at the time."

McArthur's crimson face grew more so. "Max, you realize that you've just nailed yourself to a cross here. You should have stuck it out. Explained your way out of it."

"Come on, Kenny. This Lehner guy wants my hide."

"Yeah. Well, by running, you've just handed it over to him, gift-wrapped."

"I suppose," Max sighed.

"My advice is to turn yourself in. If you want, I'll go downtown with you."

"Uptown."

"Huh?"

"The precinct is uptown."

"Oh, well. Sure, I'll go uptown too. All they have on you is circumstantial evidence."

"Enough to hold me, though."

"Maybe."

"Don't bullshit me, Ken. They can probably even get a conviction on this. I was seen loitering in the area, I'm dressed like a pulp-novel character, and I'm sure that our dear Mr. Carole would testify that I'm not playing with a full deck.

"Ken, I don't know how he's doing it, but he's running circles around me. He has to have an accomplice."

"If he does, it's someone that I can't track down. From what I gather he was a real loner in prison. Didn't have a buddy or a confidant. The other cons actually avoided him. They thought he was too weird."

"Great. How about his sister?"

"Haven't tracked her down yet. The address he wrote to her at when he was in the slam is now a vacant lot near Pittsburgh."

"This is shaping up to be a bad Hitchcock film," Max said, still dripping on the floor.

Arthur thought for a moment. "I still think it's best to do this by the book."

"I can't, Kenny. If I turn myself in, Archbishop William Rowland will be as good as dead tomorrow."

"On the bright side, though, if he's killed, the police will know that you're not the maniac. You'll be in custody."

"Thanks. But I'll still be in for cop killing."

The smile on McArthur's face faded. "Oh yeah. I forgot about that."

The two men sat in silence. Finally, McArthur spoke. "What are you going to do?"

"I'll need your help."

"Don't worry about it."

"I'll have to lay low until tomorrow. I can't let Lehner pick me up until *after* Rowland says Mass. I think our boy will hit big during some public ceremony. He's not going to kill Rowland when no one is around."

"You want to stay here?"

"I don't think I can, Ken. But I could use a couple of bucks. I left most of my cash at Debra's."

"Have you gone back there?"

"No. I figure the police will make that their first pit stop."

"How about your daughter's?"

"That's their second."

"I suppose I'm third?"

"Safe assumption."

McArthur stood, crossed the room, and removed a pair of trousers lying atop a steam radiator. He jammed a hand in the left front pocket and produced a handful of crinkled bills. He scrutinized the bills in his hand. "How does $36 sound?"

"Like heaven," Max said, getting to his feet. "Do me a favor? As Debra to stake out Carole's apartment tomorrow?"

"Any particular time?"

"How about all day and all night or . . ."

"Until someone tries to hit the priest?"

"Yeah," Max said. "Until something happens either way."

"I'll run over there tomorrow morning," McArthur said, handing the money to Max. "I won't risk using the phone. Will you be bird-dogging the archbishop tomorrow?"

Max nodded. "Yeah. I hope that Lehner will have men around too. I warned him about this, but in light of tonight's

THE CON GAME

episode he might consider me a total psycho and just ignore what I said."

McArthur frowned. "Suppose I call him and tell him that the *News* has received an anonymous tip that the priest is going to be snuffed?"

"Would you?"

McArthur grinned broadly. "Sure. I've done worse."

"I know. I read your review of *Return of the Jedi* a couple of years back. Did you even see that film?"

"I fell asleep early. But a little kid described it to me real good outside the theater."

"Thanks, Ken," Max said, extending a hand. "For everything."

The round, silver-haired man grasped Cady's paw and pumped it. "Hey. We're members of the Fleet Street Frat, remember? Just watch your ass out there, okay?"

Max smiled, sincerely moved by the older man's compassion. "Okay."

Max turned and made a move toward the door. He froze as a loud knock reverberated through the room.

Max and McArthur exchanged glances. Kenny shrugged his shoulders in a "beats me" expression.

"Kenneth McArthur?"

McArthur puckered his lips and made an angelic expression in the direction of the door. "Yeeessss."

"Police. Open up, please."

McArthur pointed Max in the direction of the bedroom and hissed, "Fire escape." He then returned his attention toward the door. "Just a min-nute. I'm nak-ked."

Max ran through the apartment, opened the bedroom window, and emerged on a fire escape as McArthur slid out of his shirt and tossed on a bathrobe. As an afterthought he ran into the kitchen and ran the cold tap across his head.

Dripping, he answered the door. Two cops in blue towered above him, glancing past him into the apartment.

"Do you mind if we ask you a few questions, Mr. McArthur?"

"No," the red-faced man said sweetly. "Come in. I was just washing my hair."

The officers noted the puddles all around the room. McArthur smiled innocently. "It's a Saturday-night ritual," he said. "Started when I was a tyke. My mother was from Dublin, you know. Have you ever heard of the Shampooing Shaunesseys? No? Well, it all started right after the great potato famine—"

"Do you know a Max Cady?" the taller of the two cops asked.

"Better than that," McArthur replied. "I know *the* Max Cady."

"When was the last time you saw him?"

"A few days ago. We had a drink together. Is he in some sort of trouble, Officer?"

"Maybe," the second cop answered, eyeing the door leading to the bedroom. A series of puddles that began at the rocking chair led to the portal.

"What's in there?" the second cop asked.

"The bedroom," McArthur said. "It's a real mess, though."

"Mind if we take a look inside?" the second cop continued.

McArthur tried to figure out whether Max had had enough time to get out the window and down the rickety fire escape. "Not at all," he said.

McArthur decided that he couldn't afford to chance it. He walked the second officer toward the door. Without warning he clutched his chest and began wheezing. He reached out with his free hand and clutched the cop's left arm, nearly dragging the patrolman to the floor.

"What is it?" the cop cried.

"My heart!" McArthur wheezed as the first cop ran to his aide. "Quick, call the paramedics!"

The first cop ran to the phone and dialed 911.

The second cop lowered McArthur to the floor. "You'll be okay, old-timer. Has this ever happened before?"

"No," McArthur moaned. "It's a complete shock. I'm a jogger."

The cop looked at the rotund man suspiciously.

Kenny continued to wheeze. "Well, I walk a lot, anyhow."

The first cop knelt down next to McArthur. "The ambulance is on its way, sir. You'll be fine now."

McArthur grinned broadly. "Thank you, Officers. You've saved the day."

THE CON GAME

Max Cady heard the approaching ambulance as he ran into the night. The rain was letting up. A cold wind ripped into his open raincoat and sent his body into a series of shivers.

He ran downtown, toward Chinatown. If he was lucky, he could find a doorway to sleep in overnight in one of the small factories near South Street.

If he was really lucky, no one would slit his throat while he slept.

CHAPTER THIRTY-THREE

A thunderclap shook Max Cady awake. He blinked his eyes as a bolt of lightning danced above the FDR Drive. He had spent the night in a gutted warehouse on South Street. He glanced at his watch. It was seven in the morning but the varicose-vein colored sky made it seem like seven at night.

A second thunderclap shook the flimsy building behind him.

When the rumbling ceased Max became aware of a wheezing noise blending in with the sound of the wind. He slowly turned his face and saw an old, scab-covered Labrador lying on the stairs to his right. Max regretted not having a bit of food to give the pathetic creature. The dog opened an eye as Max got to his feet. It offered a halfhearted growl, a prolonged fart, and a slight stretching motion before lapsing back into slumber.

Max turned his collar up and trudged back toward Chinatown and the Lexington Avenue subway. When Carole made his move at the High Mass this morning, Max would be there to stop him.

A sudden pang of fear entered his thoughts. If Lehner *did* pay attention to Max's warning and *did* attend the service, then what would prevent him from arresting Max for the murder of the shadow last night before Max could stop Carole?

Max halted dead in the middle of the street. He caught a glimpse of himself in a storefront window. He looked like hell. Good, he thought. If he looked rotten enough, maybe Lehner wouldn't notice him.

Just to make sure, though, he'd buy a pair of glasses and a large hat. Maybe he'd pass for just another New York lowlife. Max trotted down the stairs to the subway at Canal Street. The shops were just beginning to yawn to life. The coffee joints and the doughnut emporiums were serving the early risers, people

THE CON GAME

who had braved the elements to slog it to their neighborhood newsstands for a fresh copy of the New York *Times*.

Carrying their booty off into the morning, they made pit stops at the nearest eateries, proudly displaying their Book Review sections for all to see.

Max sat down on a bench and waited for the uptown local.

A black kid with a faceful of scars and a fistful of ghetto blaster sat next to him.

The kid turned the radio on. A scratch song burst forth from the speakers. The percussive, scraping sound of the music reminded Max of a robot with asthma. As the music pounded away, two small boys, dressed in their Sunday best, broke away from their mother and began break dancing on the subway platform.

Max watched in amazement as the small bodies twisted, contorted, undulated, and spun around on the concrete, turning Sunday finery into smudged normalcy.

Scar grinned and turned his radio louder.

The kids danced faster.

The mother yelled at the kids. Max thought she was speaking Spanish. With the music blasting, though, she might as well have been screaming in Venutian. She pointed at Scar and his radio and then to her dirt-stained kids.

Scar's smiled vanished.

He turned the radio off.

The woman continued to yell and point.

Scar stared menacingly.

The woman stopped her harangue mid-shriek.

Scar's lips parted. An ominous hissing sound emerged. He slowly arose from the bench.

Max watched the tableau, fearing the worst.

A roar shook the platform as the Lexington Avenue local skidded through the tunnel and to a stop before Max.

The woman grabbed her boys and yanked them into a car. Max stepped into another car and sat down. Scar sat across from him. Without any encouragement from Max, Scar burst into a spasm of giggles and explained, "I fucked with her mind good."

Max found himself smirking. "You sure did."

"Fucked with her good." The kid turned on his radio.

The funk world's answer to emphysema filled the subway car.

Max sighed to himself and began humming a tune. "Sunday in New York."

He glanced at his watch. It was 7:45 A.M. Mass was scheduled to begin at ten.

At 8 A.M., Debra Knightly was awakened by the sound of her downstairs buzzer. She slid off the couch and walked to the intercom next to the door. She was still fully dressed from the night before. She had fallen asleep on the couch, near the phone, awaiting some word from Max.

No word had come.

She had, however, heard from Lieutenant Lehner, her editor, and half the television news reporters on the eastern seaboard. A warrant was out for Max Cady's arrest.

The charge?

Murder, first degree.

Debra leaned on the intercom. "Who is it?"

"Kenny McArthur. Let me up."

"Sure, Mr. McArthur." She pushed a black button and heard the door in the hallway downstairs click open. Within seconds an out-of-breath McArthur was at her door.

"You have enough cops outside to qualify you for foreign dignitary status," he wheezed.

"I didn't notice any."

"They're disguised as people," he said, walking into the room. "Man it looks as if it's really going to come down today."

"Did you hear from Max?"

"Yeah. I saw him last night. He swears it was Carole. He also swears that Carole never left the house."

"Do you think he's cracking up?"

"I think that happened years ago," Kenny said. "I also think he's telling the truth. I don't know why, but I believe him."

"Why didn't he get in touch with me?"

"He figured that the police would be watching you closer than a chaperone at a school prom. He didn't want to call because of phone taps. So, here *I* am."

"Here you are. Is Max all right?"

THE CON GAME

"We'll know by the end of the day, won't we?"

"The archbishop."

"He still thinks that the killer is going to off Rowland. I'm sort of hoping that he does, just so Max will be let off the hook." McArthur shook his head sadly. "And me being a Catholic boy too. Disgraceful."

A thunderclap roared across the Manhattan skyline.

Debra sighed. "What can I do to help?"

"Max wants you to stake out Carole's place again."

The woman clenched her teeth and slammed the flat of her hand down onto the arm of her chair. "This is getting ridiculous, Kenny. Max is out there somewhere, accused of being a cop killer, and what the hell does he want me to do? Guard some boring ex-convict who never leaves his goddamn house. And why? Because Max is convinced that this wimp is out to *embarrass* Jimmy Ammo?"

Kenny nodded. "Humor him. Just this once. It may be the last time . . . one way or the other."

Debra stared at her knees.

McArthur got to his feet. "By the end of the day you can be sure that Lehner will have Max at the precinct house . . . either as a witness or a prisoner."

He walked to the front door.

"Where are you going?" Debra asked.

"I have to make a phone call," McArthur replied cryptically. "And I'd rather not make it from your home."

"And after that?"

"I have to make a quick stop at the office. Then I thought I might say a little prayer to St. Jude. He's the patron saint of lost causes."

"At St. Patrick's?"

McArthur shrugged. "If I'm in the neighborhood, I might stop in for Mass."

Debra shook her head. "All right. All right. I'll watch Carole. Just how long am I supposed to sit there. All day?"

McArthur nodded. "If that's what it takes."

"Shit."

"You might want to take along a radio and keep it tuned to an all-news channel. You might get excused early."

At 8:12 A.M., Kenny McArthur waddled into a phone booth on Madison and Fifty-fourth and called 911, the emergency number.

"Yes?"

"Rowland dies today!" McArthur said in a thick, Bela Lugosi accent. "Rowland is a dead man. For his crimes against . . ." McArthur drew a blank. "For his crimes against the peoples of Europe. For his not taking a stand against the Communist oppressors. His blood will mix with those of our martyrs."

McArthur slammed the phone down. "That'll give them something to think about," he whispered.

He needed a drink.

At 8:30, Debra Knightly trotted up to her desk at the *Times* building. She had left Cady's battered Toyota home. It was a pain in the ass to drive and it had already been spotted once on East Ninety-first Street. She was hoping that Ruth Malquist would be working the Sunday shift taking dictation. It was a shitty job and Ruth hated it. Still, if she wanted to be a reporter someday, the young woman felt that it couldn't hurt to pay her dues and earn a few Brownie points simultaneously.

"Ruth!" Debra found herself yelling at too high a volume.

The young, plump woman behind the computer terminal looked up, startled. "Christ," she said in a nasal voice, "you scared the hell out of me."

"Ruth. I have a family emergency to deal with. Can I borrow your car?"

"Well, uh . . ."

"For a couple of hours?"

"Well, uh . . ."

"Look. I'll put in a good word for you with Aaronson in Arts and Leisure. He's looking for a body there."

"Well . . . okay."

Debra snatched the keys and, moments later, was driving a 1984 Subaru up Madison Avenue. Seeing as how the street was deserted, when the light at Madison and Forty-eighth turned green, she stood on the automatic vehicle's accelerator. She watched with glee as the computerized dash lurched into a

THE CON GAME

bright, glowing mode and a green bar lit up like a Christmas tree.

"Turbo drive!" she laughed nervously.

She considered herself lucky she didn't hit a slow-moving pedestrian as she tried to break the sound barrier en route to Carole's. She would have laughed as the body hit the pavement. She was so scared right now, she would have laughed at anything.

She pulled up to a coffee shop on Eighty-sixth and stocked herself with doughnuts and three coffees.

Kenny had warned her that she might be there all day.

Lieutenant Lehner looked at the clock across from his desk. It was 9 A.M. The hulk Malloy sat in a chair before him. A third man, wiry and nervous, held a cassette tape player with the on button depressed. A thick Mid-European accent was droning out of the tiny speakers.

When the speech was done the wiry man flicked the recorder off.

"When did that come in?" Lehner asked.

"Less than an hour ago. I can check for the exact time. They logged it," the reedlike man, whose name was Adams, replied.

"Don't bother."

Lehner stared at Malloy. "What do you think?"

"I think it's bullshit."

Lehner nodded. "Maybe. Rowland *was* behind the Iron Curtain last week, right?"

"It's bullshit."

"Yeah, probably."

"It's Cady. It's bullshit."

Lehner sighed. "Sergeant. Let's play 'What if?' What if Cady is an innocent schmoe caught way over his head in something? What if he didn't kill Sampson last night? What if he's right about Rowland?"

"What if he's a crazy son of a bitch who killed all those people, who killed Willie and now is after Rowland?" Malloy countered.

Malloy had played directly into Lehner's hands. "Well, in that case, we should increase the number of men at St. Paddy's for Mass, shouldn't we?"

Malloy's puffy eyes narrowed into equally blotted slits. "It's bullshit."

"We can't take chances. If anyone asks for justification, we can play them this tape."

He pushed the tape back to Adams. "Thanks, Len."

"Lee."

"Huh?"

"It's Lee, not Len. I'm Lee. Len's replacement. Len's dead."

Lehner nodded absentmindedly. "That's right. I remember. I sent flowers."

"Just because we're both of the same build and because we never had much experience on the streets like most of you guys, everyone assumes that we're the same person. Well, we're not. We're as different as night and day."

"I know." Lehner nodded. "Len is dead."

"Right." Adams nodded, snatching his tape and walking out of the office. "And don't you forget it."

Lehner slid lower into his chair. "Sergeant, see who we can rustle up in the next fifteen minutes to head toward St. Paddy's. I want plainclothesmen. Grab a couple of patrols. Four people plus the two of us. Six plus the five we have there should do it . . . I hope."

Malloy nodded and slowly arose. "It's bullshit."

Malloy marched toward the door.

"Sergeant," Lehner asked, "just how did Len die?"

Malloy faced the lieutenant. "Len who?"

"It doesn't matter. I sent flowers."

At 9:15, Max Cady ran a hand across a grizzled cheek. He sat in the corner booth at a coffee house on Lexington and Forty-ninth. He'd head toward the cathedral soon. He was a ten-minute walk away. He'd time it so he'd get inside during the last big crush and sit or stand somewhere way in the back. If the police were there, they'd be up front, toward the altar. From his vantage point, Cady hoped and prayed that he could keep an eye on both the entrances and exits and the archbishop as well.

A copy of that morning's *Daily News* had been tossed on the

THE CON GAME

floor of the coffee house near the counter. Max squinted through his totally useless pair of tinted glasses picked up at Grand Central Station.

Headline: CRIMEBUSTER TURNS COP KILLER!

Cady pulled the cap down farther over his forehead and clutched his coffee cup as if his life depended on it.

Lieutenant Samuel Lehner and his men arrived at St. Patrick's Cathedral at 9:45. They were greeted by a black-and-white unit patrolling the area.

"Keep an eye open," Lehner told the uniformed cops outside. "We got a crank call. We might have some crazy here. I'm going back to talk to the archbishop now. If I can, I want to get him to call off the Mass."

The cops nodded. "We can call for backup if you'd like, sir. Get another unit here."

Lehner turned to Malloy. "What do you think, Sergeant?"

"It's bullshit."

"Thank you, Sergeant," Lehner said, pursing his lips. "Yeah," he said to the patrolman. "Get a black-and-white out by that side entrance. See if you can get someone on foot patrol on the other side. Bring out a couple of wooden horses. Make it seem like it's crowd-control time. Nothing more."

"Yes, sir."

Lehner turned to his accomplice. "Sergeant, you and the men go inside and get yourselves situated. Stay as close to the altar as possible. Make sure someone is upstairs too. I want the place scoped."

Malloy grumbled and lurched toward the church.

At 9:50 A.M., Phillip Carole, neatly dressed, left the brownstone owned by the late Eric Paine and walked to the corner of Madison Avenue and Ninety-first Street.

In her car, parked on the far corner, Debra Knightly watched him enter a newspaper store on Madison between Ninety-first and Ninety-second. A few minutes later he emerged with a copy of the Sunday *Times* and the Sunday *News*. He crossed the street and entered a Gristede's supermart on Ninety-second. He left the store a minute later with a small brown bag filled with food.

He returned to the house.

He was safely inside by 10 A.M.

Knightly bit into a doughnut and waited for something to happen.

The white-haired clergyman stared at the lieutenant. "I appreciate your situation, Lieutenant Lehner," Archbishop Rowland said, "but I can't back out of this Mass simply because you got a phone call which may or may not be on the level."

"But, Archbishop," Lehner said. "There *is* a nut out there."

"There are nuts everywhere." Rowland smiled, his horsey face taking on a kind but firm expression. "And, believe me, I've been around quite a few in my time."

"But, Archbishop . . ."

"The name is Bill. . . ."

"It wouldn't hurt just this once to—"

"I won't hear of it, Lieutenant. Wild Bill Rowland has said Mass in the middle of battle zones. I was in London during the Blitz. The South Pacific during the Big One. Korea. Vietnam. I couldn't live with myself if I let this one crank call frighten me from my duty to God and his flock."

"Awww, Jesus . . ."

"No, just Bill. Jesus is my boss, and, frankly, the worst thing that can happen, Lieutenant, is that this call will turn out to be real and I'll get to meet my boss sooner than I had expected."

"But, Archbishop . . ."

Rowland patted Lehner paternally. "It's okay. I'm wearing clean underclothes. He would want it that way."

Lehner heaved an exasperated sigh. "At least let me watch you from the sidelines."

"It's called the sacristy and you will be welcome to watch the Mass as long as you don't get in the way of my altar boys."

Lehner blinked as the archbishop slipped into his cassock. He couldn't believe how well the man was taking this death threat.

Rowland smiled one last time at the lieutenant. "The altar boys are the short people with the long robes on. Try not to step on them."

THE CON GAME

Lehner leaned against the sacristy wall and watched the archbishop say hello to each altar boy individually.

Lehner shut his eyes and waited for something to happen.

Kenny McArthur sat in the middle of the massive cathedral. It had been years since he'd visited St. Paddy's. He wondered why. It was such a beautiful place. He had loved it when he was a kid. It was a real hit with the tourists too. Maybe that's why he had avoided it during his adult years. He was a New Yorker. New Yorkers didn't like what tourists liked. They were above that.

Even if it was a house of God.

The cathedral's organ began to rumble.

A thunderclap shook the air outside.

Kenny McArthur rose with the congregation and waited for something to happen.

He glanced around nervously. He had just found something out from his researchers that made no sense. He hoped he could spot Max. Maybe Max would know what to make of it.

No one took much notice of the slightly seedy-looking character wearing green-tinted glasses and carrying his cap in his hand as the Mass began.

As the organ signaled the beginning of the service, Lehner's men didn't notice that, while they watched Archbishop William Rowland march onto the altar, the tramp glanced around the church expectantly.

As the organ began playing a hymn and the congregation joined in, no one noticed the sweat on the stranger's forehead or the way he was white-knuckling his cap.

Max Cady felt fear like he had never felt it before.

He prayed to God that he wouldn't faint.

He prayed that he could stop the inevitable before it happened.

Archbishop William Rowland, his white hair pushed back in classic matinee-idol style, delivered a stirring sermon about the Christian duty each person has to get involved in the world around him, to not only worship God in a church but through the environment, through electing good and just officials and through protecting each other from crime and moral degeneracy.

Lieutenant Lehner thought it was a good sermon, delivered in an impassioned, yet folksy, oratorical style.

No one would ever guess that Rowland, right now, was the possible target of a psycho.

An hour later the Mass ended without incident.

Rowland entered the sacristy and smiled beatifically at the lieutenant. "Wild Bill survives another one, eh, Lieutenant?"

Kenny McArthur sighed and waddled out of the church in the middle of the exiting crush of the faithful. He didn't know whether he was elated or disappointed that nothing had happened. The only thing he was certain of was his feeling of concern for Max Cady.

The cops would be on Max's case more than ever now, and when they caught up with him they'd slam dunk him for sure.

As the congregation made its way toward the Fifth Avenue exit, the man clutching the cap and sweating profusely leaned up against one of the confessional booths.

What had gone wrong?

What had changed Carole's plans?

Cady turned to a small altar on the side of the church, dropped a quarter in a metal slot, and lit a votive candle. He needed guidance. He needed help. For all he knew, he was as screwy as people said he was. He knew he wasn't a killer. He knew he hadn't murdered those hapless people. But how could he prove it? Dear God, how could he clear himself?

If they could get him, even circumstantially, for that cop last night, then they would connect him with all the other crimes. Realistically, they could hit him with several consecutive life sentences. It was classic wrong-man stuff, the kind of plots he used to wallow in.

Now he was living it and he didn't find it all that classic a situation.

The cops would be bird-dogging him like crazy now. He had seen Malloy in the crowd. The cops would feel embarrassed at this point. They had wasted a morning staking out a bum tip.

THE CON GAME

They would hate Max all the more. It would now be a point of honor to nail his ass to the wall.

Max stood in front of the small altar and watched the votive candles flicker.

"Are you coming back this afternoon for the novena?" said one female voice.

"Of course," replied another. "Nuns from Taiwan don't visit that often. They are very special missionaries. I'm sure the archbishop will have a lot to say to them in his sermon."

"Isn't two o'clock too late for you?"

"Nonsense. It's going to be very, very special."

Max spun around to see who was speaking. No one was there. Just a few stragglers heading out the door. He smiled and faced the statue of the Blessed Virgin behind the candles. He reached into his pocket and pulled out a dollar bill. He stuffed it in the votive candle box.

"Keep the change." He smiled. "You've earned it."

Outside of Eric Paine's house, Debra Knightly took a sip of cold coffee and bit into a doughnut.

Outside of St. Patrick's Cathedral, Lehner sat stewing in his car when Malloy entered.

The big man snorted, his bulbous nose flaring. "I told you it was bullshit."

CHAPTER THIRTY-FOUR

"If I were you"—Malloy scowled—"I'd want Cady's head right now."

Lehner sat behind his desk and picked at his teeth with a bent matchstick. "You have a remarkable talent for stating the obvious, Sergeant, which has gotten you to where you are today."

"Thank you, sir."

"And will probably keep you there."

"Williams," the lieutenant barked into the air.

A tall, black, uniformed cop stuck his head inside the office. "Yes, sir."

"Talk to me, Williams."

"No sign of Cady. The woman's not home. They found McArthur in a bar on Lexington. He's beyond talking to . . . unless you're into Ouija boards."

"Get someone to dry him out as soon as possible."

"Yes, sir."

Lehner continued to poke and prod his teeth. He turned to Malloy. "What did you do with those Jimmy Ammo books I bought the other day?"

"I—I threw them out."

"Get me another set."

"I thought you said you didn't like them."

"I don't. Get me another set."

"But the closest bookstore is eight blocks away."

"Get me two sets. I will read one. I will make you eat the other."

Malloy stood and lurched out of the room. Lehner sighed and shook his head. This could turn out to be the worst day of his life.

"Williams?"

"Yes, sir?"

THE CON GAME

"Stay on the horn to all mobile units. If they see anyone who even *remotely* resembles Cady, I want them stopped and checked for ID."

"Yes, sir."

"Thank you, Williams."

"Oh, sir?"

"Yes, Williams."

"The chief called. He wanted to know what progress you were making. I told him you had a hot lead and were out following it up."

"Thank you, Williams."

"You're welcome, sir."

"You'll make sergeant in no time."

"Thank you, sir."

Lehner slid down into his chair. Hopefully by this afternoon at five.

The storm had not broken. Nothing had happened at St. Patrick's. Carole hadn't left his apartment. Her coffee was beyond cold and the doughnuts were getting stale.

Debra Knightly was not in the best of moods.

The sky was dark enough now for the streetlamps to flicker on automatically.

She gazed dully at the brownstone across the street. Carole appeared at the window. He pulled the curtains closed and flicked on the television. He sat down before the flickering appliance.

"Jesus," Debra moaned. "Doesn't he ever do *anything* else?"

Max Cady sat in the back of the church as the visiting nuns from Taiwan entered.

He sighed and moved to the side of the cathedral, near the votive candles.

If nothing happened during this novena, perhaps it would be best to just turn himself in. Lord knows he had enough money for a good lawyer. Maybe he could get off with ten years with good behavior. Ten years for being at the wrong place at the wrong time.

Lehner pored over the books. He had them opened and underlined. Next to the books were typewritten notes comprised of everything that Max Cady had told him during the past week.

"Uh-huh," Lehner said, putting one of the books down. "Mr. Cady does have a problem here. A very big problem."

Malloy looked up from the comic section of the Sunday *News*. "I said Cady has himself a problem," Lehner repeated.

"No shit." Malloy turned to Dick Tracy.

Lehner rolled his eyes heavenward. By day's end he'd be religious. He was sure of it.

Abruptly he got up from his desk and walked toward the door. Malloy began to rise as well. Lehner would have nothing of it. "Stay here and mind the fort. If the chief calls, tell him I'm following a hot lead personally."

"Are you?"

"No, I thought I'd catch the matinee at the Cinema II."

"Oh," Malloy said. "Is that the Bergman film?"

Lehner marched out of his office toward the stairway leading downstairs. En route he passed Williams. "Patrolman. If anyone calls me, don't let Malloy near a phone."

"Yes, sir."

"Thank you, Williams. There is a God."

The patrolman gave the lieutenant a strange look as the man shuffled down the stairs.

Debra Knightly fought off sleep. Her head slowly tilted toward the steering wheel. She shook herself awake and stared at the brownstone. Carole was still watching the television. Her eyes began to flutter again. A chilly wind was blowing outside. She had to stay awake. She lowered the window on the driver's side down all the way.

As she did so a hand reached inside the car and grabbed her firmly by the shoulder.

"No!" she screamed.

"Please be quiet, Miss Knightly," Lieutenant Lehner said. "This is a residential neighborhood."

Knightly looked up, sheepishly, at the exhausted policeman. "I can explain."

"I know you can. Where's Cady?"

THE CON GAME

"I don't know. I haven't seen him since before . . . the accident."

"That's like the Irish calling their ongoing bloodbath 'the Troubles.' Since before a cop was stabbed to death around the corner, right?"

"Yes, sir."

"Why are you here?"

"Max thought . . . a friend of his told me that Max thought Carole might make a move today."

"And you're here to track him and, of course, report anything suspicious to me."

"Right."

"Where is he?"

"Upstairs, watching television."

"Is that a habit with him?"

"Religious one. That's all he seems to do."

"Uh-huh," Lehner said, glancing at the flickering window. "Did you notice anyone strange coming in or out of the building?"

"No. A few people. One or two patients of the psychiatrist's, I'd guess."

"You would. I wouldn't. Let's pay Mr. Carole a call, shall we?"

"Is that safe?"

"He's not a rabid animal, Miss Knightly."

Lehner swung the door open for Debra and the two walked across the street toward the brownstone.

The archbishop's sermon on brotherhood was going over well with the nuns from Taiwan. It was also producing a chuckle or two from the TV crews assembled to cover the ceremony. When Rowland was rolling, he was an excellent speaker.

"In this age of pessimism," he was saying, "it seems perfectly acceptable to say 'Good morning, maybe' as a form of greeting. But I, on the other hand, prefer to look at . . ."

Max gripped the cap in his hand and scanned the church for any suspicious characters.

He found three people staring directly at him.

He quickly returned his gaze to the altar, remembering that he was the most suspicious-looking character in the cathedral.

"Nice setup," Lehner said, looking at the front-door buzzers. "He has an apartment all his own. Eric Paine was a generous man."

Lehner pushed the buzzer.

He waited a beat.

There was no response.

He pushed it a second time.

Silence.

"Maybe the TV is on too loud," Debra offered.

"Maybe," Lehner said, leaning relentlessly on the buzzer for a full minute. "Or maybe he's gone deaf."

He reached into his pocket and pulled out a small, thin strip of metal no longer than a credit card. He pointed outside. "Look at that!" he exclaimed.

Debra spun around. Lehner slid the metal strip into the front-door lock and jiggled it. He then pushed the door open. "Well," he exclaimed, "we're in luck. The door is unlocked."

Debra smirked and shook her head. "You'd think they'd have more sense than that," she said, staring at the metal strip in Lehner's hand.

"Well, as long as we're inside, let's visit Mr. Carole."

"It's 2A," Debra announced.

The twosome walked up a thickly carpeted stairway to the second floor. They paused before the door marked 2A. "The TV doesn't sound *that* loud," Lehner said, knocking on the door.

No one answered.

"This is getting silly," he said, pounding on the door. "Carole. Open up. Police. We want to talk to you."

Silence.

Lehner sighed and stuck the metal strip in the door. He pushed it open. "Well," he exclaimed, "this is our lucky day. It wasn't locked either."

Lehner stepped inside, emitting a low whistle as he did so.

"What is it?" Debra asked.

"I believe we've just found out why Carole has struck you as a creature of habit."

THE CON GAME

A large TV screen, the size of a small wall, stood some five feet from the window. On the screen was a familiar tableau. Phillip Carole, his back toward the window, was seated in a chair. In front of him was a strobing television set.

Lehner walked over to the side of the room and approached a video cassette recorder. He punched the stop button. The screen went blank. He pushed the eject button. A video cassette popped out into his hand.

"Our Mr. Carole is into home movies. Look. A 120-minute cassette. Record on extended play, we get a six-hour program of a man and his boob tube."

He held the cassette and walked toward the window. "With the screen placed at a proper distance and with the flickering TV serving as a main source of illumination"—he examined the thin curtains—"and these curtains acting as a filter, who could tell the difference from a distance?"

He chuckled to himself. "Right out of a Sherlock Holmes novel."

Talking more to himself than Debra, he walked away from the window and then approached it again. "I walk into the room and turn on a light. I stand in front of the window and pull the shades drawn. I walk off screen and, with the light still on, turn on the cassette. If the cassette has been fast-forwarded for a few feet, there'd be minimal flicker when the picture appeared on the screen."

"But I saw him sit in the chair."

"He probably taped himself doing just that, Miss Knightly. That's probably the opening of our little charade."

He grabbed the round knob of the light on the wall. "And the light has a dimmer. So he could gradually ease the real light down and keep the taped TV flickering away for hours . . . while he went out to play. Variation on a theme by Arthur Conan Doyle."

He turned to face Knightly. "You see, there were killers out to shoot Holmes . . . Jesus! What about Cady?"

Debra shrugged. "I don't know."

"Let's hope that Carole doesn't pull a variation on a theme by Jimmy Ammo and get away with it. Excuse me. I have an appointment at a church. Don't touch anything."

"I won't. I'm going with you."

"Like hell."

"If you don't, I'll phone my paper right now and tell them everything . . . including how you ignored Max all week."

"Come on, then."

Max slumped in the cathedral pew as the last traces of incense left the air and the novena ended.

Archbishop Rowland headed for the sacristy to disrobe.

The nuns left the church en masse, leaving only Max and a few die-hard tourists in St. Patrick's. Max glanced at the sightseers. He figured that the bad weather had kept many people home this weekend.

Max remained in his pew, dumbfounded.

Could he have been wrong about Rowland being the next victim? It was possible, he supposed, but not likely. The killer had followed his books to the letter so far. There seemed to be no reason for him to change now.

But he had.

The archbishop had made it through his public day in one piece.

Max sighed. He was defeated. He might as well turn himself in and hope for the best.

A parish nun appeared from the left side of the altar with a bucket and mop and slowly, carefully wiped the steps leading up to the altar clean.

Max wondered just what Lehner would say when he walked into the precinct house.

Two of the Taiwanese nuns returned to the cathedral and wandered around the side altars of the massive structure.

The nun on the steps slowly scrubbed her way up the steps toward the altar.

Max watched as the two visiting nuns carefully avoided the wet patch at the front of the church and, genuflecting, knelt down before the altar rail to pray.

The nun with the mop moved her bucket to the side and walked slowly toward the sacristy, obviously exhausted from her work.

THE CON GAME

Without knowing why, Max stood and slowly walked toward the altar.

Work.

Work?

Max's eyes opened wide in terror. Sunday is a day of rest. No nun would *work* on Sunday.

His walk sped into a gallop and then a full run. Max charged up the center of the cathedral. Puffing past the two visiting nuns, he leapt over the altar railing, slipping on the wet stairs, and tumbled up the platform toward the sacristy. The nun, hearing the commotion, turned to face Cady.

Before Cady could react, the nun had pulled a gun. Max hit the marble floor as the air sizzled above his head. Crack. Crack. Two shots. Max raised himself to push-up position and, sensing that no more shots were forthcoming, continued to charge into the sacristy.

The nun was frozen before the archbishop, gun drawn. Max picked up the nearest object, a large missal, and heaved it as he ran forward. The book missed the nun by inches. She turned and fled toward a side exit.

Max panted after her, zigzagging past a more than startled Archbishop Rowland. "Excuse me, your goodness," Max breathed.

The nun sprinted for the exit door, Max limping in pursuit.

With one swift motion she slammed the door open and vaulted down the stairs to the sidewalk below. Max, momentum acting more than skill, flew out of the door and, accidentally missing the stairs, soared over the stairwell toward the fleeing nun.

Max saw the sidewalk approaching his face fast and clawed the air for something to break his fall.

That something turned out to be the back of the limber nun. He grabbed on to her habit and pulled her head back with a snap. The nun groaned as the veil came off in Max's hand.

Max hit the ground hard, veil still in hand. The nun scrambled to her feet and stood above Cady, hissing oddly. Max looked up. Poised, gun in hand, was Phillip Carole, dressed in a full nun's garb, minus the wimple.

Max tried to get to his feet. Carole hit him across the face with the pistol three times in rapid succession. Max tasted blood immediately. His right eye felt like it was going to come out of its socket.

Max was vaguely aware of a screaming noise coming closer. As he fell back onto the ground he caught sight of a black-and-white patrol car screeching to a halt.

A flash of lightning danced in the sky above the cathedral spires.

Carole was gone.

Max rolled over onto his side, trying to clear his head. A pair of strong, masculine hands lifted him gently to his feet. Max blinked into the face of Samuel Lehner.

"Take it easy, Cady," Lehner said. "I've called for an ambulance." He produced a handkerchief and held it above Max's eye. "We'll get you stitched up."

He sat Max down on the stairwell.

"He's gone," Debra Knightly said. "He got away. Oh, Max, are you all right?"

Max nodded.

"That was the most frightening thing I've ever seen," she continued. "A nun with a pistol running down the street."

"You've never taught in a Catholic school," Max wheezed. "Common occurrence."

Max stared at Lehner. "Thanks for attending church this afternoon."

"Don't mention it," Lehner said, easing himself down next to Cady. "Consider me a born-again cop."

Lehner chuckled to himself. "You know, I almost let my feelings about your bad writing cloud my judgment."

"Glad you didn't."

"I thought you were as mentally inferior as you were literarily. That was wrong."

"Apology accepted."

"Nothing added up at all. So, I started checking out every bit of information that I had looked at before . . . and a few things I hadn't. Nothing added up *still* . . . but I did discover a couple of weird pieces of information."

Max only grunted.

Lehner wasn't dissuaded. "For instance, did you know that,

THE CON GAME

prior to his arrest for murder, Carole had a sheet in San Francisco?"

Max rubbed his tongue along his gums. "I think I broke a tooth."

"Well, he did. Under a shitload of aliases. And do you know what he was picked up for?"

"Passing bad checks."

"Vice. He worked the streets as a transvestite hooker. That tied in with what you were saying about all these mysterious women appearing on the scene of the crime, right?"

Max got to his feet as the ambulance rolled up. "What about his sister?"

"Your friend Mr. McArthur cleared that up for us. It turns out that Carole's sister died . . . at childbirth. The guy has kept her alive as sort of an imaginary twin all his life. Wrote letters to her care of nonexistent addresses. The works. In essence, he's been playing twins all his life."

"Great." Max nodded.

"So," Lehner said, following Max to the car, "when I found that out, I figured that there had to be some way to break Carole's alibi and . . . where are you going?"

"To the hospital."

"But I haven't finished telling you how I figured out that Carole was our man."

"Tell me after my head is sewn shut. I've been telling you it was Carole all along . . . and I didn't have any proof."

Max sat in the ambulance.

"But that's guesswork!" Lehner fumed.

Max cracked a smile. "But damned good guesswork, don't you think?"

"Look, Cady . . ."

Max waved bye-bye as the doors swung closed. "Tell Debra. She'll do a profile on you in tomorrow's newspaper."

The ambulance began to pull away. Then it stopped abruptly. The rear doors opened. Max poked his head out. "And, besides, you haven't even caught the son of a bitch yet!"

The doors closed and the ambulance pulled away.

Lehner was so angry he was practically gagging. Debra Knightly put a reassuring arm on the lieutenant's shoulder. "I think he likes you," she said.

CHAPTER THIRTY-FIVE

"The thing that really pisses me off," Max said, feeling the bandage over his eye, "is that he's still out there somewhere, as happy as if he was in his right mind."

He tossed a rumpled shirt into a suitcase. Debra sat on the edge of the bed. "They'll catch him, Max. They know what he's up to now. Lehner has men guarding the rest of the potential victims around the clock."

"Let's hope they don't blow it." He paused for a moment. "Thanks for everything, Debra."

"No problem." The woman grinned. "I have a story and a half on my hands here. I filed the straight news stuff this afternoon for tomorrow's edition. My editors are doing handstands. It's the perfect lead-in for the magazine piece. You've made my career this week, Max."

Max smiled sadly. "And put an end to a few others."

Debra crossed her legs and attempted to change the topic. "Well, what are your plans?"

"I am going to load up the Toyota and return to my home in New Jersey, if it's still there."

"Prepare to be the darling of the reporting crowd for a while, Max. Your public redemption reads like one of your novels. Oh, by the way, your agent called."

"Tell him to fuck off."

"I told him to fuck off."

Max stared at the young girl on the bed. He found himself smiling in earnest. "You know what I'd like?"

Debra flashed him an inquisitive look. "What?"

"I'd like to take you out to dinner one night and not talk about anything except dumb, everyday stuff."

"You're on."

"Good."

The phone in the living room rang. Debra answered it. "Max, it's for you."

Max walked into the room and picked up the phone. A deranged Phillip Carole was on the other end. "Jimmy. Jimmy. Jimmy. I'm disappointed with you."

"Give up, Carole. The cops are onto you now. It's only a matter of time."

"Very bad behavior. Very bad behavior."

"Carole, where are you? I could come alone and we could settle this."

"Bad behavior, Jimmy."

Carole's wheezing voice clicked into oblivion. Max replaced the phone. Debra was at his side.

"What did he say?"

"He's taunting me again. He kept on stressing the words 'bad behavior.' That's the title of one of my books."

"What was it about?"

"Shit. I can't remember. I'm lucky I can recall the titles."

Max ran into the bedroom and removed a stack of books from his suitcase. He pawed through the stack until he reached the one he wanted.

Holding up the paperback, he began reading the cover blurb aloud. "A maniac decides to lash out at Jimmy Ammo in the only way now, by stalking the tough-talking detective's only . . ." Max's eyes widened in horror.

". . . child." He gazed, dumbfounded at Debra. "Sara!"

Debra raised a hand to her mouth. "My God . . . he wouldn't."

"The hell he wouldn't!"

Max ran to the phone and dialed Sara's number. It was busy. He slammed the phone down. "Do you still have your friend's car?"

"No! I returned it."

"I don't trust the Toyota. Go downstairs and flag down a cab. I want to try one more phone call."

Debra ran out of her apartment.

Max wiped the sweat off his forehead and dialed a second number. The number at the other end rang.

CHAPTER THIRTY-SIX

Sara Cady's brownstone building sat serenely as the sky above it roared and rumbled, egged onward by an approaching storm. At the front door a wiry figure carefully picked the lock.

Phillip Carole, his face illuminated by an occasional flash of lightning, jimmied the lock open without much trouble at all. He looked behind him for any trace of a police tail before darting inside. He carefully walked through the ground floor. The lights were out. No one inside stirred.

Pulling a knife from a scabbard clipped around his belt, Carole turned back toward the front entrance and proceeded to creep up the stairway.

If the living room was downstairs near the backyard, then the bedrooms must be upstairs.

Carole flicked a piece of dry skin off his lower lip as he ascended the staircase.

He hoped Cady's daughter didn't sleep around. He'd hate to kill two people instead of just one. A man in the bed would probably raise a ruckus that would awaken the little girl as well. He'd wind up slitting the throats of all three. Pity. But he supposed it couldn't be helped. Those were the chances you took in this line of work.

He reached the second-floor hallway.

A thunderclap resounded through the house.

Carole strained his ears. He heard the sound of faint, rhythmic breathing from a room nearby. He edged his way carefully down the hallway. Knife drawn.

The breathing grew louder.

A door ahead, to his right, was slightly ajar. He peeked inside. A woman stirred under her bedclothes. Carole chuckled to himself. Tonight he would commit a double homicide. He would slit Sara Cady's throat but shatter Maxwell Cady's heart as well.

It would serve Cady right. All his life Carole had been under the thumb of pompous, overblown, upright citizens. People who had no right giving orders, had no right looking down their noses at men like Carole. Carole would show them. He would show them all, beginning with Cady. He would teach Cady a lesson in humility. He would teach Cady just who was the better detective. Who was the better plotter. And after he taught Cady? Then he would teach others. He had taught Paine, who was boss. He had taught Paine that it wasn't nice to treat another human being as a pet, as a slave. Paine. Cady. Then the rest.

Carole stood in the doorway, knife poised. The woman's breathing remained steady. She turned over under the covers, from her right to her left side.

Carole moved forward, ever so slowly. He walked over to the foot of Sara's bed and stood, staring at her. This would be good, he thought. This would show Cady exactly who the master was.

He picked up the knife and headed toward the right-hand side of the bed.

Without warning, the woman stopped her rhythmic breathing pattern and sat up. She instinctively reached for the lamp on the side of her bed.

"Leave it be," Carole hissed. "Don't make a noise."

The woman sat, frozen, facing Carole.

The killer chuckled as he moved forward. "Don't worry, I won't hurt you," he teased.

"That's right," a man's voice said. "You won't."

Carole froze. An ominous clicking noise materialized from in front of him. He felt a pressure against his crotch. He looked down. The barrel of a gun was pointed directly at his spleen.

"Famous Last Words," Max Cady said, turning on the light. "Remember that one?"

Max tossed a paperback book onto the bed. "Remember the end of that one? Hendricks, the killer . . ."

". . . is caught by a double," Lieutenant Lehner said, following Max into the room. "A ringer. Mr. Carole, meet Officer Theresa Whitley."

Carole spun around and faced a uniformed police officer sitting in Sarah Cady's bed.

THE CON GAME

Lehner offered Carole a winning smile. "Theresa Whitley, this is that young author you've been reading so much in the newspapers about."

"Delighted," Officer Whitley said, deftly removing the knife from Carole's still-outstretched hand.

The hulk named Malloy and a half dozen uniformed policemen crowded into the room.

Carole narrowed his eyes and glowered at Max. Max just shrugged. "Lieutenant Lehner is a big fan of mine too," he said as Lehner launched into a coughing fit.

"Well," Max amended, "he reads me a lot. And he's an expert at dealing with sickos like you. While you were on the phone taunting me, he was already on the phone warning my daughter. He figured that, since you had finished your work, albeit abortively, on my second book, you might move on to the third."

Max grinned. "The one we chatted about? *Bad Behavior?*"

Lehner continued smiling as he watched Carole being cuffed. "I took the precaution of removing Mrs. Clerey and her daughter earlier in the evening."

"And just to show you what a literary kind of guy he is, Lehner went to my fourth book," Max said, pointing to the paperback, *"that* one, to come up with the perfect way to screw up your little vendetta. Nice piece of old-fashioned policework, eh, Carole? Maybe I'll write a book about Lehner someday."

"Spare me the honor," Lehner moaned.

Carole remained silent throughout the entire explanation. "No last words?" Cady asked. "Nothing?"

"Okay," Lehner barked. "Take him out of here."

The policewoman led the handcuffed killer past Cady. Carole went along peacefully, offering Max an enigmatic smile on the way out.

A roar of thunder shook the house.

"You did *more* than your share. Thank you for my daughter's life. When I called you I was sure I'd be too late."

"Your call only cinched what I was already onto."

The two men walked down the stairs and into the stormy night. Lehner turned up his coat. "It's going to come down but good soon."

Max walked over to a cab where Knightly was standing. "I

hope my Toyota will make it back to Jersey." Max shivered. "Want a ride back downtown?"

Debra vaguely shook her head no. Max smiled to himself. He could see that she was on the job.

Knightly ran past Max and up to the lieutenant. "Mind if I hitch a ride for an exclusive?"

"Now, Miss Knightly . . ." the lieutenant began.

"Give her a break, Lehner," Max said. "She's done more stakeout work in this past week than most of your men see in a lifetime."

Lehner smirked. "Okay. You can come back with Malloy and me."

The threesome climbed into the unmarked police car and followed the black-and-white off into the night. Cady chuckled to himself. Knightly would probably drive Lehner crazy with her questions by the time they reached the station. He shook his head in amusement. He was going to miss her. He'd have to take her out to dinner next week. Maybe the week after too.

Max got in the cab and instructed the driver to head for Debra Knightly's building. There a run-down Toyota awaited him, a battered car and the prospect of sleeping in his own bed for the first time in a week. His own bed in his own home.

Max settled into the back of the cab. "Home." He smiled.

It felt as good as it sounded.

CHAPTER THIRTY-SEVEN

Opening up a house after it has been abandoned and locked for a few days or more is like opening a memory. It's familiar yet alien. It smells weird too. Musty and old, peppered with fragrances of old dinners and abandoned cigarettes.

Max had made it home just before the big storm hit. The Toyota, in a brilliant display of mystical powers that went above and beyond anything ever conceived by a Japanese mechanic, managed to pull into the driveway just as the rain began to pummel the earth.

Max sat in his own living room in his own chair and stared at his own television.

God, ownership could be reassuring.

The rain whipped into the side of the house, sounding like machine-gun bullets as it hit the aluminum siding. The lights flickered on and off a few times. This was going to be one hell of an evening.

Cady sat next to the phone. He wondered how Lehner was coming along with the interrogation. He stared at the phone. Would Lehner consider it an intrusion if he called? Max shrugged his shoulders and decided to call anyway.

Lehner didn't answer the phone. Malloy did. "The lieutenant is still in with the suspect," Malloy said in a tone that was not the friendliest.

"Has Carole said anything?" Cady asked.

"Nope."

"Nothing at all?"

"I said he hasn't said a word. He's been pleading the Fifth since we got him here."

"The Fifth?" Max said, puzzled. "Christ, he's dramatic. All he has to say is that he wants to wait for his lawyer before he makes a statement."

"Hey, look. The guy's a crackpot. What do I know?"

"Malloy. Exactly what has he been saying?"

"He's been pleading the Fifth, Cady. Like I just told you. I got to go."

"Has he been pleading it or just repeating the words 'the Fifth'?"

"Like I told you, he's been saying 'the Fifth . . .'"

Lightning crackled overhead. Thunder roared. Max heard a loud snap as the phone went dead. The lights flickered once. Twice. They went out completely as the storm reached its peak outside.

Max sat in the darkness, sweating.

Carole was taunting the world now. He wasn't pleading the Fifth. The son of a bitch was referring to the fifth Jimmy Ammo book. Max groped his way to the kitchen, where he pulled a candle off the shelf.

The fifth book. What was the fifth book? Candle in hand, Max ran into the bedroom and flung open his suitcase. He yanked the paperback books out. The fifth book of the Jimmy Ammo series was entitled *Bronze Swords*.

Max gaped at the cover blurb. "Jimmy Ammo is drawn into a web of intrigue and danger when a mad killer blows up his best friend's home . . ."

"Shit."

Max stumbled to the phone. It was still dead. No wonder Carole hadn't put up much of a struggle being led out of Sara's house. He had planned ahead. He had a fallback plan in case his first one didn't take. He had planted a bomb in the brownstone.

He knew he had Max beaten.

Max slammed the phone down. Damn it. Carole had let Max and Lehner go on like a Dick Tracy crimestopper, flaunting their deductive reasoning. All along he had outmaneuvered them.

By this time Sara would be back home, safe in her bed.

Max threw on a raincoat and ran out of his house and into the car.

Where could Carole have planted the bomb?

The stairwell? Yeah. That would be the logical place. A section of the house that the police wouldn't notice, a nowhere

THE CON GAME

place, an area used going to and coming from the important points in the house.

Max coaxed the Toyota into running and skidded out onto the street. He headed for the turnpike as the rain slammed down onto the windshield.

He could see it. At the top of the main stairway, leading up to Sara's bedroom, a wad of plastic explosives was sitting, wired to a small, ticking detonator. One of the kid's teddy bears was probably staring right at it.

Max fishtailed onto the turnpike, narrowly avoiding a truck. The truck roared by him, inundating Max's tiny car with a wave of rainwater.

The engine began to sputter. "Not now," Max hissed at the car.

Max kept the accelerator on the floor. He continued to pick up speed. Forty. Forty-five. Visibility was poor. Max strayed dangerously close to the taillights ahead of him. At fifty-five the car began to shimmy.

Max clutched the wheel. "Come on, car."

Lightning zapped down to his left. The car in front of him braked suddenly. Max twisted the wheel and sent the Toyota careening toward the guard rail on the right. He straightened the car and continued moving.

The tollbooth was only a mile ahead. In a few minutes he'd be in Manhattan.

He pictured Sara's brownstone sitting there, unprotected in the rain.

His stomach was getting as tight as his chest. He felt like there were taloned hands raking across every nerve ending lacing his insides.

The car began to sputter again. The temperature light began to pulsate, an ominous red.

Max had to ease up on the gas pedal as he approached the tollbooth. The car sputtered to a stop not twenty feet from the booth.

As the car clicked . . . clicked . . . clicked . . . to a halt, Max's brain focused on the tick . . . tick . . . ticking of the bomb. "No!" Max bellowed.

The engine went dead.

The car rolled to a stop.

Every light on the dashboard flickered. Red lights were blossoming all over the car. Oil. Seat belts. Battery.

Max panicked.

Car horns blaring behind him, Max tumbled out of the driver's seat and began beating the car with his fists.

"You hunk of shit!"

"Hey," a voice called from behind him, "that won't help. Want me to try to push-start you?"

Max nodded dumbly, babbling a litany of thank you's as he jumped back into the car. The auto behind him, a Ford, gently pushed the Toyota toward the tollbooth.

Max said a prayer to St. Jude and turned the ignition, pumping the gas pedal frantically as he did so. The car started. Max shifted into neutral and revved the engine, glancing at the clock above the tollbooth.

It had been over an hour since he had left Sara's. There was no way she wasn't home by now.

With the engine whirring, Max slammed the car into drive and went skidding through the toll, leaving a startled attendant wet and without payment.

Max cranked the Toyota into the Lincoln Tunnel, hitting the horn. He sped into the labyrinth, a funnel that had been divided into two lanes, one heading in each direction. There was a bus several cars ahead of the Toyota. Traffic was barely moving.

Max gripped the wheel and cursed under his breath. The cars in the single lane before him moved too slowly. Punching the horn, he swerved repeatedly into the oncoming lane, keeping his free foot on the brake just in case.

The Toyota's temperature gauge was glowing blood red. The engine was beginning to knock.

Every noise the car made reminded Cady of the bomb that was ticking away.

"Fuck it," Max muttered, swinging the car into the oncoming lane for the last stretch of tunnel. His ears were filled with the wailing of countless car horns as startled drivers watched the green demon car defy every traffic law in the books. Max didn't care. He didn't care at all. The end of the tunnel loomed before

THE CON GAME

him. He raised his right foot and slammed it down furiously on the gas pedal. The little car screamed and zipped forward.

It roared out onto the streets of Manhattan's West Side, Midtown, and barreled up Ninth Avenue.

If he could time his trip the right way, he'd make every light on every block and not hit . . .

"Shit."

The light on Sixty-third turned red. Max slammed his hand down on the horn and, the Toyota bleating a warning, ran the light. He closed his eyes momentarily as headlights and horns assaulted his senses. He opened his eyes when he was safely through.

The tiny green car weaved farther uptown.

The bomb in Sara's house continued ticking.

The Toyota hit a pothole, sending one of its hubcaps spinning into space like a flying saucer. Max gritted his teeth, expecting a blowout. None came. He stood on the gas. The car whined onward. He tried to calm himself. Maybe she wasn't home yet. Maybe he'd get there in time. Maybe there wasn't a bomb at all. Maybe Max was imagining it. Maybe he was giving Carole too much credit. In his heart he knew that he was wrong. She was at home. There was a bomb. Carole was sitting comfortably in a holding cell relishing every moment of Max's agony right now, anticipating the searing agony of Sara and Peggy as the bomb tore them into small pieces.

Max swung the car onto Amsterdam at Seventy-fourth and pressed the accelerator with new vehemence. Blinking lights forced him to slow down. Road construction. Wooden horses with flashing warning lights lined the street.

"Fuck it," Max began chanting. "Fuckit. Fuckit. Fuckit."

Max pressed down hard on the gas and the car darted forward. He was up to seventy miles an hour when the car hit another pothole. A bad one. Max knew he had pushed it too far. He felt the car shudder as the right front tire blew.

"Fuckit. Fuckit. Fuckit."

He didn't hit the brake. He allowed the car to swerve and then right itself. He continued to press down on the gas, sending the valiant little auto chugging onward, riding on the rim of a blown tire.

The car whined painfully, metal on concrete, sending showers of sparks into the air. Max continued to move.

The bomb continued to tick away in his mind.

Thunder roared above him in a sudden dollop of sound. Max stiffened. That had sounded like an explosion.

He spun the wheel crazily as he hit 103rd Street. The car fishtailed onto Sara's block. Max careened to a halt across the street from the brownstone. He jiggled his door open and fell out onto the street.

He got to his feet in the pouring rain and turned to face the brownstone. He was about to run toward the edifice when he was blown back over the car.

Bright white light, peppered with shards of violent orange and blinding yellow, cascaded across the street. Hot, acrid smoke forced itself up into Max's nostrils and down into his lungs. He gagged. He reeled. He fell to his knees, stood, and fell down again.

A chunk of brick sliced into his arm.

He could hear the debris sizzle by in the air. He could hear the Toyota's metal skin being ruptured by small fragments of something that had once been somebody's home. His daughter's home.

Thunder roared. A second explosion went off. And another. And another. And another.

Max sank down onto his knees and covered his ears with his massive hands. He peered through the smoke. Tongues of flame were spiraling heavenward from the churning remains of the brownstone. He opened his mouth to shriek. No sound came out. The hot air pushed his tongue flat against his lower teeth and held it in place as concussion after concussion hammered into his stomach like left hooks from an overeager bantamweight.

Max slowly pulled himself upright. He leaned against the car. He felt old. He felt ancient. He felt beaten. Sara's building was mere rubble now. An obscenely twisted, fragmented structure. A nightmare in three dimensions. Max shook his head dumbly back and forth, trying to make sense of all this. He'd arrived too late. He had lost. Carole had not only beaten him but robbed him of the only valuable aspects left in his wretched life.

THE CON GAME

His daughter. His granddaughter. Gone. Erased. A puff of smoke. A spiral of flame. What was once vital and warm now was still and cold.

Max shambled toward the inferno. The roar of the flames licking the rooms within blended with the cries and shouts of neighbors who were now streaming out into the street. Max tilted his head toward the churning sky above. Raindrops mingled with the tears cascading freely from his eyes, streaming down his weather-beaten face.

Max opened his mouth to yell, to roar angrily at the heavens, at the Christian god who had allowed such a senseless act to occur. His mouth twisted and turned, his lungs frantically pushed the air out of his mouth to form an Olympian screech of protest. All that emerged from Max's massive frame was a sad, small, animal-like whimper.

The sound of a beaten dog. An abandoned child. A deer flattened, but not killed, by a bad shot.

Max opened his mouth wider. A wailing noise filled his ears. He shook his fist at the sky as the wailing grew louder. He closed his mouth abruptly. The wailing continued to ring in his ears. It was not a sound of his own making. Max squinted into the rain and flame. The banshee-like noise triggered a memory somewhere. This audio hallucination sounded strangely familiar.

Max listened to the screaming.

It was the sound of a car horn. *His* car horn.

Max turned and stared down the street. Sara and Peggy were standing at the far corner of the block, outside of Max's cumbersome car. Sara was beating the car hood with a tiny fist. "Goddamn you, car," she shouted.

After six rabbit punches, the horn stopped. Sara turned and stared down the block. Her mouth formed the words "My God!"

Max ran clumsily down the street toward her.

Sara and Peggy rushed forward to meet him. "Dad," Sara cried. "What happened?"

"It was Carole," Max blurted. "He tried . . ."

Max reached out and embraced them both. "I thought you were home and . . ."

Sara clutched her father, stunned. "We would have been."

She began to giggle and weep simultaneously. "It was your goddamn car's horn. I swear, if I stopped once I stopped a dozen times to keep that thing quiet."

Max gently led them both back to his car, his cumbersome, troublesome, wonderful old Chevy. "You can stay with me for a while," he sighed.

He placed them both in the car. "You'll like New Jersey."

"But my dollies," Peggy said.

"We'll get all your dollies back," Max said soothingly. "I promise."

"Well, okay," Peggy allowed.

Max slid behind the seat of his old car. Fire engines began arriving on the block. Max placed the key in the ignition. The car roared to life immediately.

So did the horn.

Max glanced at Sara. She smiled and shook her head. Max shrugged and proceeded to drive downtown toward the Lincoln Tunnel, the Chevy's horn braying full blast in the night air.

Max patted the steering wheel as the horn continued to bellow.

No hymn ever sounded so sweet.